THE COWBOY'S MAKE BELIEVE BRIDE

WYOMING MATCHMAKER BOOK 2

KRISTI ROSE

Vintage Housewife Books

PO BOX 842

Ridgefield, WA 98642

www.kristirose.net

Publisher's Note: This is a work of fiction. Names, characters, places, and incidents are a product of the author's imagination. Locales and public names are sometimes used for atmospheric purposes. Any resemblance to actual people, living or dead, or to businesses, companies, events, institutions, or locales is completely coincidental.

Book Layout © 2017 Vellum

Cover Design © 2017 The Killion Group

Editing by CMD Writing and Editing

/ **Kristi Rose**. -- *1st ed.*

ISBN- Print *978-1-944513-21-4*

ISBN-eBooks 978-1-944513-20-7

JOIN MY NEWSLETTER

AND GET A FREE BOOK

Hi

If you'd like to be the first to know about my sales and new releases then join my newsletter. As part of my reader community you will have access to giveaways, freebies, and bonus content.

Sound like you might be interested? Give me a try. You can always unsubscribe at any time.

Click here if you're interested

XO,

Kristi

The
COWBOY'S
Make Believe
BRIDE

USA Today Bestselling Author
KRISTI ROSE

WHAT'S IT ABOUT?

The Cowboy's Make Believe Bride

Searching for a new future...

Fortune "Fort" Besingame left ranch life years ago, joining the Navy to escape the shame of his father's gambling addiction and the enormity of his losing the ranch on a bet. Now Fort has returned to Wyoming, to his mother's ranch in hopes to start a new life. A former Military Police, he wants to run for Sheriff... but convincing the townsfolk Fort intends to put down roots in the small community is going to take more than words. He needs a bride.

Running from the past...

Cori Walters realizes she will never become the photographer she dreams of being in the town where her father's – former mayor turned cattle rustler – legacy taints everything she attempts to accomplish. When her friend offers her a temporary job posing as a fiancé, Cori decides going to Wyoming might be just the new start she needs. Until she realizes her pretend groom-to-be is someone she knows from high school... And hates her.

Somehow Fort and Cori have to put aside their family differences long enough to get Fort elected.

If they don't kill each other – or fall in love.

1

With the foothills of the Three Brothers Mountains behind him, Fortune "Fort" Besingame rode awestruck toward the colorful prairie before him He might be exhausted, his vision blurry, his eyes dry, but he'd never stop appreciating the view. The sun was rising and coloring the landscape in bursts of yellows, blues, and lavender. Fort scanned the flat space ahead, the last gap between him and his mother's ranch. Home. He could barely make out the dark speck in the distance, but there it was waiting for him. Like a lighthouse beacon on a stormy night. He'd only been living here full-time for the last five years but, in truth, it had always felt like home. His soul breathed better here.

Fort sat back in the saddle and let the reins go slack. He, or his trusty stead more like, could find his way to the ranch with his eyes closed. The land, the people, heck, even the cows, called to him. He felt their pull deep in his core.

A Texan by birth and for most of his formidable years, he was well aware that his inclination to call Wyoming "home" and feel that truth right to the bone were considered traitorous to others from the great Lone Star State. Yet, saying anything else was a lie.

Maybe it was the changing seasons or the granite mountains. The gray wolves that roamed the land and called out each night for their pack. He loved it all, even the wavy grass of the prairies, dry as they were this year. Mostly, it was because there were few things in life that took his breath away. Sunrise or sunset during any season in Wyoming was one. A willing and eager woman with open arms was another. Not that he'd had the latter in a long while.

Snorting at the irony, Fort rubbed the back of his hand across his brow; a fine layer of dust that coated his skin scratched both his hand and face. He was in no state to come home to a woman even if he did have one. Currently, the only woman in his life was Ma, and he'd set it up that way. After his eight-year stint in the Navy, Fort had craved the peace and solitude that came with working on the family ranch, and he wasn't tired of it yet.

Even at times like this, when one day seemed to stretch into the next, he enjoyed them. Yesterday, he'd worked the ranch in the morning, done his shift with the county in the afternoon, and returned home to quickly saddle up and ride out to the herd before sunset. He'd do much of the same today without so much as a complaint because, when he put his head on his pillow at night, he knew, unequivocally, good work had been done. It didn't matter that there wasn't enough time for anything more than work or ranching.

Nope, no women for Fort. None at the ranch, that is. He kept his dalliances to cities away from home when he went to livestock auctions. They were simple, short, and no strings. There was little free time in his life as it was, and adding a girl who required attention and affection was not how he wanted to spend that time.

The ranch house grew closer. Fort knew his faithful stallion, Diego, was as anxious to get home as he was. Lucky for Diego, he'd get to chill in his stall the rest of the day. While Fort only had enough time to wash the grime and dust from his body, wolf down a quick meal—his stomach growled in response to the thought—then grab about four hours of shuteye before starting his midday shift. Only this time as one of the county's deputies. He'd pull a twelve-hour shift before coming home and falling into bed for six hours of sleep.

Fort licked his dry, chafed lips and ignored the exhaustion. It was best to focus on what he *could* have since twelve hours of uninterrupted sleep wasn't gonna happen for him. He decided on bacon. He was a man who'd do just about anything for bacon. Diego picked up his pace, and before he knew it, he'd arrived at the house his ancestors had lived in for over one hundred years. Relaxing his thighs, he nudged Diego lightly with his heels and the horse broke into a trot.

"I'll give you extra oats, my friend," Fort promised as he rubbed his companion's neck. The horse's ears twitched.

The ride had been a dusty, dry one. Autumn had been overly wet and had carried that trend into winter, but with spring had come an unusual dryness of the land, shocking in contrast to the colder months battling floods. Fresh growth was everywhere, and normally that was a good thing since the cattle sure liked the tall, thick grass, but the underlying dry earth worried him. His mind jumped to last night's problem. A missing cow. One. Uno. No carcass to be found that would explain a mountain lion or coyote. No sign that anyone had taken off with it either. To say it was odd was an understatement. Cattle rustlers didn't make off with only one cow unless it was a prized breeding one, but this one wasn't special by any means. Just another future steak. Yet, eight years spent as a military cop, many of those years in the sandbox, had honed his instincts, taught him to listen to his gut. Over there, paying attention was a matter of survival; here it was a matter of the ranch's. With the missing cow, those instincts were on full pinging mode. Force Protection Delta, as the military used to say when they were on high alert. Something wasn't right.

Fort blew a deep breath through his nose, quelling his unease and frustration. Little more irritated the living hell out of him other than not possessing one single clue. He liked resolution. Getting to the bottom of a puzzle. No lingering questions. This missing cow? He didn't like, no sir.

As he and Diego drew closer to the large shotgun-style log cabin that was his family's homestead, he noticed the sheriff's car in the drive. It wasn't unlike Sheriff Tinsdale to stop by and chew the fat with Ma. He was her godfather, after all. In the barn, Fort gave Diego a good rub down and some extra oats. Once Diego was settled, Fort thanked the animal by rubbing his muzzle, murmuring some kind words, and then with his hands on his lower back, arched, yawning with the stretch. A grumble from his stomach broke the silence, and Fort chuckled. Fatigue and hunger were battling it out.

He eyed the heavy wood door at the far end of the barn that led to his small studio apartment, complete with ode de animal. Behind that door was his soft bed, a hell of a step up from the hard ground last night. Another growl from his stomach ended the debate, and Fort headed for the house, pushing thoughts of his bed aside. He'd pop in, say hello, cram his face full of food, and get to bed as fast as possible.

Going through the back door, Fort entered directly into the kitchen where Ma and Sheriff Tinsdale sat at the large harvest table, solemn looks on their faces.

"What's happened?" Fort asked before he'd even closed the outside door. He'd left his stepfather, Paul, and half-brother, Matias, back with the cattle near the foothills. Maybe the missing cow had been animal related after all, and Paul and Matias had come across it. Fort mentally plotted the fastest path to get back to them. "Are Paul and Matias okay?"

"Yes, they're fine. But you're correct. Something has happened, and it's both good and bad," his mom, Saira, said. "Have a seat. I'll get you something to eat." She stood and pulled out a high-back chair.

Fort eased his tired body down, then reached for the carafe of coffee sitting in the middle of the table. Sheriff T slid him a mug.

"Here's the deal, son. You know it's been hard on Bitsy and myself with the kids being so far away and not getting in any time with our grandkids," Tinsdale said, then sipped at his coffee. Bitsy, the sheriff's wife and dispatcher for the department, had recently come back from Florida where she'd helped their youngest daughter with her three children while she was in the hospital having number four. It hadn't taken a detective to see Bitsy's unhappiness once she returned.

Fort nodded. "Yes, sir." He shoved three strips of bacon in his mouth from the plate Ma put before him. He loved her for loading the plate high with eggs, hash browns, and a fist full of bacon.

"I've been speaking with your mother about it. Bitsy and I don't want your ma feeling like we're abandoning her—"

"And I don't," Ma said. Fort didn't have to look to know she had rolled her eyes. Her tone said it all. "You all were here for me after my parents died. Helped me keep this place going. I will never be able to express my gratitude for that, but Paul and I can manage this."

Ma had married Paul the summer of Fort's sixteenth year. It hadn't taken Fort long to warm up to the caring, responsible surrogate father.

"As I was saying before I was interrupted, we don't want her to feel abandoned, but we're gonna move to Florida six months out of the year. Starting this year."

Fort stopped chewing and looked between two faces of the people he loved and respected. He appreciated the kindness the Tinsdales were showing to Ma. They'd been a surrogate family to her after her parents passed. Fort knew she looked up to Sheriff T as more of an uncle, as family, and it helped that the Tinsdales' ranch neighbored theirs, too.

Saira reached across the table and took Tinsdales' hand.

"You'll be back every summer, Uncle Roy. I can't see why you and Aunt Bitsy haven't done it sooner. I'll miss you both, but that just means the six months I have you here will be all the sweeter."

Tinsdale patted her hand, his eyes glassy.

Family was important to Fort's mom. Every Sunday they ate dinner with the Tinsdales; every holiday was spent with them as well. It would be an adjustment for her, no doubt.

Fort swallowed hard. "When you say starting this year, you'll be finishing out the term, right?" This November was an election year. Tinsdale not running meant big change was coming. Doggone if Fort didn't hate change. It usually disrupted the peace and quiet he liked so much.

Tinsdale turned his attention to Fort. "I'm not finishing my term. That means there'll be a special election. I'm on my way to file papers for my retirement." Tinsdale leaned forward, his look pointed. "Words gonna be out today. Though Deke Sutton has been pestering me about it. He's figured Bitsy out, I'm guessing. Bitsy's antsy. No doubt Deke's gonna jump in the fight."

Fort slapped his fork against the table and sat back in his chair. Man, his dislike for Deke Sutton was awfully powerful. They'd been butting heads since they were kids. Deke was the one blight on Wolf Creek, Wyoming, in Fort's opinion. He'd been a punk-ass kid back when they were teens. Fort had spent most of his summers with Ma. Those times away from his dad and Brewster, Texas were some of the best of his life. Except for Deke, who lived to make Fort unhappy. Scrawny with an aversion to work, Deke used the art of con and manipulation to get what he wanted, schmoozing people with false platitudes. After college, Deke had joined the sheriff's office as a side job, though did little more than strut around with his badge out. He'd also inherited his family's insurance business, which was his primary job and employed a handful of minions, mostly made up of the troublemakers from the area. Nope, Deke Sutton as sheriff was not a situation that set well with Fort. Not one bit.

"You know how I feel about Deke, Sheriff." Fort didn't have to explain why. Tinsdale had been the sheriff back all those summers, eighteen years ago, when Deke had come at Fort with a bat and broke his arm. All over a girl he thought Fort was hitting on. Tinsdale had broken up the fight.

Tinsdale blinked his rheumy eyes. "I know you do. Why do you think I keep the two of you on different shifts?"

"Know of anyone else who might be interested in running?" Fort ran through the people in their town and the next one over, Bison's Prairie, and came up short. People were too busy these days trying to make ends meet to take on the full-time sheriff job of a huge county. Fort wasn't sure what he disliked more—Deke taking the job or a stranger coming in and doing it.

Tinsdale shook his head. "It's too bad you aren't settled with this long-distance girl of yours. You'd be a perfect candidate, but you know how these folks around here are. They want to see a married and settled sheriff."

Ah, hell, this again? The curse of a small town was that everyone knew each other's business and believed they had a right to interfere. He'd come home from serving his country, ready to give up living in various ports or manufactured, imper-manent housing in sandy countries. He wanted to forget the sounds of exploding IEDs, meals from a bag, and the unending stress of each day's uncertainty. He'd wanted to take a deep breath and not expect something bad to happen every second of every-day. He wanted to shut his eyes and not dream about being on an endless recon mission that went nowhere and did nothing, stuck in a perpetual loop of Hell. And he certainly didn't want to come home and be set up with every single female in the county, some barely over eighteen. Fort had no interest in the sort of relation-ship that required more work than one night. Out here in nowhere's land, life was hard, and he had no intention of compli-cating it with a woman who would eventually leave anyway.

Inventing a long-distance love had been all kinds of brilliant when he'd come up with it. Kept all the locals nose out of his business. And, for the most part, worked handily. Until now. Fort narrowed his eyes and looked at Tinsdale. "You saying if I were interested in running for sheriff, then I'll need to be married, first? Deke's not married."

Tinsdale nodded.

"But he was," Ma answered. "And being a widower works in his favor."

Fort nearly choked on his bacon. He wouldn't wish losing a loved one on anyone, not even Deke, whose wife died in a car accident a few months after they were married. But that was a handful of years ago, and Deke was no more attached to anyone than Fort was.

He grunted his frustration. "It's the twenty-first century. You'd think people would get over their old-fashioned beliefs about the sheriff having to be married to be fit to run." Fort kept his real thoughts to himself. The antiquated backasswards mentality of the good people of Critten County drove him nuts. He was a war veteran, his family owned a ranch, and he had been a deputy for four years now. A darn good one, too. Shouldn't that speak for itself? What did it take to earn these people's respect?

Tinsdale ran his fingers through his short gray hair. "It's more than that. It's because you weren't raised here. Born here. How can they believe you won't hightail it outta here if you get bored or a better offer? Folks like you Fort. They doubt your commitment to this community is all."

Fort snorted. His ancestors had homesteaded here, and yet, because his mother had married a Texan and then divorced him, leaving her nine-year-old behind, he was the outsider. Story of his life, never fitting in anywhere.

"And Deke looks like a perfect candidate," Fort said while pushing away his plate.

"Yup." Tinsdale nodded. "He still goes to the cemetery and

puts flowers on Laura's grave every week. No one thinks he'll leave."

"Who knew that deciding a boy should be raised by his father would work against him as an adult?" Ma put a hand on his shoulder. "I'm sorry, Fort. I feel like some of this is my blame."

Fort squeezed her arm. "How could you know the future, Ma?"

"How serious is it with this girl?" Tinsdale asked.

Fort almost said, "What girl?" but caught himself in time. "Why?"

Tinsdale raised a brow, as if puzzled Fort couldn't put the pieces together. "Getting married right about now wouldn't be a bad idea if you were wanting to throw in your hat for the sheriff's job."

Fort sat back in his chair and placed his thumb over the twitching part of his upper eye. "Ah, well, I guess we're both so busy we haven't really given it much thought." He hated lying. Hated the acrid taste that remained in his mouth for days after each lie. Hated that Deke might be the next sheriff and he, Fort Besingame, would be working for him. Hell no, he'd quit. Maybe then he'd get more than six hours of sleep at a time.

"Maybe you should," Tinsdale said. "You've been dating her a long time and haven't come across anyone else you want to date. That's something."

Fort pushed from the table and nodded. "I'll think about it right after I catch some shuteye. I've got to be at work in a few hours." He stood. "Though, I reckon asking a girl to get hitched so I can try for a job isn't all that romantic."

Ma squeezed his hand. "Sometimes, hon, a reason like that is a far better one than love at first sight. Not that I would change that, because I got you out of the deal."

Tinsdale stood. "I'd endorse you, Fort. You know I have full faith in you."

"Thank you, sir, I appreciate that." Jeez, the look of hope in Tinsdale's eyes caused Fort to cringe inwardly. He was half tempted to conjure up a bride right on the spot. As if such things could happen.

2

F ort searched the local database for two reasons: to stay current with the surrounding counties and to see if anything strange might pop up, something to explain the missing cow. Coming up empty, he checked the high priority emails from the state, looked to see if any warrants needed to be served, and then went through the call list, looking for something, anything, that might hint at his missing cow. Not that he or his stepfather had found the carcass of the animal, but he assumed it was out there somewhere. What would explain this nicely would be additional reports of mountain lion attacks.

The only call logged on the books was a complaint from Mrs. Zykowski about something weird going on around the train tracks late at night that was keeping her up.

From his periphery, Fort was aware that Deke Sutton was watching him. Fort pretended not to notice. Deke was the sort of man who didn't like to be ignored, and Fort was the type that enjoyed pushing his buttons. He didn't often have the chance since their shift never overlapped. Tonight though, Deke was pulling a second shift. For what reason, who knew? It wasn't like things were hopping around town. For Fort, business was quiet, too quiet. His trusty gut indicated something was on the horizon, and the quiet wasn't going to stay that way for long.

"You know why I'm staring at you?" Deke asked.

Fort logged off his computer and locked the screen; he didn't trust Deke to mind his own business. "I didn't even know you were here, much less staring at me. Is it because you wish you were as devilishly handsome as me?" Fort stood and considered if his perfectly tucked and ironed uniform shirt needed an adjustment. Nope, the Navy had taught him well. He was still looking shipshape.

Deke snorted. "Why would this town's golden boy wanna look like you, a dirty trail hand?" Deke raised his upper lip. "But if telling yourself those lies gives you comfort, who am I to say anything about that?" The chair let out a loud creak when Deke sat back, resting his arms behind his head. "I was staring at you and wondering if you'll quit the day I get elected sheriff or give your two weeks' notice. I'm trying to decide which I'd prefer."

Fort checked his sidearm, then picked up the manila file on the desk with Mrs. Zykowski's complaint. He glanced at the large analog clock over the front door and decided dinner was in order. It was Wednesday, and Mrs. Zykowski liked to go to the diner for the mini meatloaf and potato special. He could eat and have a quick chat with her. Not much he could do about kids out at night, but he could make Mrs. Zykowski feel that, at the very least, her frustrations were heard. Then he'd drive along the tracks.

But first he'd deal with Deke. He faced him. "So, you plan on running? Congrats." He knew Deke was not expecting Fort to be civil. "What makes you think you'll win?"

Deke shrugged. "Who's gonna run against me? You? You don't have a chance in Hades of winning."

"You seem so sure. Bribing voters already? Got some dangling chads all lined up?" Fort looped his thumb in his utility belt.

"I'm a shoo-in. I was born and raised here. I've never left.

Married at the church right across from the square. Wolf Creek is in my blood. These people know it, they know me, and they'll vote for me."

"You have zero experience. You only joined the force when I did because I did. But I've got twelve years under my belt." In a logical world, Fort's argument made sense. Wolf Creek might not be so logical.

Deke rubbed his chin. "Yeah, sure. Because that counts. None of that matters because I've got roots and you've got.... What is it you've got? No one here knows. Are you attached to Wolf Creek, or do you have an attachment to another state?"

Fort curled up his lip. "What in the heck are you talking about? What attachment?"

"Your girl lives in Texas, right? How you can be committed here when half your heart is across the country? Sure, you've got time in the Navy with law enforcement experience, but—"

"There should be no 'but.'"

"Except there is. You keep yourself detached from our community. You've got a gal we've never met, much less know her name. The veteran card will get you some votes, but not enough, because folks here see you don't belong. They see you don't have roots or act like part of the community. Nope, not you. Darn, Fort, it's like you're just handing me the job. Too bad because it would be nice if this could get sporty. I'd like an opponent, and I'd like to prove I can smoke that person. I'd prefer that humiliation to go to you. What the heck? You should run anyway." Deke chuckled and winked.

Fort guffawed. "You think I want this job? If I did run, you wouldn't be able to keep up with me. I lap you in skill and common sense."

"If you had any common sense, you'd have brought that girl of yours here and showed her around town. Now that Tinsdale's told everyone he's not running for re-election, anything you do will look like a pathetic attempt. Which it will be." Deke nodded, his smile smug.

Fort cursed that fateful day when he'd made up the girlfriend. He'd done it so flippantly and casually he couldn't even recall the specifics of when and where her inception occurred. One moment he was saying "no" to the constant bombardment of set-up offers, the next the lie was slipping off his tongue. He only wanted it to stop. And it had. The immediate cessation was wonderful. So much that, other than the taste it left in his mouth, he'd found little harm in continuing the white lie, being as vague as possible.

"I could show up with a three-headed monkey as my woman and still kick your butt in the election. You're an insurance salesman posing as a deputy. Eventually, you'll get tired of playing dress up and move along. You always do. The good people here know that." Fort let his barb sit for a second. Yeah, it was probably real immature they were holding on to grievances from their teen years, but no sense pretending otherwise. When two highly competitive men are around each other the need to come out on top is primitive. "Now, if you'll excuse me, I'm off to do some actual work." He picked up his cover, a dark brown Stetson, from the corner of his desk and fit it on his head. Following a nod, he strolled to the door.

"Mrs. Zykowski is a lonely woman. There ain't nothing by those tracks but kids. I already spoke with her foreman. He hasn't seen anything, but you go ahead and waste taxpayer dollars on making her feel good. I'll make sure to point that out once we're running against each other," Deke called.

Fort let the station door swing closed with a bang and continued his stroll down the street, whistling. Wolf Creek was the quintessential small town, and the walk to the diner was quick. Comprised of four blocks of brick and stone buildings in a square shape, Wolf Creek had everything he needed—a bar, diner, church (a Catholic one, a person had to go the next town over if they were looking for a different denomination or into the big city if they wanted contemporary religion), the courthouse and sheriff's office, a small newspaper, a woman's clothing store, and a flower shop. The feed store sat just beyond the square and provided the men's clothing as well.

The evening air was cool and refreshing, and though it was almost nightfall, the long days of light made it feel earlier than it was. He stared out at the foothills that led to Yellowstone and fell in love with the town all over again. Having spent eight years in various ports and countries, he learned what home felt like, and it was Wolf Creek. He belonged here. Heck, even Brewster, Texas felt like a place he once visited. Maybe it was all the bad memories. Whatever the reason, he didn't give it much thought. He was happy in Wolf Creek, and that's what counted. Would that change if Deke was sheriff? The man couldn't spot a clue if it was taped to his forehead. He was more concerned with looking good, feeling important, and spouting insurance mumbo-jumbo.

Fort let out a curse under his breath. He wanted to be sheriff. He wanted to keep this town safe, he wanted to help the town prosper, and a small part of him wanted to make Deke suck it.

Once at the diner, he greeted the handful of patrons. Mr. Phillips, Mr. James, and Old man Beasley from the town over, Bison's Prairie, sat in a corner, likely one-upping each other with their Vietnam stories. Old man Beasley had survived being mauled by a sick grizzly so he always won the arguments. They got together every Saturday for lunch and Wednesday for dinner.

He saw his friend Bryce Jacobson and his hugely-pregnant-with-twins wife, Hannah. A horsewoman to the bone, Hannah had found her riding restricted per doctor's orders and was driving Bryce insane. Not to mention chewing out every other customer at the drugstore they owned. To save their marriage and their relations with the townspeople, he and Bryce had concocted a plan to keep her busy. Hannah, also a whiz at spreadsheets, was compiling information regarding station calls and crimes in the area. Tonight, he was handing her information from the other cities and would later look for commonalities.

"Bryce," Fort said and slapped his friend on the back. "How are you Hannah? You look stunning."

"I look like a ginormous hippo. And you are a liar. If I had any energy, I'd slap you upside the head." As soon as the words were out, she turned crimson red. "I'm sorry, Fort. I'm just miserable, and I think it's unfair that everyone else isn't."

"If it's any consolation, Bryce is miserable, too." Fort said.

Bryce said in a rush of words, "Not because of you, dear, but because I know you are."

"Oh, shut up," she said, then buried her head in her hands.

"Hannah, I have the other town's numbers. You want them or should I—"

"Give them," she said with her hand out, fingers wagging.

Fort handed her the thumb drive. "Thanks for this."

"You want to join us?" Bryce asked with a pleading tone.

"Sorry, I'm here to see someone."

Hannah said, "Well, we know it's not a girl since you keep all that close. Just once I'd like to know about this woman of yours who can keep your attention from across the country."

Fort smiled, keeping it tight-lipped.

"Just go," she said. "If you can't even indulge a woman who is so miserable and will soon shoot watermelons out her—"

"I'm off," Fort said backing away. "Enjoy your dinner, and thanks, Hannah."

She dismissed him with a flick of her hand. Fort felt bad for his buddy but, hey, these were the consequences of messing around with women.

Fort scanned the dinner. He found Mrs. Z in a booth by herself in the back. Wednesday was a never-fail.

Her white hair sported pink tips, and he couldn't help but notice her Stetson had been bedazzled. Her colorful appearance matched her personality.

"Evening, Mrs. Zykowski," Fort said and took off his hat, dipping his head slightly in greeting.

"Evening, Fortune. Catch any bad guys today?" She'd been widowed last year, and her only son had split town for parts unknown. Poor Mrs. Z was out there all alone most days with only her hired help for company. She ran a small herd, growing smaller every year, and Fort wondered how much longer she had in her. Bison's Prairie had a nice senior resort with bingo every Thursday. He knew this because she'd told him about it once. Since her land abutted his on the east, Fort made a mental note to ride through and check on her in a day or so.

"No ma'am, no bad guys to be had. Mind if I join you?"

Her face lit up. "I would love that."

He caught the waitress Sally's eye. "I'll have the special, please," he said as he slid into the booth, then adjusted his side-piece so it wasn't digging into his ribs. Next to hers, he set his hat upside down so it rested on the crown.

She leaned forward. "Did you hear about the nonsense on the tracks last night? So loud and using filthy words."

Fort raised his brows. "You could hear what they said?"

"Occasionally, when they would yell, but mostly no. Kept me up all hours. I thought about shooting a gun out there to scare them off but"—she tapped her glasses—"with these old peepers, I was afraid I'd hit someone."

"I'm glad you didn't. I'll ride out in a bit and have a look. About what time was it last night?"

She furrowed her brow. "Well, let me see. The news had ended. I know this because I sleep with the TV on, and when they woke me, I saw that one of those bad commercials selling junk was on. What do they call them?"

Fort knew she'd stay stuck searching for the name if he didn't move her along. "Infomercials."

"Yes, those," she said, pointing a quick finger at him. "Dumbest thing ever, those infomercials. Except I did see one with a vacuum that looked good and another with an easy way to cut up salad."

"You up late a lot?"

"I think my afternoon naps are messing up my sleep," she said. "But I really like them."

"I'll go out after the news ends and hang out a bit tonight." He'd be off work by then, but Fort believed a lawman was never really off the clock. Besides, it was only a handful of miles beyond his house.

Mrs. Z patted his hand. "You're a good boy, Fortune. I appreciate you looking into this. When I called it in, that Sutton boy took my information, and I could tell he didn't believe me." She nodded several times for added emphasis. "But he was always like that as a child, too."

"Like how?"

Mrs. Z sat back in the booth and clutched the handles of her purse. "Blasé. Why shouldn't he be, though? Everything's always gone his way. Even as a child. It all came easy. He never thought he could be hurt." She shook her head. "Losing Laura was an awful way to get a taste of how life really is, but still don't see him breaking his old ways all that much."

Fort thought about her words, tapping his finger on the cheap laminate of the tabletop. "He just told me he was running for sheriff."

Mrs. Z snorted, then instantly sobered. "Well, he has been here his whole life. Maybe he's finally growing up. I'll admit he's not been in any trouble since high school, even if he does come across a bit like Eddie Haskell. Do you even know who that is?"

In a blink, Fort witnessed how quickly the mindset of the town went from disapproving to acceptance. "Yes, they still show reruns of *Leave it to Beaver*."

"It's not like he could destroy the town if he won," she said, then *oh'd* when Sally placed their hot plates of meatloaf before them.

Fort knew she spoke from naiveté. He'd seen an elected official use a town as his own bank and sit over the locals like an emperor, taking from their pockets.

They ate in silence a few bites before Fort cast his lure. "Deke said he'd love for me to run so he can beat me."

Mrs. Z smiled. "You'd be a wonderful sheriff. Much like Sheriff Tinsdale. But do you plan on staying? No one ever knows." She didn't wait for an answer and returned to eating.

"I'm planning to stay. I like it here." Had he never said that to anyone other than his mother before?

"Well, that's good news. We sure like having you around. Maybe once you get settled, you could run against Deke in the future."

Fort wasn't sure how much more settled he needed to be. Heck, the only time he left the town or county was for official business or to go to the livestock auctions for the ranch. "What makes a person settled?"

She wiped her mouth with the corner of her napkin and considered his question. "I suppose it's owning a home, looking for a wife, having some kids who go to school here."

"Deke doesn't have kids."

"But he owns his own home."

Fort sat back in the booth and repressed the urge to huff. "He inherited his family's ranch."

"True. He also has his business on main street."

"Also inherited."

Mrs. Z nodded. "He can't just grab his bedroll and hotfoot it out of town."

Now it was his turn to consider her words. He supposed from her perspective, it did look like he could just hightail it out any time he wanted.

"Too bad you and that long-distance gal of yours ain't serious," Mrs. Z said while smoothing the napkin in her lap.

"What makes you think we aren't?" He felt like a fool having a conversation about a make-believe person but, hell, it was time to chum the waters. See what surfaced.

"Fortune Besingame, if you were to bring that girl here— what's her name?"

Fort smiled coyly.

"See! That's what I mean. If you were to bring her here, maybe things would be different. Maybe people wouldn't feel like you were gonna run off to be with her."

"What? No. That's crazy. I love it here."

Mrs. Z crossed her arms over her chest. "Well, how would we know? You won't even tell us her name." She narrowed her eyes at him. "Maybe you love her more than Wolf Creek."

"If I brought her here, wouldn't it look like a lame attempt to beat Deke?" Deke's dig had bothered Fort.

"Maybe. Maybe not. Maybe it would show folks your intentions. They'd get to see a side of you they want to see."

When Sally put the check on the table, Fort reached for it as Mrs. Zykowski pushed it toward him. "I'm gonna let you treat me," she said.

"That was always my plan." He smiled at her. "Thanks for the conversation, Mrs. Z."

"Think about what I said, and don't forget to come by tonight if you see something out there. I'm sure I'll be up." She slid from the booth; her boots were bedazzled to match her hat. She then moved to stand by him and reached out to pat his shoulder. "You're a good boy, Fortune. Tell your mother I said hello." She turned to Sally and called, "Bundle me up some of that pie, Sally, and put it on Fort's ticket." She chuckled as she shuffled away.

Well, hell, he was knee deep in a shit sandwich now. His girl may not exist, but he did have a friend who might be able to produce a real one for him. And now that he had the stupid idea, he couldn't stop ruminating over it. He couldn't even see any of its flaws, and that scared the piss out of him.

3

Nostalgia. For most people, recollections came with warm and fuzzy feelings. Laughter was often followed by a moment of longing for what used to be. Sadly, Cori Walters didn't long for what used to be, but more what she never had.

Sitting in her rusty, old convertible and staring at the house that had been her childhood home, she felt as empty as it looked. Abandoned a decade ago when her father went to jail, the once grand brick two-story with its portico that stretched up to the second floor and the ionic columns was now in a dilapidated state. The windows were broken out, the grass was above her knees, and years of angry youths had left their mark in spray paint on the exterior walls. A well of sadness filled her. The house's federal colonial design stood out like a llama against the backdrop of a working cattle ranch. Cori saw the house for the harbinger it was—insight into the two adults who'd built it, both desperate to be better than the people and places around them. Perhaps the house's current state was just as indicative of who the Walters were now.

Cori sighed heavily and straightened her slumped shoulders.

She pushed open the car door, then slid from the seat to a stand. She trailed her fingers along the car door as she slowly closed it.

Did she really want to go inside?

One final farewell was what had propelled her to make the drive from town where she lived, not that it was far, only fifteen minutes. Her mom, Barbie, relocated to a swanky neighborhood on the west side of Dallas and used the hour-long drive as her excuse to not come down.

For Cori, this goodbye was as much about the finality of her family's debt as it was a personal adios. The sale was the last of the restitution her family owed, and though Cori had sold it for far less than she could've ten years ago, she reminded herself that back then there'd been no potential buyers. She'd at least gotten more for the sale than the United States Government would have. Now, the victims of her father's crimes were able to petition the government and, hopefully, get back something of what they were swindled out of. After all, that had been a key point as to why she'd stayed. Never mind that Brewster, Texas was all she'd known.

Good luck to them, Cori thought with all sincerity. The townsfolk deserved a break. She'd done the best she could to make sure the pot the government would pull from was as full as it could be. It wasn't the entire amount, penalties and fees having added an insurmountable amount. Cori could work three jobs for the rest of her life and never earn enough money. But everyone in Brewster should get *something* back. That had been her goal.

Cori shook her head, hoping to break away from the unbidden memories swarming in her mind. She turned when she heard a truck coming up the long drive and recognized it as Mr. Miller's. He was towing his zero-turn lawn mower on a small trailer.

She stepped closer to her car, uncomfortable with having been caught here. The last thing she wanted was the town to gossip about why she'd gone to her old house. That story would be easily misconstrued, a classic case of the childhood game of Chinese Operator. The first person might start the story with a modicum of accuracy, but the last person would get a version drastically different. Chances were slim there would be any sympathy for her.

The good people of Brewster, Texas were quite angry with her family, and rightfully so. Which was why Cori had done everything in her power to try to right the situation as best she could. After graduation, when most kids were off to college or the military, Cori spent any free hour at the library learning about the best way to sell off everything her family owned for the restitution pot, all while working at the local supercenter.

Mr. Miller had been caught up in her father's web and lost his small ranch, but had managed to keep his zero-turn. She was never certain how these interactions would go with someone shafted by her father. Mr. Miller had never been outwardly mean to her, but he hadn't come to her defense either. Generally, she was *persona non grata,* never mind this was her hometown.

"Morning, Cori," he said, hopping down from the dually truck. He was a portly man with thinning hair and an affinity for pie.

"You want me to make you a path to the door?" he asked as he prepared to unload the mower.

Cori wagged her head. "No thanks." Nothing was left inside. What Barbie hadn't smuggled out before her husband's sentencing, Cori had sold off first thing.

"You have to mow the entire yard?" Cori swept her hand in the general direction of the land, several hundred acres.

Mr. Miller nodded. "Just up to the Besingame land."

Instantly, images of Fort Besingame and his dad popped into Cori's mind. Man, Fort had been a ginormous pain. A few years older than her and consummate know-it-all on all things ranching. As if! Cori had made it her life's goal to antagonize the living daylights out of him and challenge him on everything she could.

Good times, she thought with sadness.

Truth be told, anything had been better than being in a stupid beauty pageant her mother forced her into. As much as Fort Be-so-lame, as she liked to call him, annoyed her, he'd was real. A welcome reminder that life was more than the stupid pageant world.

Cori patted her short pixy cut. First thing she'd done when she'd stopped participating was to chop off her butt-length hair, infuriating her mother. The next thing she'd done following Barbie's escape to Dallas after the sentencing of Cori's father was to burn her wigs and those stupid flippers. Man she'd hated wearing those false teeth overlays.

Smile big, Corinne.

Flip your hair, Corinne.

Strut girl, strut. Shoulders back.

You can smile bigger than that!

But she couldn't. There was no such thing as a large smile when it was faked. The face can only be forced to stretch so far without the smile becoming a grimace.

Fort and his dad's ranch was located behind hers and had been an easy place to escape to. Especially when she hadn't placed first in a pageant and her mother would lose her mind, screaming at Cori about all the things she'd done wrong. Without fail, Cori would sneak out and run. Sometimes there was time to saddle a horse. and she would ride to the lake that divided their land from Besingame's.

Their pretend annoyance with each other had been comfortable and safe until they moved into their late teens. Cori blamed it on Fort's ball's dropping. Once he realized the junk in his pants could be used for more than constant cupping or readjustment, their dynamics changed. No longer was their irritation faux, but morphed into the real thing. Gone was the young boy who would let her complain and help feed his cattle. He'd been replaced by a single-minded, strung out on adolescent hormones, sex-craved junkie, all while she still sported the shapeless figure of a twelve-year-old boy. Cori recalled the last pageant she did and the stupid severely padded bra her mother forced on her. Humiliated, Cori refused to participate in any pageants after that.

Now, thinking back on it, the past felt like it had been another life, a different person's story that she had read in a book or saw on TV. Cori pressed the palms of her hands into her eyes and tried to clear the past from her mind. As of today, she was technically free. Nothing held her to Brewster except the fact that this was her home, and that meant something to Cori. Roots had value; they told a story. Yes, hers was a pathetic one, but maybe now she could shift her focus and change the story moving forward. Hopefully, with the house sold and the government accepting claims, she could turn the bad feelings the townsfolk had toward her into good ones. Her motto, *keep her nose clean and mouth shut,* should help in her endeavors of finding a bright future. How hard could that be?

4

After dinner, when the sun was finally dipping low in the sky, Fort did an initial drive by Mrs. Z's, which had yielded very little. Some footprints, large like men's, and the occasional cigarette butt. No bottles of any sort, and unless the teens came out to the tracks to smoke, none of it made any sense. Wolf Creek's teens liked bonfires, cheap beer, and cow tipping. Very few smoked; instead, they preferred to chew tobacco. Something about the scene felt off.

When his shift ended at midnight, he did a second pass with hopes of catching the rowdy teens. Maybe they could provide a clue to the missing cattle. But his stakeout yielded nothing except more questions and time alone with his frustration of the town and the make-believe girl. It irked him that they, the townsfolk, didn't see him putting down roots. And since when did being private mean the same as being a flight risk?

After a two-hour wait, Fort left Mrs. Z's for home and much needed sleep. He had ranch work to do, and dawn was quickly approaching. Once he was home, he fell into bed, slept a solid four hours, and started the new day. More of the same. At least he didn't work for the county tonight, though he still planned on driving out to Mrs. Z's again to see if he missed anything.

First there were livestock to feed, salt blocks to replace, wells to check, and he was anxious to hear from the ranch's foreman, George Rockman, if any more cows were missing. Paul and Matias hadn't found a trace of anything amiss. Heck, the only way they knew a cow was missing was when they went out to tag the new heads with the GPS locator and found they were one short.

When, later that day, word came back that the numbers hadn't changed, no more lost heads, it didn't make the discomfort in his gut go away, but it had eased up some. Every animal on the ranch had a purpose, and a loss or injury to one had a greater impact on the ranch's bottom dollar than most people thought.

Since his family and George were out checking the rest of the herds, Fort did the run to the feed store, making a pass by Mrs. Z's. He still didn't find an answer to his question: who had come out and why? Maybe the answer was nothing of consequence and he was wasting his time on this, but his gut told him otherwise. He needed answers.

He drove up to Mrs. Z's house and found her sitting on the porch, cleaning her rifle.

"Something I should know?" he asked after getting out of the truck then slamming the door.

Her hair was in curlers, and a purple scarf tied around her head matched her cowboy boots. "Not really. Couple nights ago, I lost a heifer. Think it might be a mountain lion. Thought I'd ride the perimeter and check the fence line."

Fort came to her porch and rested one boot on the step, his hands in his pocket. "I lost one, too. Was thinking the same thing. Your foreman find the carcass?"

"Not yet. I'm hoping to come across it today. Hopefully sooner rather than later as I've got bingo tonight." She adjusted her scarf, then checked her reflection in the silver plate on the rifle's stock.

"We haven't found ours yet so don't get your hopes up."

"Well, aren't you full of sunshine today?" She set the rifle aside and packed up the cleaning kit.

"Yep," he said with a chuckle. "And as for the tracks and those kids. Nothing. I sat out here last night, but no one came by. If you hear them again, call me directly, and I'll be out fast as I can." He handed her his deputy card.

She stuck it in her shirt pocket. "Will do." She stared at him, her lips pursed, as if she was trying to figure him out.

Fort shifted his feet, moving the opposite one to rest on her porch step.

"Something bothering you, Fortune? You look like a man trying to solve a complex problem. You've got forehead creases, and they aren't going away, even when you laugh."

Fort looked at the ground and sighed. "Nothing in particular bothering me. Normal stuff, mountain lions, the upcoming auction, getting the herd tagged, and the dry grass."

Mrs. Z snorted. "It's awful, right. I'd come out here and dance naked if I thought it would help with making it rain."

They shared a laugh.

"I'm headed to the feed store. You need anything?"

"Of course, I do," she said, her smile large. "I have a weekly supply pickup. It's waiting there for me. I'll call ahead and tell them you're picking it up. This is a huge help. Thanks, Fort."

"No problem. I can help out anytime. I get a weekly supply as well and can grab yours when I get ours if you'd like."

Mrs. Z clapped her hands together with glee. "Oh, bless you. With Earl gone, my workload has doubled. I feel as if cattle are slipping through my fingers." She stared over his shoulder at the mountains, looking lost in thought. "So much to keep track of."

Fort's gut clenched. A sure sign that something wasn't adding up. "You missing more than the cow you mentioned earlier?"

She jerked, as if his words had knocked her from her reverie. "Not this week. But it seems I'm always one or two down each week. My herd is much smaller these days, easier for me to manage, but at this rate I'll be herd-less by the end of the year."

"That's a rate I wouldn't be happy with either. You know the cause?" Did he have something here? Was something happening under their noses?

Mrs. Z forehead puckered as she confessed, "I'm to blame. I've had some fence lines down that I took too long to fix. A mountain lion for another. Nothing unusual if you're asking. Just feels like it's gonna be one of those bad luck years. Know what I mean?"

Fort nodded. Indeed, he did. Instinct was telling him the same thing. That something was off, and it frustrated him he couldn't figure it out. "I'll be headed over to the feed store then. Be back in a few hours. If you come across any more missing head, will you let me know?" He started to turn away, but paused.

"You think there might be something to it?"

Fort lifted a hand, palm up, to indicate his uncertainty. "Hard to say, but mostly I'm just being cautious. I want to make sure there *is* nothing to it."

"Will do," she said.

With a wave, he was off and headed to the feed store, his mind going over what she'd said. He hoped the store would be busy. All those old ranchers together were just as bad as gossiping women in a quilting circle, and he might get some good information. Maybe others were experiencing the same as him and Mrs. Z. Unexplained missing cows were just that. Unexplained. They could assume all they wanted.

Luck was on his side. The store was packed. Mr. Phillips, one of the Vietnam veterans, was the loudest, spouting his latest angst against the Bureau of Land Management and Oprah Winfrey. Why the latter was anyone's guess. Phillips was the saltiest of ranchers. His skin was weathered due to endless years under the sun, his voice scratchy from years of smoking, an unlit cigarillo clamped between his teeth every waking moment, like now. He wasn't a man who kept his thoughts to himself and had an opinion about every single stinking thing. It often amazed Fort that he had the energy to do so. He started most sentences with "listen here" or "as I see it."

Fort mingled and chatted and kept his ears open. He was settling his tab at the front when he became part of Mr. Phillips rantings.

"Listen here," Mr. Phillips said and whacked Fort on the back. "I hear Deke Sutton is ready to file to run for sheriff. I hear he's the only one. Why do you reckon that is?"

Fort leaned against the counter. "Filing doesn't start for three more days. Maybe others are keeping their intentions a secret until then." A plan he'd considered himself.

Phillips grunted his skepticism. "Nah, ain't nobody here that can keep a secret, and ain't nobody interested in it except Deke and maybe you. What do you say? You thinking of running?"

Fort scratched his chin and considered his words. It would seem the town was interested in him running. Even if they thought he wouldn't win.

Phillips didn't give him a chance to respond. "As I see it, you ain't got a chance in Hades. Not that folks don't like you. But we'd like you to try. Mostly because we want to see what you'd do after you lose. Split maybe? Can't see you working for Deke."

Fort tossed up his hands. "Why would I split? My family's ranch is here. I live here." The short-sightedness of the community baffled him. Did it really take having a girl to show he was committed to the community? To him, that was straight up bullshit.

Phillips moved his cigarillo from one side of his mouth to the other. "Yep, true. But as I see it, you got this gal in Texas that none of us know anything about, and if you lose this election, maybe you'll want to go live there with her. The pull of a siren woman is serious. Hard to resist. I've been there." He started poking Fort in the chest. "You may be tied to your Ma's ranch but it's your Ma's still. Not yours, and this gal, maybe she don't like small towns. Yep, Deke's a shoo-in." He ended his words with a final poke.

"I agree," said Burt, the feed store owner. "Not that I think he's the best candidate, but he might be the steadiest candidate." A few others in the crowd nodded their agreement.

Fort kicked the toe of his boot against the ground in frustration. The entire town was comprised of fools, and clearly, he was one of them. Maybe he should leave and start over someplace where people were sane.

Stupid town. If he didn't love it so much...

Fort lifted his hand in the air to get the men's attention. "For what it's worth, I love this fool-headed town and all the nut jobs in it." He looked at Mr. Phillips. "Those eight years in the navy—"

"As I see it, you didn't even stick that out," Phillips said.

"Neither did you," Fort retorted.

Phillips straightened up. "Listen here, son, I was called up—"

"And I volunteered. Let's not fight over our time. We served, and it was an honor to do so. I appreciate what you gave this country Mr. Phillips." Fort placed a hand on Phillips' shoulder. The older man nodded and pressed his lips together, a sign that the old man's ire had receded. Fort continued, "This is my home. I love these cows, even those troublesome wild horses. I'd rather deal with the damage they're doing to the land than be away from here." He gestured to the land outside the large front store window.

"Sounds like someone is running for Sheriff," Bucky Wise said from the back of the crowd.

"I'd vote for ya, Fort, if you were settled," Burt said. "I'm not one for change, and I'd hate to vote for you only to have you run off. Know what I mean?"

Fort nodded. He did. Mrs. Z had explained it well the day before.

"We're ready to load you out back, Fort," Burt's son, Colt, said.

"Thanks, Burt. That's high praise." He gave Phillips another pat on the back and extracted himself from the crowd who were still talking about his merits as sheriff.

After his truck was loaded with both his and Mrs. Z's supplies, he drove away from the store, his mind heavy with questions. He simply needed to admit to himself he wanted to run. Being the town's sheriff appealed to him on a level deeper than he expected. With it would come an acceptance he'd never experience but longed for. A respect he was working hard to garner.

When the idea of hiring a girlfriend had first popped into his mind, he'd discarded it. Yet, it kept circling back. He made a mental list of the pros and cons, but quickly lost track of the cons since the pros of becoming sheriff and building that career were looking pretty damn good.

The stakes were high. No doubt. But maybe, just maybe, if the townspeople saw another side to him, they'd warm up to the idea of him running. He wasn't saying he needed to get married. He was only going to show them a softer Fort.

ori clenched her back teeth and stared at her coworker, a girl fresh out of high school, who used the word "like" as a noun, verb, adjective, and overall filler word.

Said girl, Mitzi, was staring at the photo-processing machine in wonder and frustration. "I, like, don't understand what happened. I, like, set it up like I always do. This machine is like a computer and should, like, do it's, like, job."

Cori closed her eyes to keep from rolling them. "Yes, well. It's not *like* a computer, it is a computer, and though they are able to do what commands we tell it, we still need to properly maintain the machine. This includes putting paper in and closing the side panel so we don't overexpose the film."

Mitzi stared at her wide-eyed. "Like, duh. But it didn't tell me to do any of those things."

Cori didn't want to point out that anyone with eyeballs, especially ones as large as Mitzi's, could see the side panel was open. As for the paper, the little blinking light on the corner of the screen was a good clue. Cori shook her head in disbelief. "I'll fix it, but that roll of film is ruined."

Mitzi smiled. "I'll, like, tell the customer that, like, the machine was, like, acting up. Like, I do it all the time." She glanced at the name on the film's envelope then sucked in a quick breath.

Cori snatched the blue and white paper sleeve from her and scanned for the name. "Crap on a cracker," she said and handed it back to Mitzi. "Good luck with that one."

The film belonged to the infamous Mrs. McAdams. Her sour disposition was what one could hope for when dealing with her. Any other day she was downright nasty. Cori hoped she'd be at lunch when Mrs. McAdams came for her photos, but in case she wasn't, she fully planned to duck and hide in one of the oversize cupboards they used to hold their supplies. She wanted no part of this mess. She still hadn't dug out from the one her parents left her with.

Cori spent every day scrutinizing her actions and calculating her risk. For her, changing the town's perception of her was imperative. She'd grown up in Brewster, Texas. Some of the folks here had educated her, babysat her, and worked on her family's ranch for generations. But fat lot of good any of that did her now. All anyone could remember was what her father did and, apparently, the sins of the father were to be revisited on the daughter. If there was ever a stranger in their hometown, Cori was one such person.

Maybe now that the government was taking applications for the restitution money, the attitude of the locals toward her would change.

"I'm gonna, like, take a break," Mitzi said, then yawned.

Cori nodded. Yep, that was about right. Mitzi had been here long enough to run one set of film through the machine, screw it up, and her day was done. She'd spend the remaining shift hours chatting with other store employees, going out for lunch, staring at the Barbie clothes in the toy aisle for fashion tips, and essentially being useless to Cori.

"Don't forget I get to take a lunch break, too. So be back in a few hours." Cori moved to the film developer and began doing a check. She wanted to make sure everything was perfect before she started any other orders.

"Like, as if. It's just a break. I'll be back in a few." Mitzi scuttled off before Cori could say anything further. Not that she had anything to say. *Keep her nose clean and her mouth shut.* Not that her nose had ever been dirty, but her mouth had gotten her in trouble once or twice. She had a problem repeating things she'd been told or overheard. There was also the time when she was eight, and her momma had entered Cori in the Little Miss Heifers pageant. Winning had been all Cori's Momma had talked about. "Just get a crown, Corinne. Just one. Smile and be sweet" had been her momma's request. Cori had tried, really. But when the judge had leaned toward her, her sour breath puffing in Cori's face, and asked, "If you could work with any of the following who would you pick? Santa, the Easter Bunny, the Tooth Fairy, or Fairy Godmother?" Cori had laughed in her face and said, "None, because they are all make-believe. They ain't real. They're a lie. When I get a job, it's going to be as a rancher. I love being on a ranch." Never mind a handful of four, five, and six-year-olds were surrounding her. Yep, she really did need to learn to zip it.

Time flew as Cori ran several disposable cameras from a wedding. She picked out several amazing shots, reprinted them, and made a collage she thought would make the bride blubber all over again. She really did enjoy working with pictures. Almost as much as she did cows and horses. Then she spent time leaning against the counter people watching. Like clockwork, as the hour reached noon, Mitzi didn't show up to relieve her for lunch.

Mr. Miller shuffled by, a bakery pie in hand. Every day he would spend time in the automotive section. He was one of the few who acknowledged her. His tiny head nod and half smile meant everything to her. Cori knew for a fact Mr. Miller had been the first to apply to the government for monetary compensation for the loss of his land. She wondered if he'd moved out of his double-wide trailer and into something with a yard for his zero-turn.

"Hey Cori, have you seen Mitzi?" Cori turned to find the store manager leaning against the counter. He pointed to her collage. "Well done," he said without so much as looking at her. Just talking to the air, like he knew she was there but couldn't see her because she was invisible.

"Thanks. I haven't seen Mitzi for a while. She took a break. If you come across her, would you please tell her it's time for my lunch break? I don't want to leave until she's manning the desk." It was against policy to leave the section unattended, so Cori hoped he picked up on her subtle hint. She wasn't about to become a narc and tattle on Mitzi, but she could leave a trail of breadcrumbs.

Joe, the manager, nodded. His lack of direct eye contact bothered her. He turned to leave, but paused. "Listen," he said, looking at his thumbnail. "You're a good worker." He nodded twice.

"Thanks," Cori said and wondered what in the heck was his deal. He nodded again and was gone before she could think of anything else to say. Her stomach growled, and she hoped Mitzi would show up soon, but like her daddy had always said, "You can hope in one hand, shit in the other, and see which one fills up first." An unpleasant image to be sure but, in this case, Cori wouldn't be surprised if Mitzi didn't show up until a few minutes before Cori was scheduled to clock out. It had happened before. Thankfully, Cori was prepared. She had tucked a few granola bars and an apple in one of the drawers and went to get them now, hoping they'd tie her over until she could go to lunch or it was time to go. Preferably the first. She had the granola bar unwrapped and in her mouth in seconds and was reaching for another when she heard the unmistakable angry tone of Mrs. McAdams.

"Is that all you do around here? Eat?"

Cori stared at the second granola in her hand. If she were a person with superpowers, she'd turn the granola bar into a wand and cast a shut-up spell on Mrs. McAdams. Maybe the entire town would thank her. She dropped the granola bar back into the drawer and turned to face the angry woman.

"Afternoon, Mrs. McAdams. How can I help you?" Darn it all and that Mitzi. She should be the one facing this firing squad.

"You want to help me? Maybe you could come mow my yard since Lloyd had to take that job over in the next county and can't help as much at home." Lloyd and Cori had gone to school together, but he'd been a few years ahead. Not the sharpest tool but considerably nicer than his mother. Mrs. McAdams, hands resting on the small of her back, glared at Cori. Crinkles of discomfort creased the corners of the older woman's eyes. "Thanks to your family. Or maybe you could give us back the money your father swindled?"

Cori was at a loss for how to respond. Mrs. McAdams words were sharp daggers to the heart. Everywhere she looked, every person she talked to in Brewster, had been affected by her father's actions.

Mrs. McAdams sighed wearily. "Are you going to help me or not?"

"Oh, right. Film." Cori forced herself into the moment, wishing she could forever forget the past.

"Well, I'm not here for tacos, am I? Obviously, I'm here for my film." She rolled her eyes and slapped her hand on the counter. "Dumb girl."

Correction. If Cori had a superpower, she would want the ability to morph into something her nemesis found scary. In Mrs. McAdams case, there was nothing that woman found frightening, but that didn't stop Cori from wanting to jump-scare the pee outta her. Like one of those pranks people play on the computer. One moment you were looking at a bucolic pasture, waiting for something to happen, and the next a crazy face flashes on the screen, appearing to jump at you. Only it goes away so fast you think you imagined it. Cori would like to do that right now.

Please she begged the universe. *Just this once.*

Of course, nothing happened. "Picking up or dropping off?" Cori asked instead. Hoping it would clue the woman in that Cori hadn't seen any pictures from Mrs. McAdams and therefore wasn't the one who overexposed them.

"Picking up," Mrs. McAdams bit out.

Cori went to the drawer where she'd filed the envelope and thumbed slowly through all the options, hoping Mrs. McAdams would simply disappear. Evaporate. Get hauled off by a Yeti. Anything. Cori held the woman's picture envelope between her thumb and forefinger and mentally scolded herself. This was not the attitude she needed to possess if she was going to change the way the majority of the town felt about her. She needed to kill them with kindness, prove she wasn't like her father.

"Here ya go, Mrs. McAdams. If you have more shopping to do, there is no need to pay here." Totally breaking store policy, but if it meant Mrs. McAdams would leave, it would be worth it.

The woman narrowed her eyes at Cori and lifted the envelope's tab as if the sticky portion had never been sealed.

Yes, Cori thought. Resistance *was* futile. Much like many of Cori's wishes. While Mrs. McAdams slid the pictures out, Cori looked over her shoulder for Mitzi. For anyone.

Mrs. McAdams gasped. "These—these, these are—are—are awful. They're—"

"Overexposed. Yes. I didn't process them, but the tech who did said the machine was acting up." The granola bar sat like a boulder in Cori's stomach.

When Mrs. McAdams tossed the pictures at Cori, they fell around her like heavy confetti. "You did this on purpose, didn't you?"

"I had nothing to do with your pictures."

"How am I supposed to believe that? Your father looked us all in the eye and lied every day to our faces. You're just like him. You have to ruin everything. This town, my family, my pictures. Everything."

Cori looked around to the other customers who had stopped to watch. "Mrs. McAdams. I had nothing to do with what my father did." How many times had she said this? She'd been in high school. The day following graduation her mother had split, leaving the responsibility of dealing with the government to Cori. Someone had to oversee the selling of the ranch and its assets. She had broken it down into bits. The more earned from the sale of the ranch and its equipment, the more the people of Brewster would get back. Not that it would ever be enough. But she'd done it, dismantled her home for everything she could get. Barbie, her mom, was too busy playing the victim to deal with it, and had Cori let the government do the selling, they would have asked for pennies on the dollar. Cori had refused to let that happen. She needed to know the people of Brewster were getting back as much as they could.

Why do I stay? she wondered for the millionth time. *Because its home*, she reminded herself.

Mrs. McAdams clutched her bag to her chest. "Every time I see you, all I can think about is what your family took from mine, and now you've even gone so far as to take away my memories." She nodded to the photos scattered between them. "I'm going to find the manager and give him an earful." After she stormed off, Cori sank against the counter.

Mitzi suddenly materialized. "Wow, that was like awful, awful."

"Tell me about it," Cori mumbled and tucked her hands under her bum to quell their shaking.

"But like, whatever, she's, like, always unhappy, and I've, like, got some really, like, good news. Like check this out. I, like, got promoted to photo shop assistant manager, and I'm, like, now your boss. And as your, like, new and super cool boss, I'm giving you, like, the rest of the day off. Like awesome, right?"

What in the flim-flam was going on? Mitzi was her freaking boss? Yes, Hell did exist on Earth, and it was right here in Brewster, Texas. Cori was standing at Hell's mouth, had been on the cusp of it for years.

"Like, I'm the bomb, right?" Mitzi smiled and kicked a photo over by the trashcan.

Purgatory. She was sick and tired of it. How long was it going to take this town to forgive her? To accept her? Across the way, Cori spotted Mrs. McAdam's chewing out the store manager. He glanced at her and quickly looked away. Coward.

Forget this. Cori looked at the clock, then back at Mitzi. "Well, considering that I get off in half an hour and haven't had lunch, you're not doing me any real favors. And where have you been *all day*?" She threw her hands up in question. Cori ran this department. Cori ran this machine and kept it going. She'd like to see Mitzi do a full day's work. Just once.

Scratch that. She couldn't care less. She was sick of it all. Sick of trying to do the right thing based on everyone else's expectations of her. Trying to undo something she had nothing to do with in the first place. She'd been a victim, too. Only difference was she didn't let it consume her. Nope. She kept trying to move forward. She'd volunteered at the hospital, took courses at the community college when she could afford it, and showed up on time for her shifts at the superstore. Yes, her dad had swindled the good people here, but Mrs. McAdams' husband was the town drunk and had been long before her father took half his herd. No one ostracized them.

Cori looked around. People were staring at her, some whispering, others shaking their heads. Why was it so easy to hate her, to constantly talk about her? Inside, she was weary. She couldn't find the silver lining to anything anymore. She hated herself every time she faked a smiled and pretended that being slighted was okay. It wasn't okay. She was a person, too. She had feelings and needs, too.

Something inside Cori snapped into little tiny pieces, or maybe she was already in those little pieces, but now they'd been tread upon so many times they were dust. She could no longer collect them up and hold them together. Or maybe it was something simpler like missing lunch and she was hangry, that magical combination of hungry and angry. Whatever the reason, she couldn't stop herself if she wanted. The next moments passed like an out-of-body experience. One minute she was standing there watching everyone, straining to hear their whispers, and the next she was whipping off her store vest and tossing it in the air toward Mitzi. Then she leapt up on the counter.

"Hey," she screamed at the store manager and Mrs. McAdams. "Thanks for all your kindness. I appreciate it," she said in a biting tone. "For what it's worth, I am not my father but y'all refuse to see that so y'all can suck it! I quit. I quit this job and I quit this town." She shot everyone the bird, thrusting her finger high and shaking it madly. She spun slowly on the counter to make sure everyone got an eyeful. Then she tapped the front pocket of her jeans, felt her keys, and jumped from the counter. She'd long stopped bringing in a purse or using her store locker since it was constantly getting broken into. All she ever carried were her keys, driver's license, money, and her phone. She strode from the store, her cowboy boots clumping loudly on the linoleum.

Cripes. She forgot how far back the photo booth was from the front doors. She kept her head high while swallowing several times to control what she knew would soon be following. She even managed to get into her piece of crap car and drive a block away before pulling over onto a side street and completely losing it.

Bent over her steering wheel, Cori cried what felt like a thousand tears. She'd tried so hard. It's not like she didn't understand why. They were hurt, too. But that didn't mean they could be so ugly to her.

Cori wiped her palms across her cheeks. Staying had been stupid, stupid, stupid. Momma had said exactly that, and for once she should have listened to her. But leaving had seemed like quitting, or worse, admitting she had been culpable, too. She sucked in several ragged breaths, but found it useless. Almost a decade of pent-up emotions wouldn't be released after one short cry. She rested her head against the steering wheel and looked out the window. Brewster was all she knew. It was home. Beyond the few houses lay pastureland that used to feed hundreds of cattle. Now only handfuls of herds dotted the horizon.

It was time to let go.

She would move. Not that she knew where she would go, but it was time. A person could only engage in self-flagellation for so long before they became a martyr, and Cori was well past that mark.

Her phone chimed, and she grabbed it from the passenger seat where she'd tossed it. A reminder. Tonight was Sabrina's book club. She thought about canceling, but darn if Sabrina didn't always have the best food, and now that she was unemployed, the free meal would come in handy. Never mind she'd have to drive over an hour to get there since Sabrina lived on the north side of Dallas while Cori lived south of the large city. She glanced at the clock, and when she saw the time, turned the key in the ignition. If she was going to cry, she could at least do it purposefully while moving toward something instead of hanging in limbo.

6

Sabrina Holloway was in the love business—making serious connections between two people so they could have the fulfilling life they wanted. She was not in the business of arranging marriages that weren't intended to last or, for heaven's sake, were "pretend," and she would never entertain such a notion.

Yet, here she was, ankles deep in a quagmire to help Fort Besingame find a pretend bride, and she was sinking fast. Though she tried to keep her business and personal life separate, she reluctantly acknowledged that she sucked at doing so. She wanted to help him. He'd been good to her all those years ago when she was a scrawny kid, stuck in the middle of Nowhere, Texas because her father was trying his hand at the poker tables at a new casino nearby. She wanted to help Fort out, really she did. But a pretend bride? How could she make that happen? Hire an actress?

"I know what I'm asking is unconventional and not really your thing, but I have few options. Placing an ad on Craigslist or some website is more public than I want this to be." He rubbed a hand down his face, sighed wearily, then sat back in the large overstuffed chair in her living room. Once he was situated, he lifted his legs and rested his feet on her reclaimed barn door coffee table, crossing one ankle over the other. His dark brown cowboy boots weren't new and shiny, but worn, soft leather. Dirt clung to the soles. Dirt and who knew what else, considering he'd just come from the Stock Exchange.

"Get your feet off my table," she said and kicked at his boots with her own, only hers were a fashionable red with a decent heel.

Fort swung his legs off the table then shifted in the seat so he could rest them over the arms of the chair. He then sunk back into the corner and pulled his straw cowboy hat over his face. She heard him yawn.

"I can't make any guarantees. The women I'm currently working with are looking for love matches. A happily ever after." She shook her head. This was a dumb idea.

"I can give them a happily ever after for now," Fort said through his hat. He sounded plum worn out, and her heart went out to him. She'd been there when his daddy had lost everything in that fateful poker game. Her own father had warned Fort's dad, Karl, about the stakes of the game. About how dirty Charlie Walters played. But Karl had been desperate, and there was no reasoning with the illogical mind of desperation.

"No, Fort. You're asking for someone to give up their life to pretend for an extended period of time to be your fiancée. It's not a simple task, and this person would not be getting a cushy life with a maid. No, she'd have to befriend the good folks of your town, pretend you're God's gift, likely help on the ranch." Sabrina frowned at him, not that he could see her with the hat over his face. "I'm not sure where I can find someone like that."

"I have faith in your skills, Sabrina," he said in a lazy, careless tone. As if he was asking her to tie her shoe with her eyes closed or something easily as simple. "So much that I filed my papers to run yesterday."

She tossed up her hands in frustration and stood before she reached across the chair and whipped the hat from his face. Sure enough, his eyes were closed and his mouth slack. His eyes snapped open.

Sabrina leaned toward him and said, "You're crazy. I'm really good at what I do, but this...this feels darn near impossible. You get that, right? Don't you dare try and guilt me by saying you have faith in my skills. What do you know about what I do?" Still holding his hat, she swat his leg. "Get up, you need to get out."

Fort sat up straight. "Wait? You're kicking me out?"

"Have you even tried any other way of solving this problem? Like maybe going online and actually meeting people? Or did you come straight to me?"

Fort had the decency to look remorseful. "Does it count if I thought about it? But honestly, there's not a whole lot of time." He clasped his hands together in prayer. "Please help me, Sabrina." He blinked those blue-gray eyes at her, and she smiled sardonically.

"Don't even try that look with me, mister. I've known you far too long to be wooed by those eyes." She didn't point out she'd seen those eyes damp with tears when Charlie Walters took possession of Fort's home after his father's ginormous loss in the devastating poker game. Or the anger that turned those blues into a steely gray when he realized his dad had disappeared, leaving eighteen-year-old Fort to bear the burden of his father's actions. She'd also seen the fear in them when she'd gone with his mother to drop him off at the recruiter's station following his enlistment.

"I'm begging here, Sabrina. Help a desperate man out." He reached for his hat, but she stepped back and held it out of range.

She softened her voice, "I already said I would, and I keep my word." She swiped at his legs again, only this time haphazardly. "Now you have to leave. I have my book club coming, and no men are allowed." She tossed his hat onto his chest.

Fort groaned and covered his face again with the straw Stetson. "Just pretend I'm not here. I'm not so sure I can get up from this chair. It's very comfortable."

Sabrina laughed, went behind the chair, and proceeded to give him a good shove forward. "Out," she said.

Fort slid from the chair, then rose slowly. He followed it with a long stretch, arms over his head. "This book club of yours? Any potential pretend brides?"

She came behind him and pushed him toward the door, his hat in her hand. "Have you given any thought to what will happen should you get elected and then your fiancée and you break up? There are bound to be some people who'll suspect they've been played."

Fort turned and stepped to the side, ceasing her pushing. He took his hat from her, brushed back his hair, and then situated the Stetson on his head, angled slightly lower over one eye. "They'll just be glad I saved them from the likes of Deke Sutton," he said.

"Answer me this. If they know what this Deke Sutton is like, why do you even need a pretend fiancée?"

Fort narrowed his eyes. "Stop with all this logic, Sabrina. Help me out. I'll cross that bridge when I get there. Besides, these things have a tendency to work out." He shrugged, nonchalantly.

"I dunno, Fort. It's got the potential to be a hot mess." When she held the door open for him, she glimpsed a car coming up her long drive.

"It'll be the price I pay for keeping Deke out of office. The more I think about him getting his hands on the town, the angrier I become. If you don't help me, I'll find someone who will." He arched a brow, likely testing how his threat was going over.

Sabrina rolled her eyes. "Mm, yes. And who might that be? I'm all you've got, so show some respect." She arched a brow of her own.

Fort chuckled. "I'm not above begging. Want me to beg?"

"Right now, I want you to get out. My book club friends are coming, and you must go."

He glanced over his shoulder and nodded. The car was drawing closer. "Fine. I'll call you in a few days to see where we are. Time's ticking." He turned to leave.

"Not if I call you first," she said and shoved at his shoulder, hoping to hurry him along, but he kept to his slow, lazy walk back to his rental truck. Nearly drove her mad. Correction, she was quite possibly mad already for even considering his idea. Where in the world was she going to find a woman who could uproot her life to go pretend to be someone's beloved? Only to walk away from it and possibly endure ugliness because of it? Sabrina chewed her lip.

Fort was getting in the large truck while her friend, Cori Walters, was parking her piece of crap convertible. Fort backed out, turned the truck around and, like his walk, cruised slowly down her drive.

"Hey," Cori said, coming up onto the porch, swinging her keys around one finger. "I hope you have some good food today because I've had a no-good, very bad day. And this book? I'll be honest. I got three chapters into it and chucked it across the room. Hated it. All that gooey romance and forever crap." She rolled her eyes and stopped in front of Sabrina.

She noticed Cori's eyes were rimmed in red as if she'd spent a fair amount of time crying recently.

She asked, "Do you want to talk about it?" Had to be something big to reduce her tough friend to tears. Sabrina gave Fort's fading truck one last look. She would have to put his problem on hold until after her book club was over.

Cori glanced over her shoulder. "Who was that guy? You know who he reminded me of? Fort Be-so-lame. Remember him?"

Sabrina jerked her attention to Cori and stared, blinking

several times as an onslaught of thoughts infiltrated her brain. "Besingame."

"I like my version better." Cori winked.

"That's right, you went to high school with Fort," Sabrina said, mostly to herself.

Cori nodded. "He was a few years ahead of me, but yeah, we went to the same school."

"He was so cute back then, don't you think?"

Cori looked back at the fading truck. "Well, it's not like there were a ton of guys. Brewster is stupid small, but yeah, he was cute."

Cori had Sabrina's full attention now. "He was so easy to flirt with, too. Fun guy. Which is probably why we've stayed friends all these years."

Cori stared at the keys spinning around her finger. "I wouldn't know. We were never really friends. Kinda hard to be when there was so much bad blood between our families. I mean, it *was* my dad, after all, who conned his dad out of their ranch." Cori's smile resembled more of a grimace, her ragged expression etched with the years of weariness from carrying her family's burden.

Ah yeah, there is that.

7

Cori stuffed two profiteroles in her mouth and moaned with pleasure. Who didn't love the little balls of creamy goodness? Nobody, that's who. Show her that person, and she'd show you someone who was crazy and found little pleasure in life. Yes, occasionally the books discussed at Sabrina Holloway's book club *were* mind-numbingly boring, but the food never disappointed.

"You want to talk about your day?" Sabrina asked and set out a plate of éclairs. She'd commented on Cori's puffy eyes earlier, and like a dog with a squeaky toy, Sabrina could be just as tenacious. She'd keep at it until the squeaker no longer worked, or in this case, until Cori spilled her guts.

Cori waved her hand dismissively as if to say it wasn't a big deal. "Not much to talk about. I lost my temper and told everyone within shouting distance to suck it."

"Oh, my," Sabrina said.

Cori scanned the room. All the book club members were staring at her. She groaned, knowing they would want the details. "Remember that co-worker I mentioned?" She tossed her head to the side in an impersonation of Mitzi. "You know, like the one that, like, never works."

The others nodded and groaned. Conversations about Mitzi had been a must at every meeting.

"Yeah, well, she got promoted to assistant manager of the department."

"Over you?" Sabrina asked.

Cori laughed wryly. "Come on, Sabrina. We all know I wasn't going to get a fair shake there, or I suppose y'all knew, and I just figured it out today."

"Or admitted it," Ronna, a psychologist said. She was always going Freudian or *Diagnostic and Statistical Manual of Mental Disorders* on them.

Cori was not in the mood. Profiteroles or not, she was still one on-point comment away from crying. "Can we talk about something else, please? Maybe the book and the douchey main guy?" Cori knew that would get at least half the room's focus redirected.

"You didn't like our main man?" Deb, Sabrina's horse trainer, asked Cori. It never failed that when it was Deb's turn to pick a book, she picked a steamy romance, apparently liking her sex out in the open and *hot*. Or a murder mystery, preferring the macabre. Often Cori wondered about the older woman. She was mostly quiet and easy-going, but Cori believed outward appearances were all smokescreens anyway. Cori was willing to bet that if she needed to off someone or wanted advice on her sex life, Deb would be her go-to person.

"I liked him okay," Cori said. *Maybe not as much as this food, though.* "It's just that sometimes I want the girl to rescue herself. Why does a man have to do it?" Cori moved away from the veggies and dip toward the éclairs.

"I'm just gonna point something out here and let you ponder it a bit," Ronna said.

Cori braced herself and grabbed a second éclair to help.

"Every time we read a romance or a book with a love story in it, on some level—"

"Which has been almost every book," Cori pointed out. She had a feeling she knew where Ronna was going with this.

"True, regardless, these are not your favorite books, and you always are disappointed in the female lead and the...hero, as Deb calls him," Ronna said.

"Yeah, and?" Cori hovered by the pastries, her stomach tightening in apprehension. She hated having the spotlight on her and, even more, anything that smacked of confrontation where she would have to dissect her emotions or behavior. She worked from one premise: do no harm and mind your own beeswax (okay, that's two), but so far, that attitude had served her well and kept her nose clean. No one could hold any *current* grievances against her. She couldn't ask for more.

"Only, it makes me curious as to why these things bother you." Ronna, a good foot taller than Cori, stared down her nose, a julienne carrot pinched between her fingers.

Cori decided a quick answer might deflect the discussion and move it on to something else. "I like my fiction a bit more realistic. I mean, seriously, what woman shaves her legs every day? You don't read about that in these books. Him sliding his hand up her prickly leg? Nope. And they're so helpless, these girls. Waiting for Mr. Six-Pack-Abs to solve the problem."

"Hey," Deb exclaimed. "I pick books with strong females." She sounded offended, but she winked at Cori, which managed to help loosen the knot in her stomach. "But I admit, I do try and pick books with hunky men. I do like me an alpha."

Cori shifted uncomfortably and pushed her glasses up her nose. That was the other thing she hated about the books. Show her a man with a six-pack and sculpted muscles, and she'd show you a man who sat on the couch and farted while scratching his belly, demanding his dinner. Yeah, she was being shortsighted, but men were all alike. Dragging their knuckles was an inherent behavior. No thank you, she was not interested.

"What books do you prefer? If I remember correctly, you had picked that one about Hemingway's wife, right?" Ronna asked.

Cori nodded. There was a realistic book about love, life, and all the bullshit that came with it.

"Cori likes nonfiction," Sabrina said and patted her arm.

"Not many surprises with those books," Cori said.

Ronna smiled and nodded. "I see," she said, as if she'd been let in on some great secret.

"You see what?" Cori wondered if she could make an excuse to leave. All the profiteroles were tumbling around in her stomach.

Ronna sighed and placed her water glass she was holding on the table. "One day, Cori, you are going to be faced with an opportunity that will require you to take a chance. Your instinct will be to run, but I hope you pause and consider staying. See it out. You might be pleasantly surprised on the other side."

Pleasantly surprised that regret isn't as painful as it seems, Cori thought. She was about ready to spill other snarky retorts, but was startled from her thoughts by Sabrina who clapped her hands in excitement.

"Oh my, I have an idea," Sabrina said. "Wow, you weren't kidding, Ronna, because I have an opportunity for you, Cori."

Cori swung her attention to Sabrina who stood next to her, hands clasped prayer-like, the tips of her fingers touching her lips.

With her dark hair and creamy skin, Sabrina looked like an angel that could work for either side. Innocent and bewitching.

"So it's safe to say you're currently between jobs. Do you have a plan?" Sabrina asked.

Cori was glad for the subject change, such as it was. "You know me, thinking of playing it fast and loose with my free time. Maybe I'll go to school full-time or something. Good ol' Babs is still trying to get on some reality TV show about housewives of convicts. If that happens, I'd like to not be around Brewster, surrounded by people who dislike my folks. Know what I mean?" Cori smiled at the group, but her lips felt stiff and she was uncertain how to make them curve. It was the same faux smile from all those beauty pageants she'd been in as a child where she'd been forced to fake-smile for hours, feeling as if her face would crack and her flippers, those stupid-ass fake teeth she had to wear, would fall out.

"Your mom's been doing that for a while, right?" Deb asked. Even though they all stood around the well-stocked and beautifully decorated table, no one was eating. For a group of women who liked angst in their books, they loved it when Cori talked about her personal life, which was rare. It never ceased to provide the drama they craved.

Cori nodded. The group knew her story. But who didn't since it had been in the state papers, even making national news? It had been huge news in Texas. It wasn't every day that a small-town mayor was convicted of embezzling, fraud with check kiting, and cattle rustling. What Charlie Walters managed to get away with was being a shitty father and an overall disappointment as a human being. After Charlie was sentenced to a decade in prison, her mom, Barbie, had shifted her one life goal. She ceased being the wife of a rich tycoon and mother to a beauty pageant winner and embraced being the victim. Now, she was the wife to a crafty tycoon, who himself was the victim of jealous people. Good ol' mom had conveniently dropped off any aspirations she might have had for her daughter. Barbie played martyr well, wearing her stiletto and tears into the prison weekly to visit her husband. Filming it for all her Facebook friends to see and sympathize. Funny how her father had been court ordered to pay back what he stole, which he professed unable to do and filed bankruptcy, yet Barbie lived comfortably in a McMansion on the outskirts of Dallas, Charlie's internment not even a blip on

Barbie's radar. Cori, saddled with the moral fortitude that had escaped both her parents, knew it was her responsibility to pay back what she could. She'd gone years without luxuries most took for granted: haircuts, meals out, and underwear without holes in them. Her one luxury had been used camera equipment, and most of that she'd been given for work she'd done.

"I have a job proposition for you," Sabrina said. "But it's a weird one."

Cori moved to the drink station and decided she would need something stronger than water. Knowing what Sabrina did, Cori couldn't imagine what this job could be. Trying to make Cori a mail-order bride was such a ridiculous notion Cori almost laughed at the thought. "Hit me," she said and pulled a beer from the silver ice chest.

"Okay, keep an open mind." Sabrina raised her brows, waiting for Cori to acknowledge the request.

Again, Cori nodded.

"There's this... ah...lawman, I suppose you could say, a county deputy who is looking to run for sheriff, but the town is small and folks are old-fashioned and they want a married man as their sheriff. He needs to be moving toward the altar for the townsfolk to consider him." Sabrina picked up a bottle of San Pellegrino and toyed with the screw top.

"What's that about?" Deb asked. "Sounds like it's the old west."

"Right," Cori said. She lived in a backward town already. Did she want to trade one in for the other? Even temporarily?

"Well, it's all about trust and showing the town you're there to stay. That you're part of their community." Sabrina gave Cori a purposeful look. "You and I both know that's still no guarantee. But this man, this lawman, he's a good one with the right intentions, and he's asked for my help."

"So I'm supposed to go marry this man to get him elected?" Cori asked and then gulped down several swallows of beer. *Liquid courage don't fail her now!* Because as asinine as this pitch sounded, Cori found she was intrigued. Not enough to get married, but curious enough to hear more.

Sabrina's laugh was brief. "No, you won't have to actually marry him. Only pretend that you're going to marry him."

Encouraging Sabrina to continue, Cori asked, "How does it end?" She took another gulp of beer.

"You'll leave him at the altar," Sabrina said, then bit her lip.

Cori choked and spewed her last sip. But, more importantly, she retained control of her plate. Dropping her profiteroles were not an option. She was going to need their comfort. Once she gained control, her throat spasms subsiding, she said in a raspy voice, "So, I'm to be a pariah in two towns. Awesome. Kinda unprecedented."

Sabrina's smile could pass for a grimace. "You're not a pariah in Brewster. Your parents are."

Cori raised her bottle in the air. "Guilt by association." She finished off the brew while sadly acknowledging there was no more courage within her, only gas and the urge to expel it.

"Maybe we can come up with something less awful than leaving him at the altar," Sabrina mused.

"You think?" Cori rubbed her stomach.

"He needs the town's sympathy, but maybe a dramatic breakup before the wedding would work."

"Either way, whoever the fake fiancé, she'll be taking it on the chin." Cori stared at the tiny, cream-stuffed puffy balls and decided something more substantial was needed. Like a pint of ice cream, or a gallon.

"I know, it's not the best situation, but you'll be helping out an entire town because the other guy running is bad." Sabrina's pointed gaze spoke volumes. "The kinda guy we are familiar with and dislike immensely. Did I mention it was also a paid position?"

Ah, yes. That got her attention for sure. Money she needed, and the opponent being a grifter like her own dear daddy had appeal, too. "So, it would be like I'm fighting crime. Kinda a superhero in disguise," Cori said.

"Sure," Sabrina said. "Stopping shysters one at a time. It's respectable, if you think about it. Going up against these sorts of people."

Cori waved her hand in the air, rejecting Sabrina's words. "Don't try to spin it. There's nothing respectable about coning a con." She would not be like her father. Nope. No way.

But the money would give her a do-over. A fresh start she longed for.

Sabrina sighed. "We both know that the only way to deal with people like this is to play their way. A pretend con is not the same as a real one. There are no rules when dealing with greed."

Sabrina was right. Hustlers were shortsighted. They rarely saw past their objective.

Sabrina continued. "It's in Wyoming. Beautiful. Imagine the pictures you could take there."

Cori pressed her lips together. Now Sabrina was just being mean, going straight for Cori's passion for photography. Just last night, Cori had been looking at the rules for the Smithsonian's Photo Contest. Not that she felt she had anything worthy to submit at this point, but crap on a cracker, she really wanted to enter. Validation she could take a good picture would do her self-esteem good. Maybe then her well of positive experiences would start to fill and balance out, and dare she hope, exceed the well of negative ones.

"How much money?" She'd be a fool not to ask, and she'd spent enough time being a fool.

"Enough to start over somewhere. Might even have some extra for college."

Cori narrowed her gaze, trying to read Sabrina's mind. It all seemed too good to be true. "This guy? He's the good sort? I'm not going to have any problems with him?" Cori couldn't believe she was asking.

Sabrina bit her lip before answering. "Well, you might get off to a rocky start, to be honest. You're both similar in personalities, but if you keep focused on the goal, then you should make it work. There's little chance you'll fall for each other so that will make leaving easier."

"That's counterintuitive for you. Must feel weird." Cori watched Sabrina closely. It was strange that a matchmaker was setting her up to fail at the match.

"You're helping a friend. I'm only involved in this because I have connections. Don't think of it as me making a match."

8

Waiting was not Fort's forte. Waiting out a crook was light years easier than waiting to meet the woman he was to pretend to love and possibly want to marry. He knew little about her except Sabrina said he'd know her when he saw her. Which he found foreboding. He'd spent one sleepless night trying to recall the mutual friends he and Sabrina shared, but his memory from those days back at the Texas ranch were foggy, likely muddled from the exhaustion he'd experienced trying to keep the ranch afloat and Dad from sinking it faster than he already was.

Fort paced in front of the escalators. He walked the width of them, paused on the other side, sighed heavily, shifted, turned, and crossed in front of them again, treading back over his footsteps. The crowd was thinning, and a quick glance at the board showed her flight status had changed from DELAYED to ARRIVED.

Any moment now.

Sweat broke out across his brow. Crap, this whole plan was suddenly real. Sabrina's warning clicked for the first time. What if this did backfire? What if the town felt played? Yeah, she'd said it all before, only now, he was listening.

Think of Deke.

That's all he had to do in order to push his reservations aside. He would take one for the team if it meant the team—in this case the town and its people—would not be at the whims of a narcissistic, greedy megalomaniac.

Waiting at the bottom of the escalators near baggage claim, Fort stopped pacing when passengers began to spill onto the escalators. He scanned all the faces of the passengers and wondered who'd been sent. Apprehension caused his stomach to clench. Hell, he'd seen some nasty stuff in the sandbox, and each nightly patrol was a tense experience. He was sure he'd come away from his stint with some PTSD, or an ulcer at the very least. But this...this waiting for a stranger was maddening. How was he supposed to convince the good people of Wolf Creek that he loved and adored this stranger when he was all jittery like a virgin on his wedding night?

Fort swiped off his Stetson, brushed his hair back, shifted his weight from one foot to the other, and let a curse roll out under his breath. With more force than necessary, he stuffed his hat back on and went to stand at the bottom of the escalators, feeling sweaty all over. This was his idea, and by God he was going to stick to it.

He stuffed his hands in his pockets and stared down at the tips of his boots, hoping he wasn't about to make things worse. Dark red dots were splattered across them. He'd helped birth a breech calf earlier today, and luckily both mom and baby were doing fine. If an animal can come into the world feet first, blinded, and still make his way, Fort Besingame could shut the hell up and do basically the same. Jump in feet first and do the right thing. Save the town. Maybe they'd see his commitment to the town then....

Lips pressed together, Fort looked up at the incoming passengers and began scanning the faces. Man, man, man, woman and child, man, man, woman, woman, woman, man... *Whoa, back it up.* He reversed his trail to the second to last person he'd seen. Something about her was familiar. She was tiny, probably could fit into the crown of his hat, but the look on her face was fierce. When their eyes met, hers widened. The man in front of her shifted, covering half her face. His mind raced to place her. The little, pert nose, dark hair cut short in that girly Disney-fairy way. Behind round, vintage, dark-framed glasses, her big eyes widened. His gut told him they were blue. When he narrowed his gaze, she rolled her eyes in response. He'd leaned in, an ineffective tactic to get a closer look when his mind finally placed her. It struck him with such a force he leaned back on his heels and sucked in a breath.

"Oh, hell no," he said, pointing his index finger right at her. The man in front of her gave him a scowl but stepped away, and Fort had his first full-length view of Corinne Walters. A large bag hung from one shoulder, a backpack off the other. She looked just like she had all those years ago, like a menace to society. Some people had a resting bitch face; Corinne's was always a challenge face. As if "I dare you" would roll off her tongue at any moment. Everything, and he meant every single stinking thing, got her dander up. He'd never met a woman so contrary. So much that she was exhausting to be around.

"You can just go back to the desk and ask for a return flight home," he said. She continued to hold his gaze, never once wavering. She dug through the bag on her side and pulled out a large camera, one of the fancy professional ones photographer's use, and lifted it. The lens already off, she pointed it at his face, and he heard the soft repeated click as the camera was set in action.

"What are you doing?" he snapped.

"Capturing this moment for posterity. Or proof." She cocked

her head to the side. "Maybe both." She reached the end of the escalator, stepped off, made a sharp U-turn, and stepped onto the one going up. She swiveled so her back wasn't to him, and he heard the camera whirl again.

"Lookey there. So much said in these pictures. Who needs words?" She winked at him, tucked the camera away, then gave him a tiny finger wave that ended by shooting him the bird as she rode away.

"What are the odds?" he mumbled. "Of course, Sabrina sent you!" he called to her. Maybe Sabrina hadn't intended to help him all along.

She nudged her chin to the space behind him. Her voice grew louder as the escalator carried her away. "Pretty good deduction considering no one else is waiting down there for you and willing to play house. Guess that's why you're a cop."

Fort quickly scanned the area and noticed they had the attention of a few passengers. No one he knew.

She continued, "But if you want me to break it down with specific stats, I think I might be able to do that, considering who our fathers were."

Children of gamblers—that was them. Only her father happened to be a crook, too, the one that had destroyed his father and what small life they had back in Texas.

"What was she thinking?" he mumbled and briefly closed his eyes. The moment needed a deep, calming breath, and he took eight of them, trying to slow the spinning, free-fall he was experiencing. One moment he was working toward his plan to be sheriff, and the next he was watching said plan crash and burn. All because Corinne Walters was sent to pretend to be his dream girl. He watched her step off and, within a blink, she was immediately gone from sight.

Fort took off, climbing the escalator in long strides. She was walking back to the ticket counter when he caught up with her.

Catching her by the elbow, he spun her toward him. A bolt of fire shot up his arm and zinged his chest.

Yeah, who was surprised that Cori produced a negative charge? Not him. "What was Sabrina thinking? Is this some kinda joke? You having another laugh at me about this?"

She studied him, as if each blink of those large eyes was seeing deep into his mind, reading his thoughts.

"I had no idea it was you until I saw you. Jokes on both of us." She jerked her elbow free, then resituated the backpack on her back.

Fort scanned her from top to bottom. "Why did she send you? Of all people?"

Cori shifted her weight and crossed her arms. "I'm sure you're hugely disappointed. I know I am. I also know I'm not your type. What was it you said about me in high school? I was a carpenter's dream? Flat as a board and never been nailed?"

Fort narrowed his eyes. "What does that have to do with anything?"

She stuck her hands out in front of her chest. "You like them big and dumb. I'm the exact opposite of that."

He wouldn't say the exact opposite. She'd filled out some in all the right places. Not that he was looking or anything.

He waved to get her to continue. "Anytime you want to make sense is good with me."

"What I mean is that Sabrina said you have one goal. Maybe she sent *me* because I wouldn't be a distraction from that goal."

Fort looked over her shoulder, focusing on something else besides her. Maybe if he didn't look directly at her, he could be reasonable. It didn't matter she wasn't directly involved with the con her father ran, but when he saw her, he saw his past. He saw his failures. How Sabrina thought she wouldn't distract him was plain stupid.

He huffed out his frustration. "Sure, I can see how the daughter of the man I despise the most wouldn't bother me at all." He narrowed his eyes. "I'm only going to think of everything your dad did every time I look at you. A constant reminder of those bad times," he bit out.

His plan was sunk. No way Cori Walters was going home with him. It was bad enough she knew his secret.

9

Sabrina stared at her phone's screen and ignored the repeated calls from both Cori and Fort. She had provided him a pretend bride, and only four days after he'd made his request. The universe had helped with that one. And she'd found an opportunity for Cori to get her pictures. They both were getting what they wanted, and Sabrina was happy to be done with the task. Now they needed to work together after they buried the hatchet. Hopefully, not in one or the other's skull.

It had been risky getting Cori to go to Wyoming, but from Sabrina's perspective, it had been a no-brainer. One of a few options could happen.

One, and the most likely, they would fight and cancel the whole thing. Sabrina was okay with that. Sure, she wanted to stop a grifter as much as the next person, but there were more ways to skin a cat, and Fort needed to see that.

Or two, they could work together. This would require them addressing the past, but everyone needed to do that at some point in their lives in order to move on, and Cori and Fort were two of the stuckest people she'd met. If this scenario were to happen, then she could rest easy that she helped out two friends.

Lastly, they could fall in love. Sabrina had endless experience, and her gut, her best asset in this business, told her Fort and Cori were perfect for each other. Yes, their histories sucked, but that didn't mean they couldn't change that. Two people looking for acceptance and roots with shared interests and no fear of hard work. Cori had the strength to be a cop's wife, and her deep love of ranching was the cherry on top. Fort's deep desire to do well, combined with his boy scout personality, was the steady quality Cori needed to feel safe.

When Sabrina's phone rang again, she pressed the ignore button. Sitting back in the overstuffed seat, she kicked her heels up onto the coffee table and said a silent prayer they would make the right choice. It was up to them now.

She'd given them the chance at something great. Now they needed to take it.

10

Cori had spent the flight trying to keep her hopes from getting out of control, but she'd created a thousand different fantasies. None of which was her being held accountable for her father's actions once again. Each daydream had been a fresh start, a chance to do something good and be considered a friend, a helper, and a kind person. Because dang it all, she was all those things, but no one affected by her father's greed could see past that. Not that she blamed them. But sometimes, she wanted to. Didn't they understand that every time she looked in the mirror she was reminded of his deeds as well?

Fort's words struck right at her center, a jab to the heart. The sight of her made him sick.

"Yep, that's me, a walking vestige. Aren't I lucky? I wear it well, don't you think?" She stuck her hand on her hip, did a model pose, and followed it with an eye roll.

He glanced at her, then quickly away, almost as if he couldn't stand to look at her. Which very well might be the case.

She reached into her camera bag and took out her phone. She wanted to lash out at someone, anyone, and Sabrina was the obvious choice. All those book club meetings where they talked about how Cori wanted to do right, wanted to be seen beyond her father's egregious acts, and here she was, an accomplice for the man who probably hated her father the most. She texted that exact thing to Sabrina.

Okay, *accomplice* might be a strong word. Fort wasn't a criminal, but he was essentially proposing to run a con. And she was his sidekick.

Irony at its finest. One day she was going to get a normal job without people like Mitzi and do all things normal. Like watch TV, have friends, and maybe get a dog.

Fort Besingame was so far from normal it wasn't funny. Take his shoulders, for example. They were so broad she half expected his shirt to rip down the back when he reached across his chest and pulled his phone from his breast pocket. How about his height? Yeah, most guys were over six feet, but not all of them carried themselves like Fort. Where they lumbered, he strolled and, for lack something less cheesy, he was essentially a pillar of strength. She knew his dark skin came from his Spanish mother, with some help from the sun; his slate gray eyes were from his father. As was that stupid strong superman chin of his, butt dimple and all. Though she supposed, on him, the dimple didn't make his chin look like a butt as it did on some others. Crap on a cracker, if she didn't find him so repulsive and, well, carrying a crap-ton of guilt thanks to dear old Dad, she'd find Fort Besingame kinda hot. Even his stupid, long fingers stabbing at his phone were appealing.

"So, we're calling this a no go, right?" She needed to make a plan soon. Maybe Sabrina would pay her some of the money. She might have to stay with her mom to get on her feet, Lord help her, but now that she had the idea of a fresh start firmly planted, she wasn't about to de-root it.

"I don't see any other choice. There's no way we could fake a friendship, much less romantic interest." His gaze swept to her chest, and Cori instinctively thrust her shoulders back, pushing her chest out.

"Give up," she said as she watched him disconnect the phone and try again. "She's not going to answer. I've texted her tons even before I saw you, and it's been silent."

"A communication blackout," he said and lowered his phone.

She nodded. "I suppose she wants us to figure this out ourselves. Maybe I'm your one-shot deal."

Fort shifted, tucked his phone in his shirt pocket, and crossed his arms over his chest. Cori watched to see if the muscles from his forearms or biceps would burst through the straining cotton cloth.

"She wants me to put my trust in you? Come on, that might be asking too much." He raised a corner of his lip in distaste.

Cori's temper flared. As had been her habit over the last decade, she went to squash it, to play nice and not add fuel to the never-ending fire, but this wasn't Brewster and she didn't have to make Fort like her. There was no chance of that. Besides, she was so very tired of keeping it all in, of being a chump. Sometimes it felt like she might choke on it all. Her only crime was being born to the wrong people. Cori stepped close to him, her head reaching only as far as his chin, so she had to tilt her head back. Way back.

"You listen here, Fort Be-so-lame." She poked a finger into his chest. "Essentially, you're trying to run a con on your entire town. Will your mom be in on it? My guess is she won't." His gaze darted away, and she had her answer. "I knew it. So don't stand there all tall and mighty—"

"High and mighty."

"That, too. But make no mistake, you're no better than me at this moment. Difference is this con isn't my idea and the end game isn't my prize." She gave one final jab into his rock-hard chest. The man was made of steel.

He placed a hand on the top of her head, holding her still,

and stepped back. "Easy there small-fry. It's not that I think I'm better. It's that I wonder how we'll pull it off. We don't really like each other much." When he removed his hand, he accidentally brushed her shoulder, and Cori experienced a ripple of goose bumps on that side.

Revulsion. Had to be. She wanted him to do it again just to be sure. Cripes, she was messed up. She was so needy for affection that even grossness felt good.

"I suppose Sabrina thought we could do it," she said, thinking out loud while picturing Fort nuzzling her neck. How would she respond? More goosebumps broke out. She jerked her attention back to him and snapped her fingers. "Oh, Sabrina sent this box to you." She dug in her camera bag and came out with a long, slender white box big enough to hold a thin wallet. Curiosity was killing Cori. She hadn't opened it on the plane. Mainly because the sides were taped, and she hadn't figured out how to peel them back without tearing at the box.

"What is it?" he asked.

Cori looked up at him and rolled her eyes. "It's kryptonite."

He glanced at her, disbelief furrowing his brow.

"How should I know? It's taped shut." She sighed loudly with exasperation. Hoping he'd realize she thought he was a moron. In case there was any doubt.

Fort dug a pocketknife from the front of his jeans, pushed the blade out, and then cut the tape. He was moving so dang slow Cori had to clench her fingers into her palms to keep from snatching the box from him and opening it. It had been forever since she'd been given a gift, and even though this one wasn't technically for her, it felt like it had something to do with her. She bit her lip to keep from screaming at him to hurry.

Once his knife was returned to the comfort of his pocket, Fort returned his attention to the box. "Wanna take a guess before I open it?"

She glanced at him. Was he teasing her? There was a slight

quirk to his lips. She made a valiant attempt to act blasé. "Maybe it's your invoice for her services?"

"Fancy way to present that, don't you think?"

"Sabrina is pretty fancy." Impulsively, she reached for the box, but jerked her hand back when her fingers touched the top. To cover her embarrassment, she said sassily, "You could just open it so we know what's inside."

Fort chuckled then wiggled the top off. When he lifted it, Cori moved in closer.

He asked, "Is that a diamond ring?" Inside were two cards and a ring tied by ribbon to a cushion. The white stone sparkled.

"Maybe it's cubic zirconia or moissanite." She stared at the large gem.

"'No Man is an Island' by John Donne," he said and lifted the first card. He turned it so she could see the poem had been printed on the back.

Cori snickered.

"This must be for you," he said and handed it to her.

The paper was heavy and thick. "I'm pretty sure it's for you." She placed it back in the box. The other card was Sabrina's business card. White card stock with the word HOPE embossed on the top, her name and information in metallic, navy ink. "Why she put her business card in here makes no sense. We know how to get ahold of her."

It was Fort's turn to chuckle. "Yeah, and she better *hope* that when I do, I keep my tone civil."

Cori went for Sabrina's card, thinking something might be written on the back, just as Fort went to replace the lid. She bumped his hand and the box flipped over, dumping everything on the floor. The ring skittered to a stopping beneath the underside of a trashcan.

Cori went for the cards and the box, Fort the ring, having to get on his knees to reach it. He had turned, put one foot on the floor to stand while handing her the ring, when they were interrupted.

"Classy Fort, asking a girl to marry you in an airport. And have you told her yet you're doing it to win an election?"

Cori turned and looked up at another tall cowboy, this one blond and a tad on the thin side. He had an even smile that would likely be engaging if he wasn't sneering at Fort. She glanced at the new guy's chest and, unbidden, pictured it bare. She mentally compared his sunken chest to Fort's broad, manly one.

Fort, on one knee, the ring still attached to its cotton bed by ribbon. His arm extended was toward her, the ring on his palm. It sure could be misinterpreted.

Cori swiped it off his hand.

"Are you following me Deke, or do you actually have a purpose here?" Fort stood and moved to stand next to her.

"I'm here picking up my campaign manager. Not that I need one. I could literally do nothing and win this race." He looked down at Cori and winked. "You're nothing like I pictured, but you're cute." He extended his hand. "I'm Deke Sutton."

"Cori Walters," she said without thinking, then quickly glanced at Fort. Had he given them another name and she'd just jacked up the entire plan? He was staring at Deke.

"You're serious that you brought in a campaign manager?" Fort asked.

"Of course. With the insurance company and working for the county, I didn't want to split my attention from those jobs. My first priority is the people." Deke dropped Cori's hand but his attention was all hers. He wagged his brows as he stepped closer, as if they were good friends and not people who had just met. With a crooked grin he asked, "So, did you say yes?" His voice was laced with happy curiosity.

She was getting the charm job. Deke Sutton was a golden boy with a twinkly smile. There was something boyish about him that was appealing, and he knew it. He used it. Yet, she saw something else. A sadness around him. Had she not spent the last decade being sad, she might not have recognized it since he covered it so well with cockiness and snark.

"Ah..." She glanced at Fort who was staring intently at her. Probably trying to melt her mind or will her into doing something. She knew from all those years back he was a control freak. "Have you decided if you are running for sheriff too, darling?" She used her best beauty pageant voice. She hoped he'd pick up on her real question. Was he in or was he out? She needed to know how to proceed.

Fort gave Deke a look that said he was sizing him up, then he turned his attention back to Cori. "I think I will run, short stuff," he said, using the nickname he'd called her all those years ago. Before everything imploded.

For a brief moment, Cori had to blink back the moisture gathering in her eyes. She gave into the impulse and threw her arms around his waist. "Yay! I'm so excited." Dang it, he smelled good. A little like camping and cows and a whole lot like she should move away quickly. She couldn't explain why, but she was glad to be staying and giving this ruse a go.

11

Her camera bag bumped into her as she held onto Fort's waist. Feeling ridiculous and like a little girl, she tried to covertly move away from the embrace, but he held on. He tucked his arm around her waist and pulled her close. Real close. Under his armpit close and, stupid as she was, she didn't mind.

One time in high school she'd seen him making out with some big-breasted cheerleader. The way he'd leaned into her, his leg between her knees, his arms around her, had been Cori's first up close and for real display of foreplay. Seeing couples make out on TV hadn't been the same after, less heated, and she'd spent many restless nights going over it all in her head. She'd always been curious about what it would feel like to have his affection and undivided attention. Sniffing his pit was likely the closest she'd get, and so be it. She'd check it off the list of things she'd been inquisitive about.

Touch alone was heady stuff, made her feel loopy as though she'd chugged a growler or something. Not that she ever had, but she'd seen people do it. When they'd stagger away, stupid grin on their face, she imagined it felt much like this moment.

For a second, she imagined how awesome it would be if Fort

was the sort of guy she could really get into. Or more specifically, she was the sort he liked, but Cori was too short and not blond enough for him. Plus, she had no boobs. Zilch. She let the fantasy deflate like a balloon.

Deke's sudden movement toward them, the thrusting of his hand toward Fort, broke Cori from her mental wanderings.

They were talking about the special election.

"Don't get it stuck in your head that I'm running because you want me to. I'm running because I'll make a darn good Sheriff and you won't. I'm running because—"

"You can't see me get something you want," Deke said and flashed a crooked grin. "I look forward to running against you."

The two shook hands, neither smiling, though there was a lift to Deke's mouth. It puzzled Cori he wasn't more upset to find out he was now running against someone versus unopposed.

She reached into her camera bag and pulled out the people seer—as she liked to call it— aimed it at Deke, and held down the shutter release. The camera hid nothing, and she couldn't wait to see these pictures.

"Smile, Deke," she said. "If any of these are good, I'll send them your way. Maybe you can use them in your campaign." She wagged her brows and kept her finger on the button.

"I would love that, Cori," he said and waved over someone from behind them.

A thick-around-the-middle man approached them. He was older, his hair combed over to one side to hide the undeniable thinning, and his eyes were narrowed slits. There was something smarmy about him. It was the same gut-churning warning she would get when her father's "colleagues" would come to the house and they'd lock themselves in his office for hours. Fort must have felt it, too, since he stiffened beside her.

"This here is my campaign manager," Deke said. "Fort, Cori, this is Conway Witty. He's going to spearhead my campaign. Con, this is Cori..." He gestured to her to fill in the blank.

"Walters."

"And Fort Besingame, my opponent." Deke made the introductions.

Cori leaned toward Deke. "Did you say Conway Twitty?" It took a lot not to laugh out loud.

It was then Cori saw the man had a wad of chew in his cheek. He produced a plastic water bottle from his back pocket and spat in it. "It's Witty. My folks were big country music fans."

Having a politically aspiring con man for a dad and a wannabe actress for a mom, her BS meter was finely tuned, and Mr. Witty was sounding it something fierce. "You don't say. They must have really loved him, and how fortuitous your family surname is Witty. Like it was meant to be." She squeezed Fort's side, hoping he'd do whatever lawman did and come away with some clues about Mr. Witty.

"And you're hanging out at the airport with your opponent because...?" Witty asked Deke.

"Oh, I happened to come upon them. Lame-oh Fort here was proposing."

"Actually, that's not true," Fort said. "I'd already asked Cori to marry me a while back. I'd just picked up her ring from the jewelers." Fort nudged her, and she sprang into action.

"Right!" She'd been clutching the ring and its cotton bed in her hand and now showed them to the men.

Deke whistled. "Look at that rock." He rubbed his chin. "I sure hope he was romantic, Cori, and glad he wasn't proposing here in this dirty, busy airport."

Cori gave him a smile. She wasn't about to create any more lies than she had to.

"Because when I proposed to my wife, it was perfect. Took me two weeks to plan out." Deke looked away, perhaps lost in a memory, then suddenly jerked his attention back to her. "It should be special and a memory you can hold on to forever. Congratulations," he said and clapped her on the back.

"Yours sounds very special. I'm sure it means just as much to her as it does you." Cori patted his arm. How wondrous would it be to have someone make a grand gesture for her? She couldn't even imagine it.

Fort took the ring from her and untied the ribbon. He picked up her left hand and slid on the heavy stone. Cori refused to look at it. Instead, she preferred to see things through her camera. After lifting it from the bag, she snapped a few shots of her hand and then went for her main target. Good old Conway.

"Say cheese, boys. I'll make sure to send you copies for posterity." She got in several shots before Conway threw his arm in front of his face.

"Lady, no one gave you permission to get our pictures," he bit out.

Cori dropped the camera back into the bag. Conway struck her as the sort who'd rip it from her hands and smash it on the ground. "Oh, well, technically I don't need your permission to take a photo, only if I intend to use it for monetary purposes, which I'm not."

Fort reached across her and slid the camera bag from her shoulder. He zipped it up and then set it over his shoulder so the bag was resting against his back. "She takes tons of photos, dumps most of them. Don't you short-stuff?"

Cori nodded.

"Now, if you'll excuse us, I need to get Cori home so Ma can gush over her." Fort steered her around the two men while shifting the bag so it wasn't in direct reach.

"It was nice meeting you both," Cori called over her shoulder as Fort hustled her back to the escalators.

They didn't say anything, just kept their large smiles plastered to their faces until they were at the bottom and Deke and Conway weren't right behind them. They stayed silent as they picked up her luggage and made their way toward the exit.

They were outside when Cori scanned the area before saying,

"Conway Witty, my aunt Fannie. That's no more his name than my dad was an honest politician." She smirked.

"Agreed," Fort said. "Something wasn't right about him."

Cori had her phone out, searching. When she found it she said, "Well, for starters, my guess is that he and Conway Twitty made their appearance around the same time. Our Mr. Witty is no spring chicken, and to say his parents were huge fans when the singer only had a few songs out...nah, I don't buy it."

"Me either. And I don't buy him being Deke's campaign manager. Those two are up to something."

"Yup. My bet is there's something going down in your town. Like my rhyme?" She grinned and pointed her finger at him. "That's the only thing that could bring Mr. Witty to the area. A guy like that lives for get-rich-quick opportunities. Like a rat on a greasy Cheetos, he'd be all over it. I should know. I've seen enough of it in my lifetime."

They were walking to the parking garage, Fort leading the way, when he stopped short. "Yeah," he said. "You would know." He looked at her as if he was working a puzzle. "Any chance you have connections that you could send old Conway's picture around and find out who he really is?"

Cori couldn't believe her ears. Did he think she knew all the crooks her dad associated with on a personal level? "Any chance you could run him through some federal system and find out who he is?" she said, trying to keep things civil. They were on good footing right now, not fighting.

Fort shook his head. "I intend to, but my gut says nothing will pop. What about asking your dad? Or any of the guys who worked with him?"

Cori stared up at him, incredulous. She crossed her arms and said, "What do you think I did for my father? Kept his books? Hooked him up with the other crooks he hung out with? I was a kid, Fort. Not his secretary or assistant. Besides, I don't speak with my dad." She rolled her eyes. "How about you? Can't you ask your dad if maybe he's seen him at any of his poker games? Maybe Conway also conned your dad. He does have a history of repeatedly being taken." She had chucked civility out the window. It was a low blow but, man so was what he'd said.

He narrowed his eyes, and like a superhero with powers to see the invisible, she watched him construct a wall between them.

"This isn't going to work," he said.

"Too late." She wagged the ring in his face. "You just told Deke you were running and we're getting married. How will you explain that to the town?"

Fort groaned and looked up at the ceiling of the parking garage.

"No man is an island, Fort. I'm here. I'm ready to help, and after meeting Nit-Witty, it looks like you could use someone." She looked at her shoe, knowing what she needed to say. Man, she wished her life had been totally different, and thus her experiences. She wished she had no knowledge about such things as cattle rustling or running cons. She wished she had a squeaky clean, blissfully naive life. Instead, she said softly, "Besides, why not get help from someone who's been down the road before lots of times? I have personal experience." She snapped her head up to look at him, or more like his chin, and poked her finger at his chest, and said firmly. "Meaning, I lived with a con man, that's my experience. Not that I ran the cons with him. Know the difference."

He leveled his gaze to her. "Maybe with our collective experiences, we can get to the bottom of this."

"There's more here than us trying to get you elected by pretending to like each other. Something's going down in Wolf Creek. You feel it, right?"

He nodded. "Yes, I do." He gave her a measured look from top to toe. "But we can't lose sight of why you're here. If we're going to pull this off, we're going to need some ground rules."

"Yes," she said, "good idea. I have one. No being a butthead. That one's for you. Now you give me one."

Fort briefly closed his eyes; she assumed he was counting cattle, or some other method to collect his cool. He'd done this before with her. Way back in the day when she would pester him about how he was running things on the ranch.

When he returned his attention to her, his eyes were still a steely gray. He probably needed to count higher.

"There's no denying we don't like each other much." He didn't wait for her to agree, but she nodded anyway. "So acting like we adore each other might be tricky, but I'm not big on public displays of affection so getting all cozy in front of people isn't something we need to do." He rubbed his chin. "Rule number one. Keep touching to a minimum. Arms around the waist, occasionally the shoulder. No hand holding."

She saw where he was going with this. "Rule number two. Kissing should be chaste. Only on the cheek. No lips and certainly no tongue." She used her finger to pretend like she was gagging herself. "Certainly no S.E.X."

"Yeah, that's a no-brainer." He mocked her by pretending to gag himself.

"Ha ha. You're very funny. That's new right? The sense of humor. You never had one of those before. I'll let you know if it's working out. And as for the PDA, who are you? I mean, in high school you were all about public displays." She looked off to the distance, pretending to search her memory. "I remember you and big-breasted Beth getting all up in each other's tonsils everyday by the lockers."

Fort smiled. "Ah, Beth. She was quite the woman." He made the outline of a woman with his hands, one that was very heavy on the top.

Cori snorted her disgust. Had someone made a wager with her that one day she'd be standing in a dark parking garage with Fort Lame-O, talking about sex and getting felt up, she'd have taken that fool's bet. Yet, here she was. Had she liked him or was a forward person, she'd consider indulging in hot, parking garage sex. As it was, she'd stick to pointing out his flaws.

"Oh, and then what about the time you and Carly McAdams were caught in the bed of your truck. Not really worried about PDA then, were you? Or what Beth might think since you were still dating her? There's also the time you and—"

"All right. Enough. That was then. This is now. I'm different." He stuffed his hands in his pockets.

"We all are," she said in a huff and grabbed her rolling case. She stalked off past him.

"But thanks for the stroll down memory lane," he called behind her. "Hey, short stuff, how do you know where I'm parked?"

"I don't," she called back and kept right on going. "But I bet I can find it. You probably have one of those stupid trailer hitches with the ball sack hanging from it." She could get a cab or something and just blow out of here. Let him deal with the consequences. This whole thing was his mess, anyway.

"Look who thinks they're funny now. Turn right at the next aisle. I'm the third truck from the end."

She did as he said and found his old beater Ford. *Second Chance Ranch* was painted on the side of the doors and the tailgate over the symbol of their brand. She rested against the back of the truck with arms crossed as he took his sweet time catching up with her.

"Rule number three," he said as he approached. "Do not get attached to anyone. You're here to do a job. Get in. Get out."

"Don't you worry, Fort Be-so-lame. That's unlikely. You and your little town probably aren't my type, anyway." Anger made people say stupid stuff, but she didn't care. Her feelings were hurt. It wasn't that she wanted Fort to kiss her or feel her up outside the sheriff's office or something. It was that he treated her like doing so was confounding, implausible, and disgusting.

"Rule number three for you. Don't get attached to this"—she gestured to herself and cocked her head to the side—"because I'm not staying."

Fort gave her a blank stare, then lifted his brows as if to ask if she was serious. "Don't worry. You aren't my type, short-stuff."

12

On the drive back to the ranch, Fort and Cori ironed out the specifics. Because he didn't want his election to be won on a lie, they decided she would leave him before then. It was unfortunate about the ring since that complicated matters. The plan was she would slip away quietly, and he would tell everyone she missed Texas too much. She thought she could leave her hometown, but found she couldn't. Funny enough, until this moment, Cori would have believed that to be true. Her love for Brewster and nostalgia for home had kept her there for a decade trying to repair everything broken. Now, watching the mountains roll by, the purple and orange sky was stunning. It captivated her like an enchantress, and as Fort spoke, she found herself agreeing to everything. She was more interested in letting the beauty of the landscape wash over her.

Maybe when she was done helping Fort, she could explore more of the West. Pack up her beat-up old car and point it away from Brewster. Picturing it made the heavy weight that had sat upon her chest lift slightly. Sabrina was right. She should have gotten away a long time ago.

Fort and Cori also worked out a schedule of when they'd be

seen together. Since conversation between them deteriorated quickly into bickering, in order to pull this off, they'd need to limit their time together. They would make sure they were seen in town often enough, but would feign an interest to be alone to avoid extended time together.

They arrived at the ranch moments before the sun slipped away for the day. Cori jumped out of the truck and took a hearty breath of air. Man, she loved the smell of a ranch. The mix of tooled leather, pine, spruce, and a tad manure. She closed her eyes and took in another deep inhalation. The scent was as familiar to her as her own. This was how she defined hearth and home.

"You have Angus?" She whiffed again and then opened her eyes. In Texas, his father had won and ran Hereford before he'd lost it all.

"Yeah, Ma's family has kept Angus for several generations."

"No dairy?" she asked while checking the landscape and structures before her. "Wow, its breathtaking here."

"I know. Makes ranching easy when you look at that every-day." He gestured to the foothills. "We don't have dairy. All beef. Some goats and, of course, chickens."

They stood in silence as the sun slipped away, leaving them engulfed in the dark blue of night. A light on the porch clicked on.

"Ma knows we're here. Come on, let's get this over with." He lifted her luggage from the truck bed then started toward the large one-story house.

"Wait," Cori said, catching up with him. "Does you mom know the deal, or are we...you know...going to lie to her?" Ugh, she hated the thought. From what she remembered of Fort's mom, she was kind and soft-spoken. "You have to fill me in on what I should know."

"Ma remarried. Boneta is her last name. I have a kid brother, Mathias." He grinned that stupid grin people do when they talk about their loved ones. "But you can still call her Ms. Saira. All the kids do."

Truthfully, Cori had often wished for Ms. Saira to be her mom instead of Barbie, who was obsessed with two things: to stop aging and for Cori to win Miss Junior Texas Pageant, the crème of the crop for pageants. Toward the end, *any pageant* would have done. Cori believed there was no way Barbie was ever pregnant and wondered if she was hatched from an egg, or the more likely scenario considering her parents, that they'd stolen her, and Cori had a real family out there missing her. Too bad she looked a lot like her father for the latter to have any merit.

"You sure you don't want to tell your mother?"

Fort paused. "Ma can't lie to save her life. Someone will ask her if she's excited or happy for us and she'll say yes, but her face will say it's a lie. I hate to say this, but I think we're better off keeping her in the dark."

Cori groaned.

"It's not my preference either. None of this is. I'd like to win the election based on my merit." He left her standing in the driveway.

She ran up to him again. "Maybe before I leave I can explain everything to her?"

"Maybe, if that's what you'd like. Let's take it day by day," he said, tromping up the stairs.

Cori stopped short, admiring the house. From the welcome mat to the boots lying on the side by the door, it made her think of family. She said softly, "I think I would feel better if speaking to her was part of the plan." She stood back and took it in.

It was a long rambler-style house, painted white with black trim. The front porch extended the length and offered seating for a perfect view to watch the sunset. Hanging baskets swung in the slight breeze with blue and yellow flowers spilling over their tops. She climbed the stairs and ran her hand over a rocking chair. She made it a high priority to watch the sun set tomorrow. Her family home was tall, made from gray brick, and not nearly as homey. It was still sitting empty, many of the windows broken.

Fort waited for her at the front door. "Off the kitchen we have a deck where you can watch the sunrise. If you're up early enough." He pushed open the door, and Cori followed him in.

Inside the house was even more inviting. Gingham, over-stuffed chairs with pillows made from ticking. Family pictures on tables and walls. Boots tossed by a closet and hats on a rack by the door. The lamp was on, giving the living room a yellow and inviting feel, as did the smell of sizzling beef and an assortment of spices and the singing that came from the kitchen.

"Ma," Fort called down the hall as he placed Cori's bags by the door.

"I thought you all were going to stay in the yard forever," Saira Boneta said.

Cori peeked over Fort's shoulder. His mother, looking exactly like she had all those years ago in Brewster except for some gray in her hair, was coming down the hallway wiping her hands on a kitchen towel.

"I hope you all are hungry. I put on the steaks."

"I'm starved," Cori said and came from around Fort.

Ms. Saira gasped. "Corinne Walters? Is that you?"

"Yes ma'am." Cori blushed, half from pleasure that his mom remembered her and half from embarrassment at what Ms. Saira would most likely say next. Everything always came back to her father's crimes.

Ms. Saira tossed the towel over her shoulder and wrapped Cori in her arms. "You sure have grown into a beautiful woman. Look at you. You're stunning." She stepped back, scanned Cori up and down, and then hugged her again.

Cori cheeks ignited with heat. She hadn't been expecting a compliment.

Ms. Saira continued, "Why ever did you keep this a secret,

Fort?" She had held Cori's face between her hands while she addressed her son.

Fort looked between the two of them before saying, "Her dad is why. Wasn't sure it was a good idea."

As if Cori wasn't already red-faced enough. Fort telling his mom he was embarrassed to be dating her was humiliating. Granted, they weren't really dating, but whatever. It implied she was desperate enough to be with a guy who didn't want to be seen with her.

"That's stupid," Ms. Saira said. "Plain and simple. Now let's go eat." She hustled them to the kitchen and went about finishing the meal.

She peppered Cori with questions about her mother, and after learning Cori still lived in Brewster, some about the small town and people as well. They ate, the conversation flowing. Cori and Fort sat across each other, and for as inviting as his mother was, a barrier sat bulky between Cori and Fort.

"You'll like Wolf Creek. I think the excessive heat of Texas has warped the minds of those in Brewster." Ms. Saira laughed. "I'm glad to see it hasn't done that to you." She squeezed Cori's hand, then tapped the ring on her finger. "Are we going to talk about this?"

Fort coughed on his after-dinner coffee. Cori stared down at the large stone. It was huge and sparkled from the kitchen light. Cori wasn't surprised at how well it fit. That was Sabrina; details were her forte.

"Um, well..." Cori searched for words, any that wouldn't be a lie.

"It's real simple, Ma. Cori and I want to be together. We're just not sure if it'll work, what with her still living in Brewster and me here. Then there's the history between our families. Why do you think we waited so long for her to come visit?"

His mother's eyes narrowed.

Cori figured she probably had a BS meter too, and wasn't

buying it. "After my dad went to jail, we had to sell off everything to pay back any of what he took. Restitution. That's been my job all these years." Fort sat forward suddenly, and she quickly cut her eyes to him, then back to his mother. "My dad hurt a lot of people and I, on some level, helped him do that. We haven't paid back near enough to right all the wrong. My past has made me slower to get involved. Fort's been patient and understanding, and though I want to be with him, I'm not in any rush."

"What do you mean you helped him?" Ms. Saira asked.

"I didn't know I was helping. It was before high school, before I could even conceive of a parent taking advantage of their own child. What I thought was a normal chat with dad while we went for ice cream was actually his way of fleecing me for information. Kids talk, and I would repeat what I heard at school, thinking maybe my dad, the mayor, could help." Cori gave a derisive laugh. "Little did I know."

Ms. Saira took Cori's hand in hers. "That's not your fault. You deserve a life, child. A happy one. You'll never be able to fix everything that he did. At some point, you'll need to walk away." She gave her hand a squeeze.

Cori blinked away the moisture gathering in her eyes. "Easier said than done."

Ms. Saira took her in her arms and gave Cori a tight hug, rubbing her back in comfort. "While you're here, you need to promise to relax and have fun."

"I can do that," Cori said as they pulled apart. She stifled a yawn.

"Jeepers, Fort. Get this girl to bed. She's exhausted." Ms. Saira brushed her thumb across Cori's cheek, wiping away a run-away tear before jumping up and shooing them from the kitchen. She hustled them down the hallway.

"I thought Cori could take the guest room," Fort said while picking up her luggage.

Mrs. Saira waived dismissively. "Nonsense. The two of you are engaged. You've been dating for years. I'm not naive and have no problem if she stays with you. It'll make life easier for you, Fort. No unnecessary sneaking in or out." She winked at them.

Cori made a strangled cry, but covered it with a cough.

"No need to be embarrassed, dear," Ms. Saira said while opening the front door for Fort. She nudged him out and then Cori. "Have a good night," she said and closed the door behind them.

Fort looked at the door, perplexed. "Ma isn't acting right."

"You think? Maybe she's on to us," Cori whispered.

Fort seemed to give her words some thought. "You might be right. Come on, we need to play this through." He turned and tromped across the yard to the barn, not bothering to see if Cori was following. His place, a small apartment, was accessed by walking through the barn and sat at the rear of the structure.

He kicked open the door, then hit the light switch before dropping her bags by the door. She moved to stand in the center of the room.

"You live in a tiny house," she said and did a three-sixty.

"What's a tiny house?" For him, he had everything he needed and didn't have to travel far to get it. A counter and sink with a two-burner hot plate made up his kitchen, and across from that was his bed. Ma had installed a curtain down the middle to separate the two spaces and give the bedroom privacy. Something he'd never needed. Until now, he supposed.

A love seat was in the middle of the room and faced the wall where a TV sat on an old iron sewing table turned entrainment stand. Because the floors were barn wood, thick woven carpets of various mismatching colors covered the area. For the first time, he saw the place through someone else's eyes. Yeah, it looked worn but homey, maybe a bit rustic. Possibly enough to put Cori off and keep her from getting attached. Ma fawning over her hadn't helped any.

"A tiny house is precisely this. They're all the rage. The only thing that's needed are wheels to tow it. And maybe minus the barn portion."

"Does the smell bother you?" He'd long gotten acclimated, but he was told it could be overpowering. Poop had a way of doing that.

Cori beamed. "Nope. I like it actually. Weird, I know."

Fort bit back a snarky retort. She was definitely a weirdo. "I'm not sure how you want to do this." When he pointed to the bed, her eyes widened. He shifted his attention to the couch. Tiny indeed. "I suppose I could sleep there." He'd have to hang his legs over the side, which would be uncomfortable as hell, but he didn't spend every night at home. Mentally going through his schedule, he figured he could reduce a few nights at home further by sleeping out on the prairie with the herd, and he could add sleeping at the station once or twice since he pulled late shifts. It wouldn't be odd to do so. OK, the couch might be doable.

"I'll take the couch."

"If you insist," Cori said and picked up her large suitcase.

As a kid, she'd been a pest worthy of an apocalypse. Always around and always had a snarky comment about what he was doing, whether it was breaking a horse, branding a cow, or whom he dated. Her dark hair had been long then, nearly to her backside, but she'd knot it up, tuck it under a hat, or braid it. The short style she now sported suited her. She'd always been a spitfire, but with her longer hair hadn't looked it. Now she did. She pushed up her glasses then swung the bag onto the bed.

"When did you start wearing glasses," he asked.

"When my vision started to decline."

"Is that why you stopped participating in beauty pageants?" He knew she'd hated them. They hadn't been her thing, but he couldn't resist a chance to tease her and pretend he thought vanity was why she quit.

She gave him a look that told him she thought he was stupid, stepped up to the curtain, and then jerked it across the room.

Dust went everywhere, and he took small pleasure in listening to her cough.

Fort wasn't sure what to do next. Fatigue helped him decide. He kicked off his boots, then hung his Stetson on the hook by the door. His hands were on the button of his jeans when she slid back the curtain with such force another dust cloud burst around them.

"Jeez, clean much?" She tossed him a pillow. There were two on his bed, and she managed to pick the one he liked best for herself. He caught the flat one and tossed it on the loveseat.

"I'm sorta busy, ya know. Working two jobs. Maybe you could make yourself useful and do it for me." He went back to his jeans, undid them, and let them drop to the floor.

She rolled her eyes. "Don't hold your breath." She tugged the curtain closed with less force this time.

Using an old Mexican blanket he got when he was in the Navy and his sleeping bag, Fort made a bed for the smallest person ever, which was not him.

Cori came from around the curtain and went into the bathroom. Her PJs were a T-shirt that reached her knees, and she looked like she could blow away in a strong wind. Or was in dire need of food. He thought back to how much she ate at dinner. A lot. He wondered what the last decade had been like for her. After using the restroom, he folded himself in half and tried to get comfortable on the loveseat. It was kinda hard with his knees higher than his ears and one of his shoulders hanging off the side.

"Dammit it all," he mumbled and tried to shift, but there was no way to go.

"Shut it," Cori called from the other side of the curtain.

"You shut it. You're not the one sleeping in a suitcase."

He never saw her coming. One minute he was trying to

balance and not fall of the couch and the next she was standing over him.

"Judas Priest," he said.

She wasn't wearing her glasses. Her hair stuck up in one spot, likely from the pillow. Holy hell, Cori Walters was a knockout. She wasn't the overdone type. She was classic, and when she smiled, like she was right now, she sucked the breath right from his lungs, the feeling equal to a punch to the solar plexus.

A giggle escaped her.

"You think it's funny?" His arm ached and was tingly from hanging off the side.

She shrugged one shoulder. "Kinda. You do look like you're stuffed in a suitcase." She hid her grin in her shoulder. When she turned back to him her smile was gone, though her lips twitched slightly. "I'm not heartless, Fort. I know we don't like each other, but I also know that working a ranch is hard, and if you don't get decent sleep, you'll be useless. I'm not going to be the cause of that. So"—she held up one finger—"I propose we share the bed. We have one thing going for us—the lack of physical attraction. So sharing shouldn't be a problem. We can build a barrier just as an extra precaution."

She wasn't attracted to him? So she said. Back in the day he'd have argued that. Why else had she kept coming around?

"Are you really thinking it over?" she asked incredulously. Then changed to a teasing tone. "Is it because maybe you find me irresistible?"

"Hell, no," he said. In one swift move, he vaulted over the couch and was on the bed in a flash, taking his pillow and blanket with him.

"Nope," she said. "We have to do this feet to head. I'm less grossed out by your feet than your face."

He sat up on his elbow and gave her a disbelieving look.

"Yes, I'm dead serious," she said and swirled her finger in the air, telling him he needed to rotate.

"You're a lunatic. But then I already knew that. Runs in the family." He flipped to the bottom of the bed and buried his face in the pillow.

"You say the town questions your commitment to them? Must see more of your father's flight tendencies in you than you counted on." She slipped onto the bed. It barely dipped. He flipped over, an angry retort ready to spill from his lips when he saw her tiny feet. He would not let this small bit of chick get under his skin.

He flat-out refused. But that didn't stop him from counting the days until she left.

13

Cori sat on the arm of the loveseat and swung her legs. Nerves were getting to her. She'd gotten up before him, switched off his alarm, and had done something she knew would piss him off. His chores.

All his life, Fort had been needed, the person his dad depended on most. It might be mean of her to show him that, for some things around the ranch, he was just another hand. Plus, he looked exhausted. Several times last night he'd sighed wearily in his sleep. She'd even accidentally kicked him in the chest and he hadn't so much as startled. His lips were dry and more than once last night she'd seen him rub his temple. A headache combined with dehydration could mean fatigue. So she threw him a bone.

Never mind that she had a good time mucking out the horse stalls and feeding the goats. When Mrs. Saira had gone in to start breakfast was when Cori woke Fort.

He had not been happy. Even now he scowled at her in the mirror. She responded by rolling her eyes.

Once Fort finished shaving, they would head into town and begin their dog and pony show. She regarded her clothes, hoping her dark wash jeans, brown cowboy boots, and light yellow floral peasant shirt said casual and cool. Not hot mess and bumbling idiot. He was engrossed in the manly task of scraping off facial hair and she took the opportunity to study his profile. Darn if he wasn't hunky. He'd filled out in all the right places. "You know they make electric razors," she said as she watched him slowly scrape a straight razor up his throat.

"Yeah, they don't work for me. My beard's too thick, and all I get are red bumps and stubble." He banged the razor in the sink and went back to shaving again.

"Okay, let me review one more time." She needed to fill the air with something. Watching him shave was...intimate, and she felt like a voyeur. He was not her fiancé, much less her friend, and sharing this intimacy was confusing. Even in the bed last night, his feet close to her face should have been gross but wasn't. Having someone nearby was comforting, and it hadn't escaped her notice that all their important parts lined up regardless of sleeping head to foot.

He glanced at her. "Is any part giving you trouble?"

She looked away, focusing on the preserved antlers of an eight-point buck that hung over the bathroom entry and tried to erase the image of him shaving from her brain. "Nope, want to make sure I have it down. We're sticking close to the truth. We've known each other since we were kids. After you got out of the Navy, you came back to Texas for an auction as part of ranch business and came through Brewster for old time's sake. That's where we ran into each other and reignited the old spark. The reason I haven't been up here is because of my job and family in Texas." She snorted with cynicism. "Because, you know, my job in the photo department at the supercenter was *so* important. Working for like, Mitzi, the like imbecile fresh from, like, high school"—she tossed her head, pretending to send hair over her shoulder—"was everything I ever aspired to."

"That's what you do. Work at the supercenter?" He was

patting his face dry with a towel. "I thought you were handling the restitution."

"That's my other job. The supercenter is what paid my bills. At least it did up until a few days ago when I lost my cool and told everyone within earshot to suck it." She picked at a hangnail, still embarrassed by her behavior.

Fort studied her, and she squirmed on the arm, looking everywhere but at him.

"I'd have liked to seen that."

Briefly, she ducked her head in shame. "No, you wouldn't have. It was awful. Remember Mrs. McAdams?"

He nodded. "I dated Carly once." He held up his index finger. "Just once because when I went to pick her up, Mrs. McAdams asked her if she wanted to live her life with a gambling fool. Like father like son, she'd said."

At least his gambling fool father had been a jovial, friendly guy who never wanted to hurt people. "And she still made out with you in your truck?"

Fort glanced at her before splashing after-shave on his face. "Carly was going through a defiant stage. She got what she wanted from me and moved on."

Even back then Cori had known Fort and Carly hadn't been well suited from the get-go. Carly was destined to become a shrew like her mom.

Cori pressed her lips together. "Yeah, well, she ran off with some guy from another town over. She never comes to visit. Can't blame her really. I suppose I had enough of Mrs. McAdams and lost my cool. When I told them all to suck it, I was really talking to her and the store manager who'd just promoted Mitzi to assistant manager of the department. Stupid girl can't even fix the processer."

Fort smiled, a slight uptick of the corner of his mouth. He finished in the bathroom and walked into the main room. He took his Stetson off the hook.

Cori sighed, her shoulders slumped in defeat. "I have no business telling Mrs. McAdams to suck it, no matter how awful she is. My dad nearly ruined her family. For generations they were ranchers and, now, because my dad swindled them out of a good portion of their herd and some land, the guys have gone to work on oil rigs and the ranching is part-time." She slid from the loveseat. "Let's keep all that out of the story, shall we?"

Fort's smile faded. "Okay. We can do that. So what are you going to say if they ask why you're here now?"

"I'm going to say I'm supporting your love for this town and dedication to the law. I'm here because I want to know what's so great about a town and its people that my man is making me choose between him and Wolf Creek or Brewster." She rolled her eyes. "I haven't been into Wolf Creek yet, but I already choose it."

"Come on," he said and held open the door. "Let's get this over with."

Cori said, "Morning" to all the animals in the barn as they made their way through. She missed working on a ranch and looked forward to doing as much as she could to help tomorrow.

The ride to town was quiet, but not uncomfortably so. In fact, today's conversation had been uncharacteristically civil. Cori smiled. They might pull this off after all.

Wolf Creek was adorable. As far as small towns went, it was tiny. Quaint, even, and she instantly loved it. Fort parked the truck a block from the diner, and as they walked toward it, he pointed out some of the businesses: the town paper, a market, a flower/trinket store, a women's boutique, and across the square was the sheriff's office and county jail. When they got to the diner, Cori froze.

"Come on," he said, hand on the door ready to open it.

Her stomach rolled with apprehension. "What if I mess this up for you?"

"You won't. Ready?"

She nodded her head but said, "No."

Fort's smil crooked up on one side. How long had it been since someone had shown her kindness? And Fort, whose life was forever changed by the actions of her father, was standing before her being gentle and understanding. She didn't deserve it.

She stepped back, and in a flash, he reached out and grabbed her hand, threading his fingers between hers. "I never figured you for a chicken," he said and tugged her toward him.

The connection to him through his palm was a lifeline, a channel of strength where she found courage. With her hand tucked firmly in his, she didn't feel alone. Instead, she was half of a whole. Yeah, a whole that was up to no good, relatively speaking. A whole that would split eventually, but for now she'd take it. She'd spent a lot of time living present day for the past. Now she was going to simply live today.

"Besides, I see Deke and Conway Witty in there. We need to figure out what he's up to."

Cori straightened. "No good. That's what he's up to. Oh, I have this for you." She took a zip drive from the front pocket of her jeans. "Here are his pictures. I don't know if you have some database or something you can run him through." While Fort was showering, she had downloaded the pictures. Man, the fury on Fort's face when he'd seen her coming down the escalator had been scary and hard to look at.

He squeezed her hand, tucked the drive in his short pocket, then opened the door and led her in.

"Morning all," he said and guided her to a booth at the back of the room.

The room suddenly grew quiet. Cori didn't have to look around to know she was being studied. She kept her eyes on Fort's back and a beauty pageant smile plaster to her face. She probably looked like an idiot; she certainly felt like one.

"Folks, that little bit of beauty Fort is dragging in behind him is his fiancée, Cori," Deke said. Cori saw him standing by the counter. He gave her a small wave.

A murmur rippled through the crowd, and Cori heard her name a few times. Fort reached the booth, then stepped aside and guided her in. Once she was seated, he slid in next to her. Reaching across her, he took one menu from behind the napkin holder and placed it open between them. He then sat back and put his arm across the back of the bench seat, his hand touching her shoulder.

An older lady, grandma material, dressed in a cowboy shirt with rhinestones, slid in the seat across from them. Cori liked her immediately. Possibly because her short bob had pink tips.

"Hello," she said and extended a leathery-looking hand.

Ranch hands, Cori thought. She glanced at her own pale one as she went to shake the woman's.

"I'm Bette Zykowski. You can call me Mrs. Z. My land butts up to The Second Chance Ranch."

"Cori Walters."

"You're adorable," Mrs. Z said, then switched her focus to Fort. "I'm glad you took my advice. Why you've kept this sweet creature from us I'll never know."

"That's my fault," Cori said and glanced at Fort. "He's been asking, but I've put it off. When he comes to see me, I don't have to share him with anyone, but here I have to share him with everyone." She gestured to the crowd. Some had gone back to eating while others were surreptitiously checking her out.

A waitress about Fort's age came up to the table. "Hey, you all ready to order?" She stared at Cori.

"Sally, this is my girlfriend, Cori. This is Sally."

"Hi," Cori said. "Nice to meet you." She didn't bother extending her hand. The waitress wouldn't take it. Cori knew contempt when she saw it, and Sally had it all over her face.

"What can I get you, Fort," Sally asked in a syrupy sweet voice.

"I'll have two eggs, hard, with two sides of bacon. Coffee, too, please."

"You want me to make sure the bacon is extra crispy like you like?" Sally asked while watching Cori.

"Sure. And get Cori the Lumberjack special."

Cori scanned the menu for the Lumberjack.

"Are you sure? She looks like the sort to eat a grapefruit and nothing else."

"Oh, she'll eat it." He turned to Cori. "If you eat it all, then it's free."

Cori found it on the menu and gulped. The special was a little bit of everything: eggs, pancakes, bacon, sausage, biscuits and gravy, and hash browns. "That looks like a lot of food," she said as her stomach growled.

He raised one brow and smiled.

"But I'll give it my best," she said.

"That's the spirit, short stuff," he said and squeezed her shoulder.

Sally stomped off in a huff.

"I hope she doesn't spit in my food," Cori mumbled.

"Oh, yes. There are going to be a handful of women in town who will be disappointed with your appearance. There was talk that he'd made you up, and I think a few of those women were hoping it was true."

Cori briefly caught Fort's eye before saying brightly, "Well, here I am. In the flesh."

"Does this mean you'll be throwing your hat in and running for sheriff?" Mrs. Z asked.

Fort nodded. "It does."

Mrs. Z hooted. "Hey Deke, looks like you'll have some competition," she yelled across the room.

Deke was still standing by the counter talking with Witty. He turned, smiled, and said, "I'm looking forward to it."

An older man, a rancher based on his weathered skin and large belt buckle, stood and shouted Fort's name.

"Yes, sir, Mr. Phillips?"

"I'd like to know why you want to be sheriff here and not some other town or her town?" Mr. Phillips asked, jabbing a finger in Cori's direction before putting his hands on his hips.

Cori was sitting close enough she was privy to Fort's initial reaction. He stiffened, and his mouth dropped open slightly as if searching for words. Cori was getting to know Fort, a different side to him, and one thing was certain, he loved Wolf Creek and the people in it. He was going to great lengths for them, and when he showed her around, he'd told her who ran what, filling in little details about the people. Trouble was the old Fort, the one from Brewster, wasn't letting anyone in to get to know him better.

Cori pushed herself up so she was crouched on the booth, looking over Fort's shoulder. "I'll tell you why Fort wants to be sheriff here and not somewhere else like Brewster. He's too shy to open up, especially to a large group of people at one time." She placed a hand on his shoulder. "But I'm not."

A few people in the room chuckled.

"Fort's always been about community. When we were kids, he'd work his dad's ranch, go to school, and then go about town helping others when times were down for them." She gave his shoulder a squeeze. "Remember Mrs. Bellows?" she asked him, then returned her attention to the crowd. "Mrs. Bellows lost her only child and husband in a car accident when we were younger kids. To stay afloat, she had her own garden and bees. Fort would go over there and help her till and plant and pull honeycomb. Every week he did something for her for years, until she passed away his senior year. He didn't do it for money. She didn't have much and paid him in banana bread. His favorite. He did it for community. Brewster is no longer a community of people united but divided. They've had some bad luck and hard times. It's no longer the home he knew as a kid. I barely recognize it myself. But Wolf Creek, wow, what an amazing town. Fort gave me a tour earlier. I know that the Jacobson's who run the drugstore are expecting twins and that Mrs. Jacobson loves to ride horses. Competes even, but her doctor has restricted her from riding. Which, understandably, is making her a little sad."

"And mean. Yesterday she called me an old coot and told me to not come back until after the twins were born," Mr. Phillips said.

"Well, you are an old coot," Mrs. Z replied.

The crowd laughed.

"Did you know Fort's teamed up with her husband and found her some volunteer work for the Sheriff's Department to keep her busy and distracted?" Cori continued.

Fort ducked his head, shook it briefly, and said, "Well, we're hunting buddies and I'm just hoping we'll be able to hunt again one day."

More laughter.

"There's a charm to this town that's palpable. I felt it the moment I came here. You all have managed to preserve a quality of life that's hard to find anywhere else. And Fort here, a man who still shaves the old school way"—she made like she was using a brush to lather cream on her face and then stretched her head back, pretending to shave her neck with a straight razor —"embodies that way of life. Will do anything to protect it, to keep this community intact. This is his home, where his soul comes alive. Even I can see it on his face. There was a visible change in him yesterday once we got away from the airport and closer to Wolf Creek. That's why he's running for sheriff, because he believes in this town, the people, the way of life, and it's his home. Of course, he'd never say all this. He's more an actions-speak-louder-than-words kinda guy." She hung her hand off his shoulder hoping her ring would catch some of the diner's light and the patron's attention.

She looked around the room, used her best pageant smile while trying to make eye contact with as many people as she could. She wanted this for Fort. Maybe in part to make up for what her dad had done, but also because he would be really good at it. She then slid back into her seat and tucked her trembling hands beneath her legs.

"Well said, dear," Mrs. Z said.

The crowd had gone back to chatting, occasionally sending furtive looks their way. Fort was quiet, so much so that it made her nervous.

When their meal came, Sally fairly tossed the dishes at Cori. While they ate, several of the locals came and made their introductions. She thought she'd be too nervous to eat, but the food was good, comforting, and she was starving. She didn't require encouragement to finish the meal; it was gone in a flash.

"Hey, Sally. Looks like my girl is getting her meal for free," Fort yelled.

The crowd laughed. "Leave her to us, Deputy, we'll fatten her right up," someone called.

"If the election were a food-eating contest, Fort's girl would win," Deke said.

Chuckles rang through the room, and Cori felt her cheeks go hot.

"Don't be embarrassed, girl," Mrs. Z said. "You've just gone from being an outsider they'll hold at arms' distance to someone they want to know."

Well, that would be a new experience for her. She wasn't sure how to handle it.

"I have to get to work," Fort said and slid his keys along the table to Cori. "Here's the truck keys. You think you can find the way back to the ranch?"

"Sure. It's a straight shot." She picked up his simple keys, one round silver ring and three keys.

"Don't forget to come back and get me at eleven."

The conversation was so civil and easy she forgot she hated him. Okay, disliked him a lot. She made a mock grimace. "Oh, I can't make any promises."

Fort gave her a stern look.

She waved dismissively. "Go try and scare someone else."

He tossed some dollars on the table, tipped his hat to Mrs. Z, and was gone.

Mrs. Z was smiling at her. "I've been around. Seen lots of people married who liked each other, loved each other, and some who couldn't stand each other. I see something in you two. Something amazing if you both take the leap."

Cori looked at the empty plates before her and searched for words.

"You don't need to say anything. Just think about it. It's not often something real is within your reach." She scooted out of the booth and was off with a clack of her heels.

In that precise moment, Cori hated who she was and what she and Fort were doing. Doing people wrong was *wrong,* regardless of the act. She didn't want Fort to be a pariah in the town he'd declared his home like she was. She could guess what "home" meant to him. It was having a land to build something permanent, a town where he fit in. Home was community. She watched him struggle back in Texas, working hard to turn the small herd and land his dad had won into a real ranch, a place they could grow roots. If she were to guess, if this plan went wrong here, Fort would personalize it as another failure and she would have played a role in it. Cori took her camera from her bag and removed the lens cap. After turning it toward herself, she snapped a few selfies. She wanted to remember what she looked like the moment she moved forward with her plan to con a town.

After she set the camera on the table and angled it to capture most of the diner, she pressed the shutter several times, hoping to catch candid photos of the townsfolk and get insight on the town vibe. The Smithsonian and Nikon photo contests were coming up, and Cori really hoped to have something entered. If she could win one of those, or even place, the accolades alone would give her the confidence to pursue photography. It would be the sign from the universe telling her what to do with her life, that photography was her path, her purpose.

Fort's money lay on the table, including an ample tip, so she made her way outside, stopping to meet and shake hands with many of the locals. Cori walked the square of the town, all four blocks, window shopping along the way. Occasionally, folks would wave at her from the other side. Here only hours, and she was more welcome than she had been in years in her hometown.

14

Cori wandered to the square center where a giant gazebo sat. A sidewalk with offshoots in the four cardinal directions circled the large building. Cori found an empty bench that faced the Sheriff's Office. For being so small, the town was bustling. She lifted her camera and took several shots. Mostly of the landscape or the wisp of a skirt from a child running behind a tree. A couple of ranchers rode horses into town and tied them up to a post outside the diner. She laughed as she captured the image. It was charm and camaraderie. Wolf Creek was community.

As she scrolled through the digital images, deleting the blurry ones, a tall woman about the same age as Cori sat down beside her. She leaned over and looked at the screen. "Wow, that's really good." It was a shot of a horse fanning itself with its tail and the rancher beside it, his back large and broad, doing the same with his hat.

Cori turned off the camera and turned to the woman. Not only was she tall to Cori's short but light to Cori's dark. She had caramel-colored hair and friendly-looking, light hazel eyes.

She extended a hand. "Hi, I'm Megan, but everyone calls me Cricket."

"I'm Cori."

"Oh, I know. You're all everyone can talk about."

Cori experienced a flash of panic.

Cricket rushed her next words. "Only because they are excited to meet you. They find you fascinating. The girl who captured Fort's heart."

Cori looked away embarrassed and a little sad that Fort was what made her fascinating. She understood, she supposed. He'd fascinated her as a kid, but just once she'd like to be the source of interest because of who *she* was, not for who she was pretending to date. "Please spread the word, there is nothing interesting about me."

"May I?" Cricket took the camera from Cori. She scrolled through the images on the screen. "I'd say these are pretty amazing. I find that interesting. You're a natural behind the camera."

"Being behind it is easy," Cori said.

Cricket chuckled. "How long did you do the pageant circuit?"

Her question caught Cori completely off guard. Her mouth dropped open with no words but "uh" escaping. How did Cricket know? Had she searched Cori's name on the web and knew her history? Was she about to pepper her with questions about her dad? If Cricket knew, then others would, too. That's how small towns work.

Cricket's smile was soft, kind. Did she pity Cori?

"I know a pageant smile anywhere. I did them all through my teens and finally convinced my mom to let me quit when I hit college. My sister did them through college."

Cori slowly let go of the breath she was holding, somewhat relieved, not that she wasn't waiting for the next boom to come.

"I did them until I hit thirteen. I flat refused to do them after that."

Cricket nodded with understanding. "Broke my mom's heart

when I stopped. Or would have if I hadn't jumped into the family business." She gestured to the building across the street that housed the local newspaper.

Cori looked between the building and Cricket. "The family business is a newspaper?"

"Yep, my great -grandfather on my father's side started it. My dad had no interest in continuing the family business and became a rancher. He hired my mom who was a journalist in Salt Lake City to come and run the paper. She took it from a one-town once-a-week rag to the only paper for the county. We cover our town, Bison's Prairie, and Elk's Pass, which is on this side of us." She gestured with her thumb to the east. "We print twice a week. Wednesdays and Sundays. It helped that my dad is a rancher since most of our stories are for the ranchers and about the ranchers. Now I run it."

"That's supercool," Cori said. She'd have liked to take over the family business, back when she thought that was ranching.

"And I'm looking for a photographer. Currently, it's me, and I'm not that good. Plus, I can't be two places at once. You're excellent. I can't pay you a lot, but I can give you a byline."

"Um..." Cori didn't know what to do. It was wrong to take a job knowing she was leaving, but this was an opportunity for experience she couldn't afford to ignore.

Cricket nudged her. "Come on, say yes. You can cover the election and do fun things like stakeout Mr. Phillips' land. He's had some cows go missing and swears it's the work of aliens."

"Aliens? You don't say." Cori lifted her camera to her eye. She'd like to get a picture of that. Not that she believed in aliens, but she wasn't about to rule anything out. Not if it could get her the winning slot in the photography contest.

"Yeah, there's no sign of the missing cows. No footprints. No carcass. Nothing."

"No crop circles? How about in the house? Cups of water

everywhere? TV signal staticky?" Cori asked, laughing at her M. Knight Shyamalan reference.

Cricket chuckled. "Yeah, none of that. That I know of. Boy, this would be fun around Halloween."

"Timing is everything," Cori agreed.

"So, how about it? I'm a family-friendly place. Once you and Fort are married, and if you decide to have babies all the time, I can work around that. I really could use the help."

Cori was nodding before she knew she'd decided. Her heart was ahead of her brain. "Yeah, okay. I'll give it a shot."

"Great! Now, get me some shots of the candidates so I can put together a spread." Cricket jumped from the bench. "Thank you so much, Cori. You're a lifesaver."

Wow. When had she ever heard that? Um, never.

15

Still in uniform, Fort exited the Sheriff's office with an hour left to the day. It had been a long shift. Mainly because he expected more to happen. What precisely, he wasn't sure, but something more than a complaint about some teens speeding off Thigpen Road. He'd driven out to the Williams' ranch, the complainers, dealt with the bored teens, and left the ranch with a loaf of fresh-from-the-oven banana bread courtesy of Mrs. Williams, who told him if she had known it was his favorite, she'd have been making him some all along.

The bread was the one highlight.

Accessing the limited database the department used had produced zero hits on the name Conway Witty or his image. If he wanted to dig into a larger database, he'd need to send the image to a bigger city like Cody and wait the seven to ten business days for the results. Only way to expedite it would be if Witty did something to get arrested.

Fort could only hope.

The streets were quiet, essentially rolled up for the night. Cori had backed his truck into the spot and was lying in the bed, her camera pressed to her face and focused at the sky. He'd spent part of the day considering her. She'd been prickly as a kid, and he still saw that in her now. But what had been annoying then was easily seen as a protective mechanism now. Far as he could tell, she'd been alone most of her life, being someone else her parent's preferred, whether it was the pageant girl for her mom or unknowing narc for her dad.

"Is there a market for inky photos?" He placed the bread next to her feet.

"I'm hoping to catch a UFO." She lifted her head. "Do I smell banana bread?"

Fort pushed what was left of the foil-wrapped loaf toward her. "Mrs. Williams made it for me."

"Yum," she said and set her camera aside so she could get at the bread.

"No one here has ever made me bread except Ma. They haven't made me anything." He sat on the edge of the tailgate and leaned against the side of the truck.

"Did anyone know you liked banana bread?" She ripped off a chunk and crammed it in her mouth. "Om, my, fiss is oh ood." She pulled off another section.

"I never told anyone, if that's what you mean. It just never came up."

She raised a finger to give her a moment and then finally said, "You're a great listener. Always have been. Probably what makes you a great deputy. But you're a crappy sharer."

"I shared my bread."

She kicked the side of his leg that was closest to her. "You know what I mean. It's easier to take a punch in the face than get you to talk."

He smirked, then reached for the bread. She pushed it to him.

"I don't have anything to say," he mumbled.

Cori snorted. "You can't see me right now, but I just rolled my eyes," she said. "Everyone has something to say. Everyone wants to be heard."

Fort grunted.

"It's true. If an animal comes down from the mountains and attacks livestock, he's telling us something. Maybe he's sick. Maybe it's a drought. What if he's been kicked out from his pack? When a coyote howls, he's sending a message. And, if by chance, you really do have aliens taking cattle—and I really hope you do and I get the photo of it—then the aliens are saying something, too." She giggled and reached for the bread, but Fort caught her hand, wrapping his around hers.

And just like earlier today, heat shot up his arm. It had been impulsive to take Cori's hand this morning, but she looked so scared, desperate for a friend, and he wanted to make that go away. He meant to grab her elbow or wrist but somehow his hand had slid into hers and he didn't second-guess it.

"What do you mean about cattle missing?"

"Cricket said a rancher wants her to run a story about how aliens are taking his cattle." She tugged her hand free.

"Hang on, I have a lot of questions here. First, how do you know Cricket?"

"I met her earlier. Funny story that. Looks like I'm the new photographer for the Critten County Rambler. Look how excited I am by that." She pointed to her face-splitting smile. It was so bright he didn't need the street lamps to see it.

"No. That's breaking a rule," he said with bite, hoping she could infer how adamant he was about her taking the job.

"Ha!" She poked him with her boot. "You broke a rule earlier when you took my hand. That, my friend, was an out and out disregard for the rules. The rules, I'd like to remind you, that were your idea."

"You looked sad," he said.

Cori sat up. "Oh, I can't believe you just said that. Are you telling me that you took my hand out of pity? A pity hand hold?" She tossed her hands in the air. "That's a low even for me. Most people get a pity screw, not me. I get my hand held." She slid out of the truck, snatching the bread as she went.

He lurched forward and grabbed her about the waist, pulling her back into the truck bed and onto his lap, the bread landing beside them. An explosion of sexual desire burst from his crotch like a million-watt Q-beam and lit him up. Like he'd been doing most of the day, he chalked it up to having not gotten laid in a long time. There was no chance Cori's tiny, bony ass was making him want to toss her onto her back and delve deep inside her. This talk about a pity screw didn't help. Now that image was burned into his brain.

"Sit still," he ground out and grabbed her hips.

"Why, so you can give me some more pity?" She wiggled again.

Yeah, if that's what she wanted to call it. He'd pity her all night long and some in the morning, too.

"I did not grab your hand from pity," he said and loosened his grip when she paused her wiggling. "It was an act of...." He thought about the word he was about to use. About how it might be true, but not entirely...yet.

"It was an act of pity!" She struggled to get away from him, her butt rubbing against him again.

He groaned with need and tossed her beside him. "I was going to say friendship."

She was scurrying to get away but suddenly went still. She looked at him over her shoulder. "But you didn't."

"I'm not sure I'm ready to call us friends, yet. But we're getting there. I just have to accept that you're going to be the most annoying friend I'll ever have." He smiled and hoped she could see it.

"Not there yet, huh?" She moved back to sit next to him.

"No, but close." He elbowed her.

"Ow!" Cori said, and then laughed as she pretended to fall over from the force of the nudge. "Friends don't hurt friends."

"I said almost friends." He picked up the bread and opened the foil. After breaking off a chunk, he offered her more.

"But we're good. We can acknowledge you broke rule number one, and we've survived, so me breaking rule number two is no biggie."

"I don't know about this. What—"

"Think of it this way. It's not so much as breaking a rule, but an opportunity to help you figure out what Deke and Witty are up to. Working for the paper, I can get inside information. I can be around Witty without suspicion."

"Like the aliens," he said.

"Well, sure. That's not a true story, though. There are no aliens, much to my sadness. I could use the big break." She finished off the bread and, after taking the foil from his hand, balled it up.

"There aren't aliens, but there seems to be cattle missing more each day. Ma called today to tell me they found three more head missing." He crossed his arms over his chest. "Mrs. Z said she's missing one as well. Did Cricket happen to mention who thinks aliens have visited?"

"Yes—"

"Phillips, right? I don't know why I asked." He slid from the tailgate. "Come on," he said, pulling her by the ankles to the edge. "Let's take a ride."

Inside the truck he tucked his gun and holster under his seat.

While buckling her seatbelt, Cori said, "I hope we didn't jinx anything with us getting along here a moment ago and you almost being my friend."

"It doesn't mean you can finish off my bread like you just did," he teased.

Cori, ever sensitive to being the reason anyone might feel slighted, sat ramrod straight. "You only have that bread because of me and what I said at the diner. Not so much as a thanks from you. Not that I'm surprised, considering how stubborn you are and your natural tendencies to be an ass." She turned her back to him.

Fort chuckled. "And now we're back to being snarky."

She clapped her hands together in pleasure and laughed. "We are good at snark. So, where are we going? Do we have a second mystery?"

He settled back in the seat before peeling out of the parking lot. "If I have a natural tendency to be an ass, you have one to be a constant pest."

"I'll accept that," she said, "because you said it so nicely. Are we trying to solve the mystery of the missing cows?"

He grunted his agreement and then asked, "What's the first mystery?"

"The mystery of the man with a bogus name. Conway Witty. It's like he's asking to be caught. With the cows, how do you know it's not nature or an animal? The earth is pretty dry. I'm guessing it's a problem for not just the ranchers."

"No carcasses."

"Hmm. Interesting." She tapped her index finger to her lips.

They rode in silence until Fort pulled onto a dirt road and parked a mile down. "We're going to walk from here. In the glove box is a flashlight." He cut the engine, fumbled under his seat for his sidearm, and then jumped out of the truck before she had the large Maglite in hand. Outside, he hopped onto the truck bed and opened the toolbox, using only the glow of the truck's interior light as his guide.

"You still know how to shoot?" he asked, jumping down.

"Do dogs like to hump human legs?"

"Grab the shotgun from the truck. There are shells under the passenger seat. Ease the door closed when you're done."

She did as he asked, hanging the shotgun from her shoulder by its strap, extra shells in her pants pocket. "Crap on a cracker, its dark out here. I can't even see you." When Fort touched her shoulder from behind, she jumped but didn't squeal.

"Mrs. Z complained of some kids near the tracks the other day and also mentioned her missing cows. When I looked, I didn't see anything out of the ordinary, but the more I think about it, I didn't see the typical either."

"That being?" She turned and leaned toward him.

"You can turn on your flashlight. Keep the beam close, though."

She did as he said, and when the beam broke between them, there was little else in the space, she was that close. She stepped back.

"The typical for teens might be some beer or booze bottles and a fire. Thank God whoever was out there had the good sense to not start a fire, but there was no sign of a party. Just cigarette butts." He slipped on a headlamp then flicked on the red beam. "What's odd is there aren't any footprints or tire tracks in the area where these animals go missing. Our animals are tagged with a GPS system. The ones that have gone missing still show like they're with the herd. It's bizarre."

Cori held the light beneath her chin. "It's not aliens. It's a ghost. You're being haunted by cattle."

"Come on, smart ass, we're going to walk out there and see if we can stumble upon anything." He set the GPS locator on his phone and hers, then showed it to Cori in case they got separated or lost.

With the light still under her chin, she narrowed her eyes. "You have your gun on you, right?"

"Of course." He flashed the light on his under-the-shoulder holster.

"Then take the lead."

They walked in silence. A couple of times he heard her stumble and catch herself by putting her hand on his back. Every time she did, he experienced a zinger of a shock that spread across his back and straight to his dick.

He definitely needed more time with women if Shorty, The

Annoying, was charging him up. Which didn't make sense. She'd been correct in saying she wasn't his type. For starters, he liked a little meat on his women. Shorty was a stick. A cute twig. He found her energy contagious, as was her smile.

They walked along the railroad tracks for over a mile, and Fort's gut told him they weren't going to find anything tonight. That's when the idea struck him.

He stopped short and Cori ran smack into his back.

"Shush," he whispered and hunched down.

She squatted behind him, her breath on his ear. "What is it?" she whispered.

"Do you see that light? Way off in the distance there?" He pointed down the line of the tracks.

She gripped his shoulder. "Is it a train?"

"Can't be. No train comes through this late." It was a train. A hauler that the town called the midnight crawler due to its slow pace. Often it would stop for a spell. Fort reckoned that's what it was doing now, it's light a hazy glow far away.

"It doesn't look like a fire. What do you think it is?"

He could feel her small breasts pressed into his back, and he briefly lost his train of thought. "I don't know what it is. I mean, it can't be what I think it is. That's impossible."

She stood up. "Maybe we should go?" She tugged at the back of his shirt.

"Come on, you're not scared, are you? It's not like there is such a thing as a cow ghost anyway."

Cori squeaked. "You think it's a ghost?"

"Do you believe in ghosts?" He faced her and nearly laughed at her large owl look.

"Don't be silly. It could be anything like....okay, I think it could be anything, including aliens or a ghost or an alien ghost even. I don't rule anything out. Let's go back." She stepped away and pulled his upper arm, coaxing him to follow.

He looked over his shoulder, then glanced at his watch.

Almost one. The Crawler might start moving soon. "Okay, we'll head back. I don't want you to be scared."

"The hell, you say. I'm not scared. I'm terrified." She turned and started hoofing it down the path they'd come, her light swinging quickly.

"Wait up," he said. "Let's be reasonable. There has to be a perfectly good explanation."

"Yeah, like a train, but you said there aren't any trains." She was practically running, her words coming in a pant.

Fort looked over his shoulder and saw the light moving toward them, albeit slowly. "Holy shit." He feigned panic.

"What?" she screeched.

"It's moving!" He almost laughed and gave away the game.

She stopped short and spun around. "Sweet Jesus," she cried. She grabbed his shirt and screamed, "Run!"

A second later, she was off like a lightning bolt, her light swinging madly around her, mumbling what sounded like a prayer as she ran. She was like a maniac, a confused rabbit darting between the tracks and the grass on the side. She was going to get hurt.

"Cori, wait! I'm joking," he called. When he glanced over his shoulder, he saw the train was moving faster than he thought. The night was hazy, which made the train light look eerier than normal. No wonder she'd been spooked. He dashed off behind her, surprised at how fast and far those short sticks of legs took her.

"Turn here," he cried as she came to the path for the truck.

She made the sharp left turn without losing speed.

Impressive.

He caught up with her right as they broke into the clearing where he'd parked the truck. Right as the train came roaring closer and became obvious what the light was.

Cori spun on him as fast as she'd taken off, her chest heaving from exertion. "You asshole," she cried, lunging at him. "How could you do that to me?"

He did a quick sidestep. "I tried to tell you, but you were running so fast you couldn't hear me with all that wind whipping past your head." He cracked, and a laugh escaped him. "Damn, girl, you can run." He smothered another laugh and turned his back to her so she couldn't see. His shoulders shook.

"You think this is funny?" she yelled.

Next thing he knew, she was on his back like a monkey, legs wrapped around his waist, arm around his neck in a mock choke-hold. "I should clock you with this flashlight." She wiggled on his back.

"What are you doing?" He reached back, trying to swipe her off.

"I'm trying to wrestle you to the ground."

He dropped to his knees and did a quick jerk to the side, effectively tossing her to the ground. "No such luck, short stuff."

How she retained her grip on the flashlight was anyone's guess, but she shone it directly in his eyes, blinding him. "Apologize."

"No way, it was kinda funny until I thought you might go off the path and get lost." He blocked the light, but she angled it, keeping the beam in his eyes.

"Come on with that," he said, lunging for the light.

He fell on top of her and trapped her hand with his, wrestling the light from her grip and tossing it aside when he got it. "See how it feels!" He shone his headlamp on her.

Her short hair was wispy around her face, her cheeks pink from her run, her skin dewy, her glasses askew, and he was entranced. When had Cori Walters become such a beauty? She might be the size of a large child, but she was most certainly not one. His hand found her breast and cupped it. What was the saying, "More than a handful was a waste"? There was nothing wasteful on Cori. Without further thought or hesitation he kissed her.

It started out a soft, nudging sort of kiss that asked the question, would she invite him in?

Her lips were soft, just like she was. And "welcome" was her answer.

He saw her acceptance as a gift, a chance to know her on a level he never considered. She smelled like vanilla, and when he dipped his tongue into her mouth, she tasted like bananas. He wanted more. One kiss led to another, and all Fort knew was that he wanted to learn more about her, preferably with their clothes off.

She slid her legs up, one on each side of him so that he fit snugly between her. Much like last night, even at odd ends, they lined up.

The train roared by, rumbling the ground, and they matched the tempo. Gentle, exploring kisses became hungry ones. She ripped his headlamp off, letting it fall to the side. His hands never leaving her, he ran them up her body and wrapped his arms around her. She trapped him with her legs, her hands in his hair. Fort flipped them over so he was lying on the cold, damp ground and she was straddling him. She sat back to look down at him. He slid her glasses from her face and dropped them over his head.

"We shouldn't do this. What's wrong with us?" Where her hands rested on his chest, heat ran into his body. He moved his hands up her legs.

"I'm only doing it because I'm still hungry and you taste like the banana bread you finished off."

"If it wasn't for that..." She gasped when he spread his hands around her waist, his thumbs stroking her ribs.

"I'd find this completely disgusting," he said, moving his hands farther up.

"Totally gross," she murmured. When he grazed her breast, her head fell back, a deep sigh of pleasure escaping her. He desperately wanted to hear it again. He cupped her, exploring her nipples with his thumbs. This time she moaned, grinding her pelvis into him.

"Christ," he said and sat up. He took her chin in one hand and brought his mouth down hard against hers.

"This doesn't mean I like you," she said when they separated for air.

"I kinda think it does," he replied.

"Then it means you like me, too," she responded.

He leaned away from her, far enough that he felt the magic bubble around them pop. Not that he wouldn't lay her on the ground right now and do everything in his power to make her howl like the coyotes. He got stiff imagining it, and he was pretty hard already. Stiffer was inconceivable. Yet here he was, practically bursting from his pants, his hands cupping her tight ass, and her so willing. And he was about to jack it up like the idiot he was. "Maybe this is a moment. A mood. I dare any two people with a modicum of attraction to come out here and not get swept away."

Truth was, whatever this was couldn't happen again. The waters with Cori were too muddy to swim in. When the time came to settle down, it wouldn't be with someone like Cori.

She pushed away, sliding off his lap and to the ground with a thump. "You're right. I could have come out here with Deke, and this might have happened. I think, for us, it's because we've been stuck together for the past twenty-four hours." She rose, picked up her flashlight and the shotgun, and then went to the truck. Fort was still sitting on the ground when her door slammed.

16

Fort woke the next morning disoriented and frustrated. He'd had indecent dreams most of the night. Many of them had Cori underneath him writhing in pleasure. The others were with him under her. She hadn't talked to him since leaving the tracks last night. He wondered how today would go.

He rubbed a hand over his face and tried to get his shit together. There were jobs to be done around the ranch that required his lazy ass to be out of bed. Just like him, the animals were hungry. The sun was just beginning to break, bringing with it a dusty yellow light that painted a swath of color across his bed. Rolling softly onto his back, he glanced toward Cori, wondering if she was awake. He expected to find her dead to the world, but she was blinking back at him.

He dropped his head back onto the pillow. "You don't have to get up," he said to her foot, extending an olive branch.

She said nothing, so he searched for the right thing to say. He knew he'd hurt her feelings yesterday, but it had needed to be done. She was hired for a job, but last night they'd forgotten that. Let things get carried away.

"Cori—"

"I think you're right about the rules. We were smart to make them. We should stick by them."

"So no more of what happened yesterday," he said. They needed to stay focused.

"Right. We call everything a wash and start over."

He nodded and stared at her tiny feet. She carried so much on her shoulders. It was nice to see her laugh, and here he was an ass for trying to make it out like something it wasn't.

"Cori, calling it a wash is not the same as calling it a mistake. You see that, don't you? I don't think anything that happened last night should be a regret."

She sighed so heavily the bed moved. "But I'm so good at regret."

"Did you really have to sell everything when your dad went to prison?" he asked her, or more like her foot since that was closest. "What did you do when you all lost the ranch?"

"It would seem that good old Pops made sure to provide for Babs but not for the kid, so I worked at the supercenter and picked up odd jobs when I could. The thing for me was to get the most money possible. His lawyer told me if I let the government do it, they'd sell it for pennies. Since the money was going back to the city, I thought it only fair to do my best."

When everything had gone to shit with his dad, Fort was free and clear to walk away and never look back. Something he'd done without hesitation. So had his dad, and Fort had no idea where he was. Leaving had been easy. A clean slate ahead of him had been refreshing. In the Navy, he hadn't been known as Gambler Karl's kid. Even in Wolf Creek where people knew about his dad somewhat, it was all-superficial, and he liked it that way. Liked that part being in the past.

Cori had experienced the exact opposite. "So you took this deal with Sabrina because...?"

"The money. I'm going to get a fresh start. A do-over. Also, I came to get pictures." She said it so wistfully he wanted her dream, too.

"Are you going to open up your own studio or something?"

Cori sat up on her elbows, and he did the same.

"One day. But for now, I'd like to enter a national competition and maybe win some money. I'd like validation that I'm good enough. Might even finish my degree."

He looked at her legs, stretched out beside him and thought about what it must be like to be here. To go through what she did. Now he knew why she was so skinny, because she gave to everyone first. Probably even her money for food. Damn that Charlie Walters. He'd loathed the man something fierce when his dad had lost the ranch, but now, now he was disgusted by him, too.

"I'm sorry, Cori. Your parents suck." It was a pathetic attempt to say the right thing, but did such words exist in this situation? Doubtful.

She laughed and fell back onto the bed. "Boy, do they ever." She looked back at him. "But thanks for noticing. How about we stop talking before we ruin the moment with another fight or something?" Without waiting for him to reply, she rolled off the bed and padded to the bathroom.

He was working again tonight so having Cori's help would go a long way. If he worked alone, there would be no way he'd get his share of the chores done before leaving for town, which meant he was making more work for Ma and Paul.

When she stepped out of the bathroom in bare feet, towel drying her wet hair, face fresh from makeup, dressed in jeans and a loose top, he forgot what he wanted to ask her.

"Take a picture, Be-so lame, it might last longer," she said.

He picked up her camera and did just that.

"Hey," she called, lunging for the camera. "No one touches the camera!" She laughed as he held it over his head, far out of her reach.

"I have a favor to ask," he said.

"If I say no, will you harm my baby?"

He quirked a brow and grinned. "Try and see."

She punched him in the stomach.

"Oomph," he said, but stayed upright. "I was wondering if you would help me with the chores. I'm running behind and don't want to leave Ma and Paul in a lurch."

Cori rolled her eyes. "Of course, I'll help. I have nothing to do today and would love to spend my time on the ranch. Now, give me my camera."

He handed the heavy piece of equipment to her. She cradled it lovingly. "Never threaten my camera," she teased.

"Wait for me, and I'll find you a jacket." He escaped into the bathroom. He dressed quickly, brushed his teeth even faster, and skipped shaving. When he stepped out into his place, Cori was gone. Outside he found her feeding the goats.

"I'm almost done here. Stalls are next," she called when she saw him coming. She was swarmed by goats and laughing as she hand-fed a few. His Carhart jacket hung off her.

"You should borrow a jacket from Mathias. He's more your size," he said, coming up behind her and then leaning on the fence.

"I saw your mom. She said you need to ride out with Paul. Go grab some food before you go. I got this."

Fort was instantly alert. "Did she say something was wrong?"

"She didn't. Sorry. Do you think it's the aliens?" She chuckled and worked her way out of the goats.

"I'll let you know. Are you sure you're good if I do this?" She looked good, fresh with bright energy pulsing off her. She climbed up on the fence he was leaning against and sat on the top rail, looping her legs threw the one below to give her stability.

"I miss being on a ranch. So I'm better than good with doing all this." Her camera hung from a post and she lifted it, aimed the lens across the yard, and began capturing pictures of the horses.

"There are wild horses up near the foothills. We could ride out sometime and try to catch them. You might get some amazing shots of them fighting. They can be brutal."

Cori sucked in air, her eyes large. "That would be awesome."

Judas Priest, she was adorable. She could easily distract him from...well, everything. He blew out a deep breath and searched for his bearings. He caught sight of Ma near the house and remembered he was needed by his step-father. "I should eat before I ride out," he said, restating the obvious.

"Better hurry on then Be-so-lame."

The sound of a truck coming down the lane caught his attention. He frowned. "Looks unlikely," Fort said and pointed to the truck. "That's Bryce. Either Hannah's had the babies last night or something's up."

"You know that simply because he's coming down the drive?"

"I know it because he's going faster than normal and is supposed to be going to a livestock auction today in Cody. Considering the time, it's too late for that. Something's stopped him from going." Fort pushed off the fence and went to meet the truck, Cori behind him.

Bryce brought the truck to a quick stop, and the passenger door flung open. Hannah leaned out. "Don't make me come to you," she hollered.

Fort chuckled and went to her. "Bryce, Hannah. Is something wrong?"

"Yes," she said and handed him a stack of papers. "We've been at the library all morning. The big one in Elk's Pass."

Big was subjective. Elk's Pass was the town to the east and boasted a population of a few thousand more people than Wolf Creek and Bison's Prairie combined, hence the "bigger" library.

"If some of the smaller papers would archive online, then we wouldn't have had to go. Don't get me started, though." She crossed her arms.

"Yes, please don't," Bryce said, then winked.

"What do these mean?" Fort asked while flipping through the pages. There were maps, and he figured he needed to spread them out to get the full scope.

"I did a sheet on those numbers you gave me and something odd popped up."

"I'm listening." The familiar pinging in his gut kicked in.

"Apparently not only in our county but the next one over, ranchers are reporting weird cases of cows disappearing. Not large numbers either. Some as many as fifteen. Others as low as two. At the library, I found similar stories throughout Wyoming. I even found an article about this happening to a rancher in Montana. "

"Aliens?" Cori said with a laugh.

"No explanation," Hannah said. "No clues either. Like the cows just up and vanished. Here's the thing, though. When you add up the numbers, it's pretty substantial. We're talking a couple thousand cows in the last six months alone. That's statistically significant. It's not even a blip when considering individual ranchers. A cow here, a cow there, but combined... Something is going on."

Fort rubbed his chin. "Okay, thanks Hannah. I'm gonna take a look at all this and see if I can find anything from other states."

"If you get me numbers, I'll run them through the sheet, look for something to pop." Hannah rubbed at her belly. "Sooner than later, too. I think these two aren't going to stick to the schedule."

Bryce crossed both his fingers. "I'm ready for the next stage."

"Anyone else locally been complaining about losing heads?" Fort asked Bryce.

As the local vet, he heard all kinds of stories. "Not specifically. Usually when I'm involved, we have bigger problems. But I'll ask when I see people."

Fort nodded then faced Cori. "Do you think you might have time to go to town?"

Her grin gave the bright sun a run for its money. "Sure, I need to get some photos of Deke for the election. I was planning that for tomorrow, but I can go today. I also figured while I was in town, I might stop by the diner to tell everyone about your awful prank last night and casually drop that y'all are missing some cattle and see if anyone pipes up."

"That's my girl," Fort said and slung an arm across her shoulder.

"What prank?" Hannah asked.

Cori wagged her finger. "No spoilers. You'll have to come to the diner to hear it firsthand or wait for the rumor mill.

17

C ori found Deke at his insurance office. She'd dressed the part of innocent newcomer by wearing a flowy floral skirt made of different patchwork fabrics, a solid T-shirt, a jean jacket, her cowboy boots, and paired everything with a confused expression. She'd gotten to be a master of controlling her features while living in Brewster.

She was undeniably nervous. Insurance and those that sold it were a trigger for her. Her father had sold insurance before getting elected mayor. Good old Charlie Walters had used the guise of "he's got your back" to woo the hard working, gullible people of Brewster to spend their money with him. It was after he'd been elected mayor that he continued to sell insurance and use their trust against them. He passed laws with buried restrictions that would require ranchers to buy insurance they didn't need, or didn't exist, or else they paid a fat tax. Sometimes the tax was confiscating portions of their herd.

Prior to entering the building, she pushed back her shoulders. Once inside, she was instantly confused by the setup of his office. Instead of a large secluded space in the back of the building, Deke's desk, a worn, ratty piece of furniture from the sixties, was in the main room. Even more confusing was that his secretary sat across from him. She hadn't expected him to share space with the help. Her father's office had been grand, his secretary far away with walls between them. She supposed if her father had Deke's setup, he might not have gotten away with what he did for as long as he did.

"Hey," Cori said as she set her camera bag on the corner of his desk.

"Well, if it isn't the future Mrs. Besingame. Sure you wanna do that? It's an awful last name." His smile was smooth, like melted butter on a pancake.

Cori's stomach growled. "Excuse me," she said and made a mock grimace. "It's not so bad, Fort's last name." It felt disloyal to tell Deke she called him Fort Be-so-lame.

"What can I do for you? I don't have much for food, but I do have some of these great snickerdoodles Mrs. Williams makes for me." He produced a tin of cookies from his desk and offered her one.

As hungry as she was, she did not do snickerdoodles. They reminded her of dear old dad. They were his favorite. "I'm on my way over to the diner for some lunch. I popped in because I'm the current photographer for The Critten County Rambler, and we'd like to get a picture for the paper to use for election articles. If you have a head shot you prefer to use, we can do that instead."

Deke stood. "Nope, I want you to take the picture. I'll go to the diner with you. Gives us a chance to get to know each other." He turned to his secretary, an older woman Cori had seen before. "Mrs. Williams, I trust you to hold down the fort."

Cori went through her mental Rolodex, trying to place how she knew the name aside from the cookies. Mrs. Williams had made Fort's banana bread. She'd eaten half of the loaf last night. Unbidden images of their make-out session flashed through her mind. Her body heat rose as she recalled all the places he had touched.

Her nipples puckered.

Crap.

She blew out a slow breath. Time for a distraction. "This is a cozy office," she said. "I expected a big office in the back."

Deke was shaking his head. "I like to be where people can reach me. They have to know their insurance man is there for them. Just like I'll be when I'm their sheriff." He stepped around his desk and gestured for Cori to precede him.

Bile rose in her throat. Deke was just like her dad, and it was going to give her great pleasure to bring him down. Oh, yeah! Any fallout would be worth it.

He reached for her camera bag, but she shifted it to the other shoulder. "I got it. But thanks. So, where's Conway? Maybe I could get a picture of the two of you. The ones I took at the airport were out of focus and, I'm embarrassed to say, poorly done."

"Conway likes to stay in the background. He's always saying this election is about me. Not him." The walk to the diner was a slow, easy stroll.

"How did Conway come about being your campaign manager?" She hoped her questions sounded innocent enough, simple curiosity. At worst, she could say she was passing the info along for the article.

"I was in Cody, spent the day at the livestock auctions, and was out with a bunch of other ranchers from various areas. Subject came up and Conway, who was with someone, I'm not sure who to be honest, offered me some free campaign advice. Told me if I had any questions I could call him. I figured your beau would be entering the election and would give me a run for my money so I reached out to Conway and asked if he might be able to help."

"What does your wife think of him?" She was curious about the woman who would marry a man like Deke. Her vapid, wanna-be-famous mother was the perfect match for Charlie. Who was the perfect match for Deke?

He stopped walking.

When Cori turned to face him, she was confused by the sadness on his face.

"Why do you ask about my wife?" He stuffed his hands in his pockets, the corners of his mouth downturned.

"You mentioned your proposal at the airport. I was just curious how she felt about Conway."

Deke looked across the square, and Cori followed, trying to see what he was looking at. Trying to get into his head. All she saw was the church and attached graveyard, the library, and a quickie-mart.

"My wife, Laura, died five years ago. I think if she was still here, I might not need the help of Conway. She would be all the counsel I'd seek."

Aw, poop-cicles. Her distrust of him wavered. "I'm so sorry, Deke. I didn't know."

"How could you? I'm sure my love life isn't something you and Fort talk about. Not the most romantic of pillow talk." He smiled slightly and nudged her with his shoulder. "What are you gonna do?" he said, appearing to accept there was no changing the hand fate dealt him.

"I'd hug you, but I'm sure that would get back to Fort pretty quick, and that wouldn't go over well. So how about I buy you some pie? Not that I'm saying pie will fix this, but it might make you feel better. Not that you need to feel better, but it's better than booze, which you can't take back the aftermath of a bender. Not that I know about—"

Deke tossed his head back and laughed. "Cori," he said. "Stop. I'm not offended in case you thought I might be, but I'll let you buy me that pie so your conscience feels better." He nodded forward with his head for her to start moving. "Let's go before the crowd gets there."

Relief washed over her. Last thing she wanted to do was offend someone, especially a guy who was a widower. Two steps later, she reminded herself that Deke was the enemy. He could potentially be the one who was organizing the theft of his neighbor's cows and was planning to use a public office for other nefarious activity. She was here to thwart him, after all.

No matter how nice he seemed.

Cricket was inside the diner and waved Cori over. Her smile fell when she saw Deke step in behind her. She led him to Cricket's table anyway.

"Hey, Deke's joining me for food, and I'm going to get some shots of him. Did you have any questions for him?" Cori asked and slid into the booth.

"I'm not talking to him," Cricket said and put her hand up to the side of her face in what Cori assumed was an attempt to block out Deke.

Startled, Cori chocked back a laugh. "What? How are you going to interview him?" She slid into the booth, Deke following after her. Something peculiar was going on here, but Cori couldn't place it.

"I sent him an email. Feel free to share anything he says with you. Or better yet, record it." She handed Cori a menu and smiled like a southern belle with a deep secret.

"Ah..." Cori didn't know what to say, but she was totally curious as to why they weren't talking.

Deke filled in the void. "She hasn't spoken to me for six months. Woman can hold a grudge." He extended his arm across the back of the booth.

Cricket began to hum.

"Okay, then," Cori said and looked for the waitress. Sally was working, and she pointedly ignored Cori. "I don't think we're gonna get service anytime soon, and I also think it's because of me."

Cricket tried to flag Sally down, but the waitress wasn't

having it. Clearly, she wasn't over Fort bringing Cori to town. Cori faced Deke. "You might want to order for us. Apparently, Sally doesn't speak to me. I'd like the buffalo burger with extra fries and surprise me with the pie."

He looked at Cricket, who pointed at what she wanted on the menu.

Deke slid from the booth and made his way to the counter, stopping to talk to people along the way. Cori snapped pictures, anxious to look at them later.

"Wanna share why you haven't talked to Deke for half a year?" She kept the camera on Deke.

"It's a long story. One I'd have to be waterboarded to share."

Cori glanced at her. Her thin pressed lips were no joke. "Noted," Cori said. "Are you going to be able to eat with him here? I can move."

"Nope." She waved her hand like it was no biggie. "I do it all the time."

Cori wanted to probe further, but Deke returned. Maybe the silence wasn't awkward for them, but it was for Cori. Of course, she wasn't used to it like they were. She'd intended to share a watered-down version of last night with folks in hopes of shining a light on Fort that didn't show what a tight-ass he was. A more carefree side.

"So, last night, Fort played the worst prank on me. I was so mad, though it's kinda funny today." Cori noticed the two tables closest had stopped talking.

She painted a story of two lovers out enjoying the stars, not ready to end the day, who found themselves by the railroad tracks. She laughed as she imitated Fort's frightened face, telling her the light was a ghost. The chatter in the diner was quieting as more patrons were listening to Cori. She had their rapt attention. Then she bragged at how she beat him back to the truck and made up the part about making him sleep on the couch. The last part earned her an ugly scowl from Sally. She had the room laughing when she told them the size of the couch and how his legs hung over the arm to nearly touch the floor.

She let the story float around the room for a few minutes before broaching her next topic. "It was nice to see him relax. Aside from the election"—she elbowed Deke good-naturedly —"his family has had some cattle go missing. One here. Another there. It's weird and"—she lowered her voice—"kinda spooky. Where I'm from, there's usually a sign of what happened. Fort says there's nothing. Not one clue."

"Don't I know it," Mr. Phillips said. "I have my suspicions."

Cori looked at Cricket who mouthed "aliens."

"Recently?" asked Cori.

"Another went missing last night," he said. "Poof. Gone." He did his hands in a dramatic mock explosion.

Deke squirmed beside her. "Listen, I have to go. Thanks for the pie, Cori." He turned to the rancher. "I'm sure there's a logical explanation, Mr. Phillips." He tossed down a twenty and was gone before Cori could protest.

"The Williams had it happen, too," said Sally to the crowd.

Others were chiming in with their thoughts. A few of the ranchers left, plates barely touched, likely heading out to check their herds. Cori turned to Cricket with a brow raised. "What do you think?"

"I think something in Wolf Creek stinks, and we've got us a story."

"I would agree." Cori glanced at her watch. "I'm gonna head over to the sheriff's office and try to catch Fort before he starts his shift." She hung her camera bag across her body, messenger style. "You need me anywhere soon?"

Cricket pursed her lips in thought. "Nope. Pop over and give me those photos when you get the chance."

"Done," Cori said. As she left the diner, a few people called out their goodbyes to her. Here only a few days, and she'd smiled more than she had in the last ten years. Wolf Creek was more home than where she grew up. Cori exited the diner and stood in the shadow of the door, biting her lip. She would not get attached to Wolf Creek and its people. She reminded herself that she could have this nearly anywhere. It just meant starting over, and doing so wouldn't be all that awful. She was about to step out of the shadows when she caught Deke stalking across the town square toward his office. Left behind in the parking space in front of the church was Conway Witty. He was leaning against the door of a pickup truck talking to someone. Cori couldn't make out whom. Moving swiftly, she fit her camera with a high-powered lens made for long distance shots. She brought it to her face, finger depressing the shutter, hoping to get an image before the opportunity was gone.

She knew the shots weren't likely to be in perfect focus. Sometimes a person could miss a shot and sometimes they got lucky and snagged the perfect one. The man in the truck leaned farther out the window, and Cori got the shot she needed. When she saw him up close through the lens, she gasped. She captured some more then quickly tucked everything away. She tugged a sun hat from her bag and placed it on her head at an angle, hoping to hide her face. She shuffled from the diner toward the sheriff's department, head down and away from Witty and the man. She reached the sheriff's office as Fort was walking in.

"What's up short stuff? What's with the hat?"

She snagged him by the elbow and dragged him into the office. Once inside, she removed the hat and moved away from the windows. "I have lots to tell you. First, Mr. Phillips had another cow disappear last night. Said it vanished without a trace."

Separating the offices from the waiting room was a waist-high wall and swinging door. Fort sat on the edge of the wall and stretched his long legs out in front of him, crossing his feet at the ankle. He looked delicious in his uniform, all strong and capable, like an alpha hero waiting to come in and save the day. Her mind got off track as she pictured being swept up and carried in his arms, fireman style would work, too, to a remote field where he'd lay her down, slowly work on her buttons and...

"Cori, where'd you go?" Fort was snapping his fingers in her face.

She coughed then cleared her throat. "Sorry, was trying to recall if any other ranchers said anything." She fanned herself. "Is it hot in here or is it me?"

"It's seventy degrees in here." His lips twitched, leaving her wondering if he could read her mind.

"Hm, must be all the food I ate." She sat down in one of the waiting room's plastic chairs and set her camera bag in front of her. "After I mentioned the Mystery of the Missing Cattle, a few ranchers hustled out of there. I don't know who they are."

"If they find heads missing, they'll probably report it now that they know it's happening to everyone. It's a small community, but it's amazing what people don't say. How'd it go with Deke?"

Cori groaned. "I don't think I can be unbiased where he is concerned. I think he's up to something." She told him about his behavior when they started talking about the missing cattle and how she'd seen him storming across the square minutes ago. "But that's not all. I got some shots of a stranger. Witty was talking to this person, and I'm guessing Deke was, too." She lifted her camera and turned on the screen, then scrolled through the pictures.

"This guy look familiar to you?"

Fort took the camera and studied the image. She liked how he took his time. That he wasn't impulsive...much. He'd been rash about bringing her here, but she liked to think it was working out for him.

Fort leaned closer to the image. "Can't say that he does. He look familiar to you?"

Cori blew out a breath, lunch sitting in her stomach like concrete block.

"You okay? You look kinda pale." He pushed from the wall and came to squat before her. After setting her camera aside, he pressed his palm to her forehead. "You're sweaty. Here, tuck your head between your legs"

She did as he said. She had to tell him. "I don't know the guy's name, but I've seen him before," she said as she stared at the under seat of her chair at a large pink blob. "Someone stuck gum under here."

"Who's the guy, Cori?"

Feeling much like that blob of gum, chewed up and left in the dark, forgotten, she said, "He used to come around my dad. I think they did some work together, and by work, I mean cons."

18

Fort kicked the toe of his boot against the red clay, his hand resting against the post where the salt lick was nailed. Eventually, old cantankerous Lester Phillips would shut up, so Fort held his tongue and waited for his opportunity to get a word in. It might be when the man was finally put into the ground, but the time would come, and Fort had enough inner reserve to dig deep and wait him out.

They stood in Phillip's east pasture, ankle deep in brown and green grass with the foothills behind them. It was an idyllic view, bucolic, only thing missing were the cows. They should have been surround by a small heard of ten heifers, but instead it was just Fort and Phillips.

And the salt lick.

To the casual observer, it might have looked like the two were shooting the shit, or maybe one was selling the other something. Fort touched the badge on his hip and stared over Phillip's shoulder to the intact fence line twenty feet away. This was serious business, and Fort was getting sick of these cattle disappearances. Rustlers, it had to be. How they were doing it was the million-dollar question.

The old man paused to take in air, and Fort had his moment.

"You aren't being targeted by aliens, Mr. Phillips. I promise." He held up his hand when the man began to bluster. "I know this because we aren't the only town losing cattle around here. Far as I can tell, nearly everyone's seen some heads disappear. Bison's Prairie, Elk's Pass, and as far as the outskirts of Cody."

"Without a trace?" Mr. Phillips asked wide-eyed.

Fort nodded. "Yessir. No tire marks or hoof prints from horses that anyone can find."

Phillips harrumphed. "Then how you reckon it's not aliens? A giant UFO comes down and sucks them up in their beam." He narrowed his gaze at Fort.

Fort suppressed a chuckle. He knew there'd be no changing Mr. Phillips mind, a man who'd long preached conspiracy theories with such sound arguments he made pastors look inept and the Bible like a fiction novel. Fort knew what he'd have to do. He pulled out the big guns and hit him with science.

"Well, sir. I was doing some research, and even if a UFO had come down to suck up the cows in their giant beam, there'd be some trace of the beam. Maybe the grass would be a shade lighter? A tad crisper, perhaps. But some sign. This brown grass is from how dry it's been, not a beam. You can see because it's all over the pasture. I've taken pictures of every area. I've studied them till my eyes burn. I'm not seeing anything. I've asked other law enforcement, and they can't see anything either. They've taken pictures, but nothing."

"So then how do you explain this ain't no aliens? Maybe their technology is so far advanced there wouldn't be any telltale signs. Hm? What do you say about that?" When Phillips raised his overly bushy eyebrows, Fort couldn't hide his slight smile.

Phillips frowned.

"Maybe I'm naïve, but I'm fairly certain that it doesn't matter how advanced the technology is. It can't change physics. Maybe change how it presents, but not hard and fast rules."

"And there's no crop circles." Phillips scratched his cheek with his thumb, lips pressed together in thought.

"That, too," Fort said.

"I reckon you might have a point or two."

Fort let it slide. "I'm gonna tell you what I told the others and what we're doing at Ma's ranch. Mix things up with—"

"What in the Sam Hill does that mean?"

"It means you have a predictable schedule. We all do, and these thieves have watched us long enough to know it. They're taking advantage."

"Bullshit," Phillips said.

"Mr. P, you eat lunch every Monday, Wednesday, and Friday at the diner with three other Vietnam veterans and ranchers. You're away from your ranch about three full hours. All four of you have been targeted. Let me take a wild guess and say these heifers were new to the herd and not yet branded?"

Phillips shoulders drooped.

"Yeah, that's been the same in most places. So, moving forward. I'll get in touch with livestock auctions, but it's pretty much impossible when the animals aren't tagged or branded. You change your schedule. Be less predictable. Brand the new ones as soon as you can. Any chance any of these cows had some distinguishable marks?"

Phillips frowned and glanced at his feet.

"Any chance you've registered your branding with the county?" Fort already knew the answer but thought perhaps if asked, he might plant a seed of an idea in Phillips head.

"Hell, no. You think I'd let the man into my business?" Phillips brows pulled down and inward until they looked like one long, bushy line.

"I can respect that Mr. Phillips, but right now the man"—Fort pointed to himself—"could use just one element to be in our court to help out with this. Think about it."

Phillips spat on the ground. "Well, shit."

"Yup."

They walked in silence the hundred yards to the dirt road where they'd left their cars.

"If it's not aliens, then the next commonality is your gal. She showed, and cows started going missing."

Fort stopped at the hood of his deputy SUV. "Cows started missing before Cori came to visit."

"True, but that doesn't mean she wasn't doing it from afar. Tell me when your heads are next to each other in bed you don't engage in pillow talk?" Mr. Phillips upped his voice several octaves. "Tell me what's going on in Wolf Creek," he said in what Fort thought was an impersonation of Cori. He then dropped his voice low. "Mr. Phillips got in some new heads. Old fool doesn't even register his cows." Fort assumed that last bit was him.

"I would never tell her about you getting cows." He leaned closer to the older man. "Because when our heads are close together, I've got better thing to say and do than talk about an old fool like you."

"Ah-ha," Phillips said, "so you *do* think I'm an old fool."

Fort nodded. "Yes, I do. With technology the way it is, today there's no reason for you not to be protecting yourself. On our ranch, we're old fools, too. We like to think that we can take our time. That nothing's gonna happen. We even have that fancy GPS system and we tag them right away but brand when we can." Fort pointed to the mountains. "There's an epidemic out there. Meth, and we might think it's not affecting us here in Wolf Creek because we don't see it, but it is. My guess is that we're experiencing rustlers, and its likely for drug money. Trick is I can't figure out how they get the cows out of here."

"Maybe the meth heads built a spaceship. A hovercraft."

"Maybe," Fort said and got into his truck. Some people never changed. Never saw what was in front of them, that their actions were not helping their situation. Cori had shown him that. Since he got home from Afghanistan, he'd held everyone at bay. It wasn't easy letting people in. Sometimes it was annoying, but Mrs. Williams had made him more banana nut muffins today, and that was a perk.

19

The following day, while Fort was out talking to ranchers, Cori spent her time with Cricket at the newspaper going over photos to use for articles and making a list of what others she needed to get for upcoming stories. The newspaper offices were housed in one of the original buildings. Brick walls and large windows gave it charm. The front room were the offices, the back held the antiquated-looking printing press that Cricket ran with the help of some high school students.

"You're really good," Cricket said as she held a candid of Deke talking with others at the diner. He looked nothing like the guy Fort had said he was. In Deke, Cori saw a warmth and genuine interest for his town and people. Her father had always feigned that. His smile had always been too small or too big. Engaging with the people who'd elected him mayor was one never-ending beauty pageant for him. All fake smiles and what he thought others wanted to hear.

Cori's gut told her something wasn't adding up. No, sir.

Fort texted her that he was coming to town in a few hours and would pass off the truck keys. She would try to talk to him then if she could get him alone. She texted back and asked him to meet her at the station. Hopefully, the walk to there could provide some alone time to think everything out.

Cricket slid another photo from the pile, Deke with this manager. It wasn't a close-up like the previous one, but she could still make out the expressions. Cori had caught them in conversation. On Deke's face was the largest, fakest smile she'd seen him make. But his body language spoke the opposite. Arms were crossed over his chest, shoulders were back in defiance, and he was leaning away. Witty looked much the same, but when Cori lined up a sequence of the photos, Witty never looked at Deke.

"Something's not right here," Cricket said.

"I agree. Just wish I knew what."

Cricket sighed heavily and flicked the photo. "I've known Deke my entire life. Hiring Witty is out of character for him."

What a perfect moment to dig into Fort's past. "To tell the truth, Fort paints a different picture of Deke."

Cricket snorted. "I'm sure he does. Those two are like oil and water. Competitive as hell. When we were growing up, Deke had the town's attention. He was great at sports and liked to help out with the rodeos. He's good with animals. Then summer would come and Fort would show up. Anything Deke did, Fort could do better. And man, Fort is amazing with animals."

Cori nodded her agreement. That had always been true about Fort and animals. She was confused; the math on Deke wasn't adding up. "Deke wasn't a troublemaker?"

"Yeah, sometimes he'd raise a little hell, but because he could always talk his way out of it, he was never held accountable for anything. Drove Fort berserk. No one here is surprised he's a cop."

"Fort says Deke went after him with a bat."

Cricket looked away, chewing her lower lip, as if lost in memories. "That was over my sister, Laura. Deke had been in love with her since elementary school."

Cori put the pieces together. "Wait, your sister was Deke's wife?"

Cricket turned her attention back to Cori. "I can't believe she's gone. A deer ran in front of her car."

Cori gasped and covered her mouth. "I'm so sorry. I had no idea."

Cricket reached for a book on the shelf behind them, a school yearbook. She flipped through the pages until she found what she was looking for. "This is Laura. She was the best big sister a girl could have. I miss her every day."

The picture was the famous "senior year photo" with the girl looking over her shoulder. She was stunning. It was easy to see she and Cricket were sisters, though where Cricket had darker hair, Laura had been blond. Laura was totally Fort's type. Cori could easily imagine him getting in a fight over a girl like her. "She's beautiful."

"Mm, and the kindest heart. The day she was killed she was driving to the assisted living place."

As a human, this is where Cori fell apart. She didn't know what to say. Were any words the right ones? Instead, she closed her hand over Cricket's and squeezed. Cricket squeezed back.

"I think I need a pastry or something," Cricket said. "You wanna come with?"

"You bet. I never turn down food."

"Me either," Cricket said. "Hey."

Cori was packing her camera up and turned to face her new friend.

"I'm glad you're here. I like you, and I look forward to getting to know you better." She bumped Cori with her elbow.

"Oh," Cori said, uncertain what she should say. What she wanted to say was the same thing, to make plans for the next day or week. But, she reminded herself, she wasn't staying. "I'm glad we met, too. This"––she gestured to Cricket and then herself––"has been very nice." She hoped it would convey to

Cricket that she appreciated her friendship, something Cricket might recall after Cori was gone.

Cori finished packing up, and they walked out the newspaper office together. Cori waited while Cricket put the sign of return on the door and turned the lock. Outside was hot, and the dry air made Cori glad she wore a light skirt and a tank top. Summer here would be a scorcher.

"Just curious, but do you all have a date set?" Cricket asked.

"A date for what?" Cori adjusted her camera bag and kept stride with Cricket's long-legged pace.

"For the wedding," Cricket said.

Cori stumbled, but quickly recovered and feigned concern over the heel of her cowboy boot, as if the footwear was the culprit.

"Oh, I think it would be hard and unfair to ask Fort to focus on a wedding and an election at the same time."

Cricket held open the diner door and waved Cori through. "Take the back booth," Cricket said and pointed to the far corner.

Cricket picked up the conversation after they took opposite sides of the booth. "Do you imagine something big or small?"

She pulled the menu from behind the napkin dispenser and played with the edge. "I dunno. I've never imagined anything."

Cricket barked out a laugh and wagged her head.

Mrs. Z, sporting freshly dyed purple-tipped hair, slid into the seat next to Cori. "What are you girls talking about?"

Cricket pointed to Cori. "This one just said she's never imagined her wedding when I asked if she was planning something big or small."

Mrs. Z gave a toothy grin. "I have ten bucks that says she is lying."

Cori gasped.

"That's a fool's bet," Cricket said. "Of course, she's lying." They turned their attention to Cori. "Come on, we all have planned a thousand weddings in our heads. You can't tell me you never dreamt about it."

Cori never dared. To do so would have been one more crushing blow. One more thing she couldn't have. One more hopeless dream. Even now, she dared not pretend because once she left Wolf Creek, those dreams and memories would follow her.

Cori rubbed her arms in hopes of keeping away the pessimism. She would not give in to their pushiness. Besides, doing so probably fell into one of the rules she and Fort had made and swore not to break. They had to at least keep one rule. "Honestly, I'm not picky. It's not the event, but the commitment. That's what counts."

"I'm gonna lay it out for you, dear," Mrs. Z said and patted her hand. "You and Fort should tie the knot before the election."

Cori moved to the corner of the booth, shaking her head. "Oh, no. No. Absolutely not. Bad idea. That's asking too much of him."

Cricket leaned across the table to Mrs. Z. "She doesn't think it's fair to have Fort split his attention between the two events." She glanced at Cori. "Right?"

Cori nodded.

Mrs. Z shrugged. "Fair enough, but what if all he had to do was show up?"

Cori felt like a bobble head with her maniacal shaking. She already knew this train was about to derail.

"What about your momma? Would she need to have a say?" Mrs. Z was fumbling through her purse as she asked.

"Um, no. Not my mom. But this is not a good—"

"Hush, child. We've got this covered." She pulled a sheet of folded notebook paper from her purse and went about straightening it on the table. "I've already spoken with Fort's momma and got her input. We figure, Cricket and I, that you and Fort move too slow."

"Look how long it took him to bring you here," Cricket interjected.

"And left to your own devices, you'll both be old and gray before you tie the knot, so we're gonna help you out." She pointed to the paper. "Ten days before the election will be the rehearsal. That way y'all can go away for two nights into Cody or somewhere for a quick honeymoon."

On the wide-rule paper was the sequence of events leading up to Cori and Fort's nuptials.

"Um..." Backing away from this would take finesse, a delicacy Cori wasn't sure she possessed. "Um..."

"Is that a look of pleasure? I hope so. Fort's momma has run through this list and approved it. In fact, she's split half the tasks with us and started on them."

Cori's mouth fell open, her eyes darting from Cricket to Mrs. Z. "I can't have you all do this. I have to talk with Fort. He may not want to get married so soon."

Mrs. Z waved an indifferent hand. "Then he wouldn't have put that ring on your finger. It's all relative, and you said so yourself, it's not about the event but the commitment. This town needs to see that."

"But we are committed." She waved the ring around.

Cricket leaned closer and whispered, "Many think that if Fort loses, he'll leave with you to go back to your hometown. They want to see you all settled here. That way if Deke doesn't work out, they can vote Fort in the next election."

Cori let the words sink in around her. "Wait, so is Deke going to win this election anyway. No matter what?" Would Fort ask her to leave if that was true?

Mrs. Z gave her a sad smile. "He's got a strong lead. There are still some gun-shy where Fort is concerned. Which is why we thought we'd ease their anxiety with a wedding. Who doesn't love a wedding?"

Cori resumed her head shaking. "That feels dishonest." Look

at her, the kettle calling the pot black. "Besides." She tried to image a big fancy wedding and couldn't. "The more I think about it, the more I'm sure I'd elope."

Cricket and Mrs. Z gasped and sat back away from her.

"Elope?" Cricket said.

"You can't do that. This town would be so hurt," Mrs. Z added.

Cori looked around the diner. She was starting to put names with faces and could add little facts about people. Like Mrs. Williams baked a lot, every day, and Mr. Phillips, for all his weird theories, was lonely, she could see it in his eyes. Whenever she mentioned little tidbits about Fort, the locals enjoyed it. He'd held himself back, and Cori understood why, but the good people of Wolf Creek had been asking him to join them for years. Eventually, the invitation would be withdrawn. People did get tired of waiting around. Mrs. Z was right. If Fort shut them out any longer, he would always be an outsider.

Maybe she couldn't get the people of Brewster to forgive her, to move on, but she could help Fort move forward. He deserved to be happy, too.

"Okay," she said, more for herself than for them. Okay, she was going to help Fort really win over this town.

Cricket and Mrs. Z squealed with pleasure.

"All you have to do is say what flavor cake you like, Mrs. Williams is baking it, what flowers you love, I'm handling that, and pick out a dress."

"Wait, I was saying okay that we wouldn't elope. Not okay we'll get married in"—she slid the paper from Mrs. Z, scanned it, and then gulped—"three weeks." No way in hell.

"Too late," Cricket said. "You agreed."

A wild panic was rising within Cori. "But no, I can't," she blustered. The train had not only derailed but tipped over as well and was spilling its wares all over the place. "I mean, I have to talk to Fort."

Mrs. Z smiled coyly. "His mom's already cleared the date. But here's your chance to finalize it all. Here he comes."

Cory looked to the door and watched Fort enter and then stop to talk to a few people along the way, occasionally glancing at her, a small smile on his lips. Poop on a porcupine, he was hot. Looking all trim and manly in his uniform. For a second she imagined what it would be like to be married to Fort, to snuggle next to him every night. A flush of heat burst from her girly parts and swarmed her body.

Cori was glad they hadn't had time to order because suddenly she wasn't hungry at all.

"Good afternoon, ladies. How are you today?" Fort said with a smile for each of them.

Cori tried to signal a message to him. *Run! Duck! Brace yourself!* she screamed in her head, making her eyes go wide and crazy, hoping her look would convey the words as the warnings ran a loop in her head.

"Fort," Mrs. Z said while tucking the paper in her purse. "Remember that old honey shack that sits between your momma's place and mine?"

"The hunting cabin?"

Mrs. Z cast a coy glance at Cori and Cricket. "Every time Earl and I went there, very little hunting was done, if you know what I mean." She elbowed Cori. "Yes, that place. Can you be a dear and go by it sooner than later? My foreman thought maybe it was being used. Maybe those kids who like to hang out by the tracks. I'd like a trained eye to look at it."

"I can do it today," he said.

"You're a dear," she said and winked at Cori. "Also—"

Cori jumped up on the bench seat. "We need to go," she said in a rush of words.

"Are you okay?" Fort asked.

"I'm fine. Great." She stepped cautiously over Mrs. Z.

"What's the rush, dear?" Mrs. Z asked. "We were going to tell Fort—"

She blurted out, "He has to be at work soon and promised me a quickie."

Both Cricket and Mrs. Z's mouth dropped.

Cori continued. "You know how it is. Working all those hours, we never get any time." She faced Fort then leaped into his arms. "Run," she whispered in his ear.

He slid her slowly down his side, his steely eyes twinkling as he tried to read her.

Cori did some fast thinking. She needed to get them outta there. "Thanks for the conversation, ladies. I'll make sure to get back with you about everything. Come on," she said and grabbed Fort's hand. Making a beeline straight for the door, she dragged him from the diner with all her might. Once outside, she kept up her pace until they were a good half block away and Fort jerked her hand, pulling her back toward him.

"A quickie? Really? What's going on?" His brow was furrowed, but bemusement played on his lips.

Cori looked around him and saw that no one was within hearing distance. "Something terrible has happened," Cori whispered.

He automatically reached for his gun.

"No, nothing like that. Worse," she said while swiping at his hand. She needed to tell him, just needed to blurt it out. Like ripping a Band-Aid off a gaping wound that would likely spurt blood. "They are planning our wedding. Your mom is in on it. We're getting married at the town gazebo in three weeks. Wear your gray suit." She had read that note jotted out to the side on Mrs. Z's paper and realized Ms. Saira must have written it.

The smirk was gone, replaced with a tight-lipped grimace. "The hell you say?"

"No joke. I tried to get around it. They say that being hitched will go a long way with the election."

Fort looked over her shoulder, his face impassive, like granite. "We need to work this out someplace private." He took her by the elbow and led her toward the sheriff's department. At the door, he told her to wait then stuck his head inside.

"Bitsy, I'm headed out to check out something for Mrs. Z. I'll be back soon. Call me on the radio if you need anything as I'll be in the back forty," he said and then stepped out without waiting for a reply.

He reached for her arm again, but she pulled away. "I know how to walk and can make it to the truck on my own accord. No need to drag me there."

He pointed to the passenger door. "Get in," he bit out.

As if this was her fault. But then, according to everyone affected by her dad, wasn't everything her fault anyway?

ort couldn't believe his rotten luck. Having Cori "break up"
with him before the election had been a plan he could live
with. Now? Now he was going to have to marry her. Or come
close. He needed to tell his mother the real deal. She was going to
be pissed, which meant his step-father would be ticked off as
well, and life on the ranch would suck for a while. Not only
would Cori be gone, but he doubted his mother would make him
extra bacon.

With the way his luck was going, he wouldn't be surprised if
they ended up hitched, had three kids, and a dog. He could see
them saying on their twenty-fifth, "We don't even like each other.
This was all pretend." But odd how it wasn't hard to imagine Cori
with his kid.

Fort's right eye began to twitch, and he shook off the vision.

Okay, maybe she wasn't hard to look at or touch. She could
kiss like a champ and, frankly, he liked her better with her mouth
preoccupied with anything but talking, preferably her lips on his.
But that wasn't enough for the long haul. Ranch life wasn't easy,
and it took a special person, plus he was asking said special

person to live with him being a cop. Double negative whammy for putting stress on a marriage.

Fact was, those days of living like a monk were wearing thin. He'd been fooling himself to think he was doing all right. Those infrequent trips out of town were, in hindsight, not enough. Obviously, since he was getting a woody thinking about Cori Walters, the evidence spoke for itself.

She sat next to him, chewing her thumbnail.

"Start at the beginning."

"It happened so fast. One minute I'm telling them 'no' and the next they've mistakenly thought I agreed. I did not agree. I know I didn't." She explained what Mrs. Z had planned out.

"And my mom is involved?" They'd been traveling along the main road when Fort took a turn onto a dirt road, extending his arm in front of Cori to keep her from rocking forward when they hit the bumpy road.

"Yup, everyone is already signed on and involved. This is bad. Real bad."

"Yeah," he said. "But let's not panic. We had talked about you leaving me at the altar initially, right. Maybe we just go back to that?"

She groaned, briefly covering her eyes. "I think if I left you at the altar, it would kill your chances of winning. They'd wonder if you'd be so upset you'd take off. Maybe I should go now?" She chewed her thumb some more as they rode in silence.

If she left now, he'd have his bed to himself. Not that she took up any space, and her toes were awfully cute. Fort wanted to slap himself upside the head. Her toes were cute? What the hell was wrong with him?

"You could say your mom was sick." He cut off the dirt road onto a path that typically was hard to find, but the grass was matted down. He leaned forward and slowed the truck.

"Yeah, she could be really sick, which would keep me away for a long time. You could break up with me because you pick the town over me." She leaned forward as well. "What are we looking at?"

"The grass is down. Someone has driven on this path."

She looked out her window. "I don't see anything out of sorts over here. Mrs. Z said her foreman had been out here. Maybe it was him?"

"True, but this is repeated. Look, there's more than one path." He brought the truck to a stop and jumped out.

Cori climbed over the console and sat in his seat. She stuck her head out the window and looked at the ground. "What can I do?"

"Not obligate us to anything more. Like two-point-five kids or a house or anything." He pointed at the truck. "Stay put."

"I knew you would think this was my fault," she said and crossed her arms. He bent down to look at something in front of the truck, then popped up quickly and pointed a finger at her. "Don't lay on the horn with me in front of it."

She raised her hands over her head. "As if." But the lack of eye contact confirmed she'd been thinking it. He jabbed his finger in her direction one last time for good measure and went back to look at the various footprints in the dirt. None were complete as the ground was too dry, but he could make out difference. One set was cowboy boots, and the other looked to be steel-toed boots.

Not that any of this meant anything yet, but it might. Fort went back to the truck and pushed Cori over. He climbed in and drove slowly toward the cabin before coming to a stop twenty yards from the front door in a makeshift space nestled between two trees. There was no driveway, but that didn't take away from the place.

The little three-room house was located on a stunning piece of land, surrounded by an outer rim of trees. Cori slid from the truck and stared at the log cabin structure. It was simple in design, a slab foundation with the house on top. No extras like a porch or trim around windows or doors. "Wow," she said and pointed to the view behind the cabin.

Beyond the trees, the prairie broke out, spreading wide and far before butting up against Three Brothers Mountain. The view was vast and breathtaking, and he was used to it, but Cori gazed slack-jawed.

With his index finger, he gently pushed under her chin, closing her mouth. She made a half-hearted swat at his hand.

"Can you imagine looking at this every day?" She sucked in a deep breath and held her arms wide. "Why doesn't someone live here?"

Her face was lit up with pleasure as she took in her surroundings. He'd seen her like this before, and the memory of it made him feel closer to her than he had felt to anyone else in a long time. She's been barely a teenager then and had come upon him on the side of the road, helping a cow birth a calf. She'd seen birthings before, that he knew. Yet, when that little calf came out and blinked its large brown eyes at them, Cori had stared back with the same enchanted awe he saw on her face right now.

For all the annoying habits Cori possessed, and he could tick them off on two hands, maybe one, she loved the land, the animals, and the lifestyle of ranching, and he had to give her that. She lifted the camera that hung from around her neck to her face, and the two became one, snapping him from his thoughts.

"Hey," he said. "When you get all the pics you want, think you can get some of these?" He pointed to the footprints by the front door.

She glanced at him and then where he was pointing. "Sure."

Fort slowly walked the perimeter and came back around to the front with nothing solid by way of clues. Yeah, there were footprints, human, bovine, and horse, but that was nothing out of the ordinary. Cori was snapping shots of the ground when he opened the door.

"I used to come up here and hunt with Paul. Both Ma and

Mrs. Z own the cabin." He scanned the interior before stepping in. He felt Cori come up behind him.

"Any chance this is a vagrant or something?" she said, looking around him.

"Not unless the homeless travel with candles and champagne," he said and stepped in, opening up the doorway for her to see. Someone had gone to the trouble of setting up the table with a picnic of sorts: a red tablecloth, wooden candle holders with candles, and a bucket of half melted ice and champagne. A basket sat on the edge of the table with a note hanging from the side.

Cori was the first to reach it. "Oh, no," she said and handed him two sheets of paper.

Congratulations! It read. *Welcome to your new home. As a gift for your impending nuptials, your mother and I are gifting you this cabin to set up as your own place. Your ranch. A place to grow as you both grow in love and marriage.*

Behind the note, was the deed to the property signed by both Mrs. Z and his ma. Made out to both him and Cori.

"Fudge sticks," Cori said and resumed her nail-biting.

"Yeah," he said and placed the paper on the table. A place of his own. A ranch of his own. He liked the idea. And Cori didn't look out of place in the cabin either. One large room made up the kitchen and living space with the bedroom and bath off to the side. It was in good condition. The land was wide enough to add more rooms and the septic was in place and was piped for running water. The cabin could become a home.

"I think you're right. I should leave right away. Maybe in a few days. If I left today, it would be really obvious. I don't mind giving Barbie some crazy illness." She was backing toward the front door.

"Cori," he said.

"Fort, I like these people. I can't—"

"You broke a rule." He stepped toward her.

"They're stupid rules. I'm human. It's only natural that I like at least some of the people here," she said, arms raised halfway, palms out as if daring him to disagree. "I need a drink." She skirted around him, then snatched up the champagne, immediately going to work on peeling off the foil around the cork. "It's one thing to be associated to a con because your father did it. But I was always above that because, even though he was a crook, I wasn't. But now I'm the crook." She tucked the bottle between her legs and cinched up her face in effort as she wrestled with the cork.

She was cute. He took the bottle from her. "You aren't a crook." He eased the cork out so not to spray the drink over both of them.

"But I'm no better than him now. Fooling people." She took the bottle from him and took a large swig. Then another.

Fort raised a brow and didn't bother to hide his smile. "You're doing it for a good cause. Tell yourself that." He took the bottle from her and placed it on the table.

"I'm not sure about Deke being bad. Besides, people are still going to get hurt. Feel like they've been conned. This was a stupid idea." She reached around him for the bottle, but he blocked her.

"Then why did you agree to do it?" He chuckled when she thumped him on the chest in frustration.

"You mean besides the money? I thought maybe I could score one for the good guys if I helped you out. But it was misguided. A con is a con. People get hurt," she said, watching him with those large owlish eyes of hers.

"You should have thought of that beforehand. You're in too deep," he said.

"You should have thought about it before you even went to Sabrina." She whacked him again, but this time on the arm. "I blame you."

"Me? You're the one hanging out with Cricket and taking jobs. Had you just stayed on the ranch like I said, going to town with only me, none of this would have happened." He grabbed her hand to stop her hitting him.

"Me?" she said incredulously and followed it with a bitter laugh. "I should have known you would blame me." She tugged at his hand, but he wouldn't let go. He saw her eyes narrow, and before he could anticipate it, she stomped on his foot.

"Ouch," he said and let go of her hand so he could grab his foot. She'd caught him good with her heel.

"I'm out of here," she said and ran for the door.

He had her over his shoulder before she got more than four steps. He slapped her ass hard.

"Hey," she cried, "that hurt." When she punched him in the kidney, her glasses fell to the floor.

Fort arched to the side in reaction to the back pain. He slapped her ass a second time.

"*Yowl!* Stop that."

"You stop hitting me. I don't like it any more than you do." He spun around the room, looking for a place to dump her.

"This is all your fault. You and your stupid ideas. All I wanted was to start over somewhere else. Somewhere like here, but I can't because you're here and I'm pulling a con on these people. Thanks a lot." She pinched his waist.

"Christ, Cori. If you don't stop..." He sunk his teeth in her thigh. Gently at first, and then adding pressure slowly.

"Oh, my word," she groaned, and her body went slack.

The energy around them changed. Sparks still flew, but instead of crackling with anger, they arched with sexual tension, going from red-hot to blue. It took Fort five long strides to the small bedroom off the main room. The full-size bed was made with what looked like clean linen. It stood tall on an old brass frame. In one swift movement, he dumped her onto the bed and spread her legs.

"You aren't going anywhere," he said. "We're in this together, and we'll figure out a solution." He dropped forward, one arm on each side of her. She lay before him, eyes on him, lip between her teeth, breath ragged. Her tank top had ridden up some, showing a sliver of belly. He bent forward and pressed a light kiss above her navel. Cori groaned and grabbed at his biceps.

"You're an idiot," she said in a whisper.

"No more than you are," he said against her skin, then nipped a bit of skin between his teeth.

"Undeniably," she said and moaned again.

He traveled more kisses up her belly, pushing her shirt up with his nose. She trembled beneath his lips. He stepped closer, the lower part of his thighs against the edge of the bed. Her legs closed around him, her fingers clenching his arms.

He kissed the valley between her breasts. Her bra, made from fabric thin like a tissue, was held closed with a clasp in the front. With a flick of his thumb and index finger, he released it and swept the material to the side. Revealing her. She was glorious. He'd never seen her in the light and as he blew air around her breast, a gentle lick around the underside, he committed this vision to his memory. When he took her hard nipple in his mouth, Cori arched and whimpered his name.

That was all the invitation he needed. As if someone had cranked up the volume, he whipped her tank up over her head, her fingers working madly on his uniform buttons. He stopped to kiss and suckle at her collarbone before traveling to her other breast when he felt her hands on his buckle.

"Cori?" He needed to know.

"Undeniably," she said and lifted her hips so he could pull off her tights. With their clothes on the floor, he eased himself on top of her, both moaning as they became fused. Skin to skin.

"We need a condom," he said, hating the words because the odds of either of them having one were slim.

She reached over her head to the end table and slid open the drawer. Inside was a box, a new box. He didn't want to guess who might have placed them there. The truth was too awkward.

Once sheathed, he situated himself to press against her and snuggled his hand there, too, stroking her from the top, his fingers damp with her want. She was putty under his hands, her head tossed back, and he wanted to keep her here forever, like this, moaning his name. He pushed at her, gently asking to come in. She raised her hips and clutched tightly to him.

There was a resistance that gave him pause. Was he really her first? Did he want to be? Not that he could stop if he wanted to. He'd been thinking about this moment since that night they made out in the pasture.

"Babe," he said, "are you sure?"

She didn't say a word, only raised her hips higher and pushed him past the barrier, expelling a long hiss in the process. After a brief pause, she moved once more, fitting him farther inside her.

In the past, he'd been with women who didn't care to know him beyond the good time he offered. Cori, she knew all parts of him, the good and the bad. He wanted this moment almost as much as he wanted to win sheriff, if not more.

"Wait," he said, "give it a moment." He throbbed to move, desperate to feel her come apart in his hands. He reached between them and stroked at her center. She bucked against him, calling his name.

Slowly, he began to make her his. With each stroke, she unfolded and opened up to him. He felt her tighten, knew what was coming, and with his arms under her, holding her in place, he drove harder, pushing against her before pulling back and starting again. She rose up, sunk her teeth in his shoulder and began to quake. He nipped at her breast, then took the nipple between his teeth, his tongue teasing it. Cori tossed her head back and cried out his name. He thrust one last time and held onto her with everything he had, letting himself go and joining her in the free fall of their release.

21

They lay beside each other on the bed, her head tucked against his shoulder.

She didn't know what to say. Maybe, "Wow that was good." "Can we do that again?" seemed wanton, and she wasn't sure that was the message she wanted to send. Though it kinda was. Argh, she didn't know what to do. She was woefully unprepared for this. She closed her eyes and prayed for wisdom. This was not only new territory for them, but for her.

Fort rolled toward her and kissed her forehead. "Are you okay?"

She nodded.

"Do you have any regrets?"

She shook her head.

"Can I ask you a question?" he said softly in her ear.

She buried her face in the bed and groaned.

"How have you gone all this time and not...? Why are you...?" He ran his finger from her shoulder down her arm.

Cori peeked up from the bed. His question hadn't sounded judgey or like he was about to brag. "I've spent the last several years trying to make amends for my father and what he did." She looked away and then dipped her head back onto the bed.

"You can't put your life on hold for something that wasn't your fault. No one blames you."

Cori jerked with surprise. She pushed up on her elbows. "You're kidding, right? Because of all the mean things to say, that's one of them. So what, we just had sex. You don't need to start being nice and lying to me now." She rolled her eyes and went to sit, grabbing the comforter to cover her chest.

Fort, who apparently didn't care that he was naked, sat up, too. "I mean it. What happened is not your fault."

"Says the man who blames me for what went down between his father and mine." She moved to sit on the edge.

Fort groaned and flopped back on the bed, covering his eyes. "You're right," he said.

The admission caused her mouth to drop open. He sat back up and looked at her. "You're right and you're wrong."

She snorted.

"I mean that, logically, I never blamed you for your father's actions." He held up a hand. "But I did take it out on you. Which may have felt like I was blaming you. Used to be every time I looked at you, I thought of all my own failures with my dad and that last year in Brewster. But look around me. Life here is great. I'm not sure I would have this if the past hadn't gone like it had. Maybe I should look at you and think of all the good things I have."

"That would be a first."

He winked. "Or, and this is my favorite so far, remember you with your head back calling my name as I bury myself deep inside you."

Cori buried her face in her hands. "Just shut up already."

He kissed her on the shoulder, his arm snaking around her waist, his hand tugging the comforter out of the way so he could reach her breast. "Let me see if I can make you call my name again."

"Wait, what?" she cried as he jerked her back by her waist, then in one swift motion flipped her on her stomach.

One hand dug in the drawer of the side table, the other pressing down on her back, keeping her in place.

"Fort?" she asked. The excitement made her voice warble, and a nervous giggle escaped her. All he had to do was touch her. Anywhere. His thumb stroked the small of her back.

"I think you're going to like this even more," he said, fitting himself over her between her legs. He dipped a kiss where his hand had been, then gently lifted her backside up by her hips.

"You can tell me to stop anytime," he whispered. As his hands stroked upward, his mouth traveled south. She was powerless against him, yet felt safe. His touch was gentle and strong.

He showed her how talented he was with his mouth and his fingers as he explored all parts of her. When he took her from behind, Cori nearly wept at the tenderness he showed her. They found their release together and collapsed as one on the bed, Cori tucked against him.

"This," he whispered in her ear as he held her from behind. "This is why you should stay."

A few more weeks of this would be glorious and heart wrenching. She didn't have to have eons of experience to know she was falling for the big doo-doo. At least he'd warmed up to her, found her appealing even. She'd take what she could get.

"We're starting to confuse the real and the pretend. Maybe me leaving will give us clarity," she said on a sigh.

He pulled away, and rush of cool air ran up her backside. He dropped a kiss between her shoulder blades. "If you must go, then you'll have these memories to take with you," was his reply, then he was off the bed. When he disappeared into the bathroom, Cori jumped up, using his absence to dress. She'd clean up when he was done. She had her tank and denim skirt on but was searching for her panties when he came back. He lifted the comforter and pointed to her hidden garment. She slid them on as fast as she could, and not knowing what to say, went for the safest topic she could pick. "Guess there are no clues here."

Fort was buttoning his shirt. "I'll have to talk to Mrs. Z's foreman to be sure, but my guess is we might have found something. Too many footprints, and I can't imagine why they would be bringing cows here. And there's this." He held up a glittery gold matchbook with the name Bruno's Honky-Tonk written next to the silhouette of a big-breasted woman, much like the ones she'd seen on mud flaps of tractor-trailers.

Men.

"What? You think Mrs. Z wouldn't go to Bruno's?" She was joking, of course. "Couldn't it be from her husband? Or your step-dad?"

Fort smirked and tossed the matchbook over in his hand. "This is fairly new, as is Bruno's. Opened about a month ago. If Paul had the time to go to Bruno's, he'd probably not take the chance that Ma would find out and skin him alive. It's a titty bar."

Cori made an O with her mouth.

"And Mr. Z died before Bruno's opened." Fort opened the pack and showed half of the matches were missing. Not that she knew what that meant.

"Those could have been used before they got here?"

"Doubtful. Look at this." He went into the kitchen, then pulled out the trashcan from under the sink. From inside, he lifted out something white and stubby. It was the last few inches of a candle. "There's no other trash in here. My guess is that whoever set this up"—he gestured to the picnic—"found the candles and tossed them. But why would candles be used when the place has electricity?" He flicked a switch, and the light over the sink came on. He turned it off. "Because that can be seen from further out, and if one doesn't know the billing cycle, an increase in the power bill for here would be another tip-off."

"But it wouldn't be that much." Cori wasn't sure the dots were connecting. "Not a waving red flag."

"The breaker is turned off until someone comes out and flips it. Like if we're expecting a freeze, I've come out before to heat the place to make sure the pipes don't burst. My guess is Mrs. Z flipped the breaker when she set up our lunch."

Cori could faintly see the connection now. A squatter wouldn't risk getting caught, and turning on the electricity could give him away. The candles indicated someone was hiding out. Regardless of that person's intention, she couldn't help believe they weren't good. She looked at the cabin through new eyes, rubbing her hands over her arms. It grossed her out to think they'd just done what they had in the same bed a crook was probably sleeping in. She was going to need a long shower.

In the distance, a train whistle blew.

Fort looked at his watch and nodded. "That's the two-thirty."

"Sounds closer than the other one we saw."

"It is. About half a mile from here are the tracks. Run past some good pastureland and a pond. Good and bad qualities of the cabin."

Cori shuttered. "Can we leave? It bugs me to think someone has been hiding out here. What if they came up and saw us, you know, through the window." She looked over his shoulder out the window. "I'm freaked out."

Fort chuckled and dropped an arm around her shoulder. "Officially we own this place now. You should be more concerned with the fact that someone's illegally using your property."

"I am. How about we let the law handle it?" she teased as they walked out to his truck together.

Fort chuckled and opened the door for her.

Before getting in, she glanced back at the little house and pictured adding to it. A wrap porch and hanging flower baskets would be charming.

A heaviness settled over her heart. False pretenses. That's

how all the good things were coming to her. None of it was real, and she would be wise to remember that. "I'll sign over my half to you." She couldn't bear to look at him.

Once she was inside, Fort closed the door. He walked around the front of the truck, looking as if he didn't have a care in the world. Not an impending wedding to a girl he didn't love, some missing cattle, and now a squatter.

What did they say in the adventure movies? She needed an extraction plan.

They took the same dirt road out they'd come in on, riding in silence, but his hand on her knee felt as if it belonged there. She could picture this long-term, ranching with Fort, occasional lunches with Cricket, being a part of something more. She thought about the little cabin, a place that could be her home. Being in Wolf Creek was more than she imagined, yet was everything she'd dreamt of when she pictured herself starting over. Having Fort by her side was a bonus she never dared let herself hope for.

All the more reason she should leave sooner than later. Everything was getting too confusing.

Fort radioed in, checking with the station to make sure everything was quiet. And it was. Cori gave him a grimace when she realized he'd been on the clock, technically, while they were fooling around. Mrs. Z might not care, but others certainly would. When they turned onto the main county road, Cori resisted the urge to look behind her at the fantasy she was leaving behind.

Fort sat forward, and the truck slowed. He gave the siren a short blast. *Bleep. Bleep.* Then he pulled onto the shoulder. Cori glanced at him then followed his path, wondering what had caught his attention. She spotted a truck on the side of the road, hood open, and she half expected steam to be pouring out.

Fort called it in, asked for a run on the license plate, while coming to an easy stop in front of it. "Stay here," he commanded without so much as looking at her.

Cori pulled out her camera and grabbed a few shots. Behind the truck was a dilapidated barn, and the image spoke of a past lifestyle. When Fort slammed the truck door, two men popped up from the truck bed, looking half asleep or three sheets to the wind. One was Conway Witty. The other she couldn't make out clearly because of the angle. He looked to be the same dude she had managed to capture in film a few days ago, which made her sit up straighter.

Fort walked slowly up to the side of the truck, one hand on his firearm. "Engine troubles, fellas? Need some help?" His tone was friendly enough, but Cori heard the caution.

"We ain't sure," Witty said while swiping at his eyes. "Well, lookee here. It's the wanna-be sheriff." He stood, walked down the bed, and eased off the tailgate. In doing so, the truck rocked slightly to the side and a flash of silver on the dashboard caught Cori's eyes. She lifted her camera and zoomed in. It was a matchbook from Brunos. She pressed the shutter button several times before dropping the camera to the floor, out of sight.

"You wanna try and start it for me? Maybe I can determine the problem." Fort stepped away from the truck, giving Witty a wide path to the driver's seat.

While Witty was getting into the cab, Fort moved toward the truck bed, resting his hand on the edge. He glanced at Cori and slightly tilted his head toward the bed.

She'd place crisp cash that her squatter was one of these guys.

"You all been drinking?" Fort asked and walked to where Witty sat in the driver's seat, door open, one leg dangling out.

"So what if we were? We ain't driving," Witty said. The engine gave a grinding sound.

Cori chuckled. Nitwits. They must have been wasted to not realize they'd run out of gas.

Fort went to the hood, removed the safety bar, then let it slam shut. The guy in the back popped up.

Yep, it was him, the guy she'd recognized as having worked with her father. Cori wished she could get a better shot, but the glare on the windshield would ruin the shot.

"I have gas in my truck," Fort said. "Can't give it to you until you take a breathalyzer."

Cori smirked and hid her smile. It was well past noon. For these two to be still feeling the effects of booze meant they'd really tied one on.

"Aw, come on. That's just you harassing me," Witty said.

"Let me see your driver's license." Fort held out his hand. "Both of you."

Witty dug in his back pocket and produced his. The other guy didn't move. "Musta left it somewhere," he said.

Fort cut his eyes to Cori. He walked to the truck and called in Witty's Tennessee license and asked for a Wants and Warrants check. He said nothing while waiting for Bitsy, the dispatcher, to come back. Witty was watching them.

After Fort was given the all-clear from dispatch, he negotiated with Witty to walk a straight line and complete the touch-his-nose test, both done without issue. Fort then put enough gas in their tank to get them into town.

Fort let them drive away first. The other guy tucked in the passenger seat was asleep before Witty pulled out on the road.

Cori waited until they were traveling down the road before asking, "You think they're going to the cabin?"

Fort's forehead was wrinkled in thought. "I'm going to drop you off at home and go back and check."

Cori lifted the camera and pulled the matchbook up on the viewfinder. "Look at this. It was on their dash."

"You didn't get a better picture of the drunk in the back, did you?" Fort glanced between her and the road, his lips a fine line.

She wished she'd had. "No, the angle was bad. There was a glare." That didn't stop her from feeling like she failed.

"Cori, it's not your job to solve this," he said as if reading her mind.

"It is if my dad's involved." She prayed that was not the case.

"What are the odds?" Fort mumbled. "It's not like he's the only cattle rustler."

"True, it's just weird seeing this guy. And my dad was never one to be idle. I can't see him in prison playing Jenga or Scrabble."

Fort drove up the ranch drive faster than normal, likely anxious to get back to the cabin. They were near the house when his phone vibrated in his shirt pocket. After removing it, he gave it a quick glance followed by a groan of frustration.

"What's happened?" she asked.

He tossed the phone on the console between them. "It's from Paul. They found the GPS tags that were on the missing cows buried by a salt block where the herd was last."

Cori's eyes went wide. "They snip off the tags and bury them. So simple."

"At least now we have the answer to that question. I'm meeting Paul at the station to see if there might be any fingerprints."

She wanted to caution him to expect the tags to yield nothing. The cow thieves, whoever they were, weren't lazy enough to not wear gloves.

When he stopped outside the barn, she pushed open the door and picked up her bags.

"Hey," he said, grabbing her by the arm before she could slide out. "Today was amazing. Thank you."

Heat coursed through her. Embarrassment? Sexual attraction? Maybe both. Regardless, she appreciated him saying so.

"You know what this means, right?" She jumped out of the truck.

"We're going to have to do it more often?"

Cori laughed. "Okay, now I understand the single-track mind of a man, but we're gonna have to go to Brunos."

Fort shook his head. "Pointless. I can't walk in there and find out anything new."

"No, but I can. All I need are some heels and a good wig." She thought of Cricket and wondered if she still had her pageant stuff.

Fort pointed a long finger at her, a determined set to his jaw. "Nope. No way."

"Okay, good. It's decided then. Why not try for tomorrow since you're off?" She slammed the door and gave him a finger wave before hotfooting it to his place. They could argue about it later.

22

Cori knew Fort wasn't happy. He'd made his dislike for the plan clear, but since he hadn't come up with another that didn't require him marching into the bar and roughing up some guy, they were going with her idea.

Both Cori and Fort were hesitant to involve Cricket. But in a game of who-was-more-stubborn, Cori won. She used Fort's sense of justice and strong desire to protect Wolf Creek as her trump card, and he caved. Bringing Cricket in was a necessity. She had all the accouterments that Cori needed. Fort tried to get around it, but finally admitted that sending Cori in was the one plan that had the highest probability of succeeding.

They were holed up at Cricket's, the women in Cricket's spare room where her pageant goods were stored, making choices about Cori's disguise while Fort waited outside in Cricket's living room ready to wire Cori.

"Thanks for helping with this, Cricket." Cori looked at the wigs before her, wondering which would be the best.

"Anytime. Pick the red. It'll be a contrast. It'll work and get you some attention." She pulled a box off the shelf. "Are you scared?"

"I think I'm more pissed off than anything. Cattle rustlers, if that's what we're looking at, make me angry." Cori snapped the eyebrow pencil she was holding in two.

Cricket's eyes grew wide. "Yeah, I can see that."

"It cuts close. Cattle rustling."

"It happens." Cricket handed Cori the auburn-colored wig. "Sadly. My folks consider themselves lucky if they go a year without incident."

"But they shouldn't feel like that." Cori stomped her foot. "Makes me so mad."

"I'm guessing you were the victim of cattle rustlers?" Cricket pushed her to the chair in front of the vanity and pointed to the contact lenses Cori had brought with her.

"Sorta." Cori knew she would have to share something with Cricket, and she couldn't stand to tell any more lies. Omitting some facts would be the best plan. Not looking at Cricket made telling the story easier so she focused on inserting the contacts while she talked. "Do you know how Fort got his name?"

"Nope," Cricket said as she spun Cori around to face her. Cricket picked up a makeup sponge and began applying the foundation.

"On the night Fort was born, his dad won twenty-five acres and twenty-five head of Angus cattle from my dad. Fort's dad, Karl, had put up a little swath of land as his final bet. My dad wanted that land. It was prime real estate, only Karl didn't know that. The land was in a direct line from where oil had been found on our land. My dad had kept it a secret as he tried to buy up all the surrounding parcels. Karl's was one of the last. So my dad put up those acres to woo Karl into the game. Charlie, that's my dad, never expected Karl to win. The guy wasn't very lucky. But he did. He won, and when Fort was born a few hours later he convinced Saira to name him Fortune because he had made his fortune that night. His luck had changed. Little did he know he was sitting on a bubbling crude of money, but Karl thought he'd struck it rich by becoming a rancher in one night, after one hand of poker. Over the years, my dad's anger grew, often screaming about how it was a chump's bet. How he shouldn't have lost."

Cricket listened, mouth agape. "Did Karl ever find out about the oil?"

Cori tilted her head up, eyes closed while Cricket worked on her eyeshadow. "Yeah, a day after he lost the land and cattle to my dad in another high-stakes game eighteen years later. But the ranch had been struggling for a while. Karl wanted instant riches and often embarked on these schemes that would result in him losing more money, which meant they'd have to sell cattle or land to cover the losses. Usually to my father."

"Sounds awful. It's amazing you two are friends, much less romantically involved."

Cori was glad she couldn't see Cricket. "It's been a struggle."

Life after her dad had been a never-ending hardship. Creating a relationship with Fort, however it was defined, had been the easiest of it all. "My dad was a real bastard. Greedy. He's swindled many of the ranchers from their hard-earned money through insurance policies and taxes. He would swoop in like a good guy and offer to buy off their land or cattle for less than market to help with trumped-up fake diseases or federal charges. Essentially, he used the town of Brewster like a piggy bank, constantly dipping his hand in. He bought a big house for my mom, put me through all those stupid pageants. I lived in luxury while he was stealing from his neighbor. All his neighbors."

"Jeez." Cricket took Cori's hand in hers. "'Is that why you're so adamant about doing this?"

Cori opened her eyes and nodded. "I can't let anything happen to Wolf Creek. Even more so if my dad is involved. And if Deke is involved—"

Cricket said with force, "He's not. I know he's not. He's not the sort."

Cori was skeptical. "He's running with a bad crowd. How do you explain that? He's not that naive that they're taking advantage of him." They would know more tonight, hopefully. Cori picked up the red curly-haired wig, running her fingers over the mesh lace inside the cap.

"I know. And there's a perfectly good explanation. We'll find it. Now, let's get you finished." She waited while Cori wrapped the wig cap over her head. Cricket set the wig on Cori's head, then went about styling it.

"What do you think?" Cricket asked.

Cori stared back at the stranger in the mirror. She looked like a bombshell. Her hair was a seductive auburn and hung in heavy waves around her shoulders. Her blue eyes popped and sparkled. Tucked into the waist of her tight jean skirt was a clingy purple T-shirt. But what made the outfit remarkable was the push-up bra. It was amazing because, unless she grew breasts overnight, which she knew she hadn't, her perfectly sized chest had exploded and was straining against her shirt and bra, spilling over the top. She couldn't wait to see Fort's face. Cori slid on the three-inch heels and stood.

"Cripes, I hope I don't break my neck." She walked around the room in an attempt to get her "stiletto legs." "Okay, let's do this." She opened Cricket's bedroom door then strode down the hallway. The plan was to try to eavesdrop but have enough oomph to use it to her advantage if she had to. Fort had grumbled about the plan, but couldn't offer an alternative. Knowing he'd be in a truck in the parking lot was a small comfort.

When Cori stepped from the hallway, his eyes went wide. Fort growled. "Nope. No way," he said, standing. "We'll find a different way. I'm calling this off."

"What? What's wrong? You don't think I can pull it off?"

"Have you seen yourself?" He stepped toward her and spun her to the mirror hanging over Cricket's entryway.

"Yeah, I think we did a good job. I look nothing like me."

"That's correct. You look like you're wanting some trouble. I don't like it."

"Or maybe you like it too much," Cricket said.

Cori nodded. "That's got to be it. He's always had a thing for showy women."

"Those heels make your legs look a mile long, and the short skirt shows *way* too much thigh. No," he said again, then licked his lips while staring at her cleavage.

Cori rolled her eyes. "Don't be stupid. I have a stun gun in my purse and you waiting outside the bar. I'll be fine."

He crossed his arms over his chest and set his jaw in determination.

"Do you want to know what's going on? Put a stop to the cattle rustling? 'Cause, if not, then we need to tell the good folk of Wolf Creek that you haven't done everything in your power to stop this. Seeing as how you want to be their sheriff and all." She stuck a hand on her hip, but his eyes never wavered from her breasts.

"This is a bad idea," he said, then looked at her. "I could make it worth your while if we stayed home."

Cricket gave a discrete cough. "That's a good offer," she mumbled to Cori.

Cori sighed. "So, to be clear. You *don't* want to be sheriff?" She gave him a pointed look, one telling him to prioritize.

"Fine," he said. He fit her with the wire, brushing his knuckles over her sensitive parts, probably on purpose to distract her. "You sure you don't wanna come up with another plan?"

She shook her head, focusing on steadying her breathing.

"Okay, then, let's go." He gestured to the door.

"Shotgun," Cricket said, laughing as she pushed past them both.

Cori teetered out, the heels causing her hips to sway.

"Jesus," Fort mumbled. He held the door open for the women. He'd brought the ranch truck to give them more room.

They rode to Bruno's in silence, Cori quietly going over the plan in her head. When they pulled into the gravel parking lot, she got nervous, sitting forward with her arms around her belly.

Bruno's was a honky-tonk in the truest sense. Motorcycles lined the front, pickups as well, many with horse or cattle trailers. Music was bleeding through the tin rafters and shook the neon sign that touted the bar's name.

"You're just trying to eavesdrop. If you get drawn into a conversation, try to find out the connection with that guy and Witty."

"And my father." She desperately needed to know if he was behind all this.

"Don't focus on that. Your dad can't be wielding too much power from—" His eyes cut to Cricket.

"You don't know that."

"Cori, stay on point," Fort warned.

"Sure, sure." She nodded. If her father was involved, she would kill him. With her bare hands.

Fort helped her out of the truck from his side. He reached for her, a tiny microphone in his hand, but she stepped away. If while touching her he asked her to cancel the plan, she wouldn't be able to say no.

"I'll do it," she said and tucked the small recorder and cord between the valley of her breast, and then hid everything in the padding of her bra at the bottom of the cups. "Can you see it?" she asked and moved her head away so he could look down her shirt.

He barely glanced at her chest. "Cori—"

She didn't wait for more but walked off toward the bar.

Inside Bruno's was loud, smelly like body odor and cows, and packed, clearly exceeding fire marshal limits. There was no way Fort was going to hear a single thing from the wire unless she pulled it out and screamed into the microphone. She was flying solo.

A large stage broke the room into two halves. On the stage, women in various states of dress danced.

She had a hard time finding her target, believing for a

moment she and Fort had picked the wrong day and they would have to do this again. And she really didn't want to.

That's when she spotted Witty by the bar on the far side of the stage. He looked to be with three others and already heavy into his drink, but not one of the guys with him was the stranger Cori was hoping to chat up.

Disappointed, Cori decided to get close anyway. Maybe they'd say something, anything, to help Fort.

As she wove through the crowd, she had to slap away two wandering hands and push a drunk in the chest with a threat to stab her stiletto in his eye if he didn't back away. When she finally reached the side of the bar where Witty was, the stranger was there, too. She caught his eye and smiled.

At the bar, she asked for a beer, and before the bartender could produce it, stranger-guy was next to her.

"Hello, beautiful," he said in a wave of foul breath. If he was staying at her cabin, he should at least make use of the bathroom shower and sink. She turned her curled lip into a smile.

Her cabin. As if. But she couldn't help that she felt that way. She just did. Even if it wasn't true.

"Hello, cowboy," she said and turned to face him, putting her hand with the bottle in front of her like a glass wall.

"What brings a pretty girl like you here?" When he swayed forward, she leaned away.

"I was meeting someone, but it looks like he stood me up." She stuck out her lower lip in a fake pout.

"You from around here? Cuz I ain't seen you in here before." He balanced himself by leaning against the bar, shoving a person out of the way.

Cori's gut told her to go with no. She knew he wasn't a local either, and that might appeal to him. Plus, if he were cattle rustling, he wouldn't take them to a livestock auction nearby; he'd go miles away. Like her dad had done. Her father had actually established a second residence in Oklahoma for trafficking cattle.

Cori smiled coyly. "I'm from Montana. Billings. Came to see a friend and meet a guy who I was chatting with online. Looks like I'm meeting you instead. I'm Co—Coral." Fudge-cicles. She'd forgotten to come up with an alias.

"Coral, pretty. I'm Brody Fant, and you smell like the beach." When he whiffed her neck, nausea nearly knocked her aside. At his smell, it all came back to her. Brody was his real name. That she was sure. But the last name was new. She remembered her mom pleading with her dad to turn in a Brody to reduce his sentence, but her father refused, saying he, Brody, was his right hand, and there were things Brody would need to take care of while he was in prison.

Brody was mid-thirties and had probably been handsome once upon a time when his sandy blond hair and dimples were fresh. But now, he looked weary. Road hard and put up wet, as they said. The lifestyle he led was coming through his weathered skin, his yellow teeth, and when the odor of booze leaked from one's pores, it wasn't from the drinks he was currently imbibing. No, it was from a lifetime of them.

No doubt, her father was involved. There was no such thing as a coincidence.

"What do you say we leave and have some quiet time?" Brody suggested.

Cori cocked her head to one side and bit her lip, as if she was sorely tempted. "I wish. I see my friend waving to me over there by the door. I can't go anywhere without her following." Brody teetered to a twist, looking over his shoulder. Cori waved to some random lady by the door that happened to be looking their way. The woman waved back, a puzzled look on her face.

"I could entertain the both of you," he said, facing her again while hitching up his britches.

Cori seriously doubted he could entertain himself with the state he was in.

"Maybe, if you're ever in Billings," Cori said and set her beer on the bar top.

"I'll be in Billings Thursday," he said with a cocky smile. "Got me some business up there."

"At the livestock auction?" It was a stab in the dark, but she wasn't raised by a rustler to not know *something*.

Brody didn't answer, but stared at her slack-jawed.

Cori ran her index finger down his plaid western shirt. "Are you a cattleman? I have a thing for cattlemen." She swirled her finger near his belly button.

Brody's slack mouth went into a wide smile. "As a matter of fact, I am. I'm in the cattle broker business."

I bet you are, she thought.

"I can meet you at the auction. Maybe a little afternoon delight?" She suppressed a gag at what she was suggesting, swallowing it instead.

"Yeah, sure." Brody came in for a kiss, but she quickly turned her head and he caught her at the neck.

"We'll save all that for Thursday. Okay dokey?" She patted his chest and tweaked his nose. "See you then, sexy." Not waiting for a response, she pushed through the crowd like a mad woman with fire at her backside. Once out the door, she rushed to Fort's truck. He was standing outside the driver's door with his hands on his hips, a serious frown and mean ass glare on his face.

"Two more minutes, and I was coming in," he said when he saw her.

"Worried, were you? Too loud to hear anything I bet?" She scooted around him and then climb in the truck through the driver's side. "Let's get outta here. Where's Cricket?" The other side of the cab was empty.

Fort pointed over his shoulder. "Talking with Deke."

"Deke's here?" Cori looked in the direction he was pointing and saw Cricket with arms waving madly in the air. "I think she's yelling at him. Those two are weird. I thought she didn't talk to him."

"It drives me insane the way she defends him. I know he was married to her sister, but still."

Cori gasped as realization dawned. "Oh, no."

"What?" Fort spun around to look at Deke and Cricket.

"Something is going on between them." Cori moved to the back seat and ripped off the heels. "Something like what we did in the cabin."

"What? No way." Fort harrumphed "I don't believe that. Cricket is smarter than that."

Cori rolled her eyes. "The heart wants what it wants Fort Be-so-lame." Man, hers really wanted him.

When Cricket turned around and pointed in their direction, Cori waved at her to hurry it along. She was anxious to get the hell outta dodge.

Cricket had grabbed Deke by the arm and was dragging him from the truck and toward them.

"Incoming," Cori said as Fort let go of an expletive.

"Deke here has something to say." Cricket let go of his arm, then shoved him in the shoulder.

"Can it wait? I really want to get outta here. The guys are already drunk, and I may have promised one an afternoon of pleasure on Thursday. I'm nervous he might come looking for me now, ready to collect."

"You did what?" Fort bellowed.

Cricket twisted Deke's arm. Deke said in a rush of words, "Witty isn't my campaign manager."

"A-ha, I knew it," Fort said and pointed a finger at Deke. "What scam are you running?"

With her free hand, Cricket punch Fort. "Tell him, Deke."

"I hired him under the pretense of being my manager. What I was really doing was trying to get to the bottom of a cattle rustling ring in the area."

Fort snorted his disbelief.

"It's true," Deke said.

"And I should believe you, why? Maybe you know you're caught so you're trying to save your own neck."

"I'm not a dirt bag," Deke said and took a step toward Fort, hands balled into fist.

"You broke my arm with a bat because I gave Laura a ride home." Fort met the challenge and moved closer to Deke.

"I was swinging it to try and scare you. You weren't supposed to bum rush me. Fool."

"You're the fool," Fort growled.

Cricket stepped between them. "You're both idiots. Can we please focus on now and not the past?"

Fort stepped back and spread his hands wide. "Okay, if this is true. You think you might have told us at the office?"

"Oh, no," Cricket said, her tone heavy with sarcasm. "And give up his dream of being Insurance Commissioner for the state? Not a chance. Dick Tracy here thought he could single-handedly solve this crime, and he would be escalated to the top of Wyoming Government."

"Do you even want to be sheriff?" Fort asked.

Deke gave a slight sigh of defeat. "Only because it'll help me become commissioner. Plus, I needed you to run. If I do become Insurance Commissioner, I didn't want my rise to the top to be easy. No one respects someone when the job is handed to them."

Cricket and Cori shared a look of disgust. The things men would do to get their way.

"Can we take this discussion elsewhere?" Cori asked. She was itching to take the wig off.

"Yes," Cricket said. "My house. I'll make sure Deke gets there." She steered him back to his truck.

Cori climbed over the console and into the passenger seat. "If you could step on it, that would be awesome," she told Fort when he turned over the engine.

"You think we could squeeze in a little late-night delight?" he asked, then leaned over and dropped a kiss on the top of her breast.

"Aren't you thinking about what Deke just said?"

"Sure, but I'm thinking more about what's right in front of me. There's time for Deke later."

Cori smiled and tossed a curl over her shoulder. "So long as you can make it fast. I've never had a quickie, and I'm interested in seeing what all the talk is about." She needed to get what she could before she no longer had it.

Fort gunned the truck and peeled out of the parking lot. "I know of a little secluded area just down the road from here. Used to go fishing there."

23

The fishing spot Fort was talking about had two paths. They took the one to the left, and Cori discovered just how much fun, and how awkward, having sex in a truck could be.

When they were leaving, they almost collided with another truck that was exiting the path from the right.

It was Deke and Cricket.

"Still think I'm crazy?" Cori asked as she brushed out her own hair, happy to lose the wig.

Fort blocked their exit and jumped out, leaving his door open.

"What in the hell is going on here?" Fort stood before Deke's front lights.

Deke turned off the truck and climbed out. Cricket did as well.

Deke said, "It started after the holidays. Tinsdale was out of town, and some of the guys were coming in, asking about their policies, talking about making claims for a few head of cattle. Most weren't looking for immediate payout, but if their heads kept going missing, then could they make a claim? I told them not without a police report and paper trail, but none were filing claims. I finally asked Mrs. Williams, and she said her husband hadn't because none of the cows were tagged or branded, and there were no signs of them being taken. They were all wondering if they'd miscalculated or the error was on them."

Cori was sitting in the driver's seat, listening, and perked up. "That's what we're seeing, too. It's still happening."

Deke leaned against the truck hood. "I'm not surprised. It's happened in Bison's Prairie and as far up as Bozeman."

"I'm seeing signs of it throughout Wyoming and Montana. Even a few reports in Idaho," Fort said.

"It's like they take just enough to make people wonder, but not enough to make them outraged and do anything."

"Plus, the cows aren't marked, so it's an uphill battle for the rancher," Cricket chimed in.

"That's not all. Couple of the guys over in Elk's Pass came in, wanting to file claims and were pissed when I couldn't do anything without a police report. They mentioned having a secondary insurance they got off some salesmen they met at a few auctions."

"Let me guess," Cori said, "the insurance is bogus."

"Yeah, how'd you know?" Deke asked.

"What tipped you off?" Fort asked Deke, changing the subject. Protecting Cori was more important than getting *all* the clues. He had enough to piece the puzzle together.

"I was at the insurance convention I mentioned earlier. Lots of brokers were talking about it. It's not the first time something like this has happened. There was this guy in Texas—"

"Charlie Walters. That's my dad," Cori said and looked at Fort. "He's the guy in Texas."

Fort didn't have to shine a light on her to see her panicked expression. "Cori," Fort said. "Your dad's in prison. He's not doing this."

"Except that it's starting to look more like he is."

Deke looked between them. "I don't know about your dad, but what I do know is that Conway isn't the brains. There's a guy

I'm thinking is in charge. He's been in town a few times. That's who I'm trying to get to. By hiring Conway, I thought I might, but Conway protects the hell out of him."

Cori reached under the passenger seat and withdrew her camera. "Is it this guy?" She found Brody's image and passed the camera to Fort who showed it to Deke.

"Yeah, that's him."

Cori covered her face. "His name is Brody Fant. Fant isn't his last name. That I'm sure of. But Brody is his real name," she said between her fingers. A memory tickled at her brain, and she closed her eyes, trying to picture it. It was her mother telling someone her father wasn't home. After she'd closed the door, she'd shuddered and said, "That Mr. Brody makes me nervous."

"In fact, I almost think Brody is his last name." She opened her eyes and looked at Fort. "I know this because he worked with my dad or for my dad or whatever. The Feds were going to reduce my dad's sentence if he gave up Brody. I remember my mom begging him to do it, but my dad refusing, telling her that Brody needed to stay out of jail if she expected to keep up her spandex and highlights habit. Tell me again why you think my dad isn't involved?" She brushed tears from her cheeks.

"Babe." Fort went to her, stood next to the seat, and then pulled her into his arms. "Even if he is, we'll get to the bottom of this. We'll stop it."

"Can he ever be stopped?" She rested her forehead on his shoulder. Her weary sigh could have broken his heart. "I made plans to meet Brody at the Billings Auction on Thursday. He was planning on going up there. That's how they do it. Probably have local tags on their car, say their working for a ranch, and bring in the stock to sell."

Fort kissed the top of her head. "That's in three days."

"That means they'll be doing a roundup of the last few over the next few days," Cricket said.

"I wish we knew where they were hiding out," Deke said while rubbing the back of his head in thought.

Cori lifted her head and looked at Fort.

"We know where they're staying," he said, staring back at her, reading her mind. He then shifted so he was facing the others, his arm around her shoulder, and explained about the cabin.

"I know the place," Deke said, chin in hand, lost in thought.

"We need a plan," Cori said.

Fort nodded. "Hannah Jacobson has been running stats for me, and one thing keeps popping up. Heads go missing quickly after they're brought to the ranch, before they're tagged or registered. When I added the number missing to what is sold at auctions days later, its relatively close."

"No identifiable marks makes tracing nearly impossible," Cori said.

"Anyone know of anyone bringing in a few cows?" Cricket asked.

"Mrs. Z said she was bringing in some for breeding since her herds gotten thin," Cori supplied.

"She's an easy mark," Deke added.

"We need to find out if anyone else has brought some new cows in," Fort said.

Cricket said, "Cori and I are meeting some of the women this week to nail down the specifics for your wedding. We'll just move it up to tomorrow and see if we can get info out of them."

"Wait, y'all are getting married...soon?" Deke asked.

"Apparently in a few weeks," Fort said.

Deke threw back his head and laughed a deep, belly one. "Oh, that's rich," he said between fits of mirth. "Town won't let you drag your feet this time Besingame."

"Also means they aren't sold on you," Cricket pointed out.

Deke's laughter faded but his smile stayed. "I don't care, Cricket. Fort's the better candidate for sheriff anyway. I'll be all right if I don't get the job."

Fort held up a hand in question. "All that trash talk—"

"Was to get you to run. I'll take the job and try my best, but I won't stay in it. I'll move on."

"Up," Cricket said with heavy sarcasm.

"Yes, Cricket, I have aspirations. I also have feelings for you that, apparently, I'm only allowed to display under the shadow of darkness."

"You were married to my sister," she cried.

"Laura has been gone five years."

"Doesn't matter. What will people say about us being together? What will my family say about us? Can you imagine reading your bio if you were commissioner? 'Married all the girls in one family.' It could never work." Cricket looked like she could cry.

"You're being ridiculous," Deke said, throwing his hands up in exasperation.

"This is all very interesting," Fort interjected, "but can we get back to the real issue? Cattle thieves."

"I've been trying to work it out," Cori said. "How are they getting the cattle out without a trace?"

"The train," Deke and Fort said in unison.

"How?" Cori asked and glanced at Cricket, whose puzzled expression matched Cori's confusion.

"The midnight crawler stops for about an hour. Sometimes more. They could load then," Fort said. "I should have put it together yesterday." He grunted with self-disgust.

"I don't get it," Cricket said.

Deke said, "When you go in with guns blazing, so to speak, and take as many cows as you can get in one swoop, you bring all the attention to you until you're caught or the trail runs cold. If you do it in pieces, quietly, at night, people are slower to react. A person could make away with a good number, a few hundred head, before anyone is the wiser."

"Try over a thousand. Between us, Bison's Prairie, and Elk's

Pass," Fort said. "I have a number from four different counties. We're well into the thousands overall."

Deke gave a low whistle. "So they take the cows, how?"

"By walking them out of the herd. Broad daylight. The dry earth leaves no sign. They know the ranchers schedule and work around it. Lead the cow out like a kid walking a dog," Fort said.

"Let them graze down in the valley behind the cabin, which is great pastureland," Deke added.

"From there I bet they transport them to the train." Fort was looking at Deke.

"Tomorrow, you stake out the cabin, and I'll take the pasture and train," Deke said.

Fort nodded. "We're gonna need to collect as much evidence as we can before we spring into action. This crew is crafty. I imagine we're looking at a crew with about..." He paused to calculate in his head.

"Including Conway and Brody, there were four others at the bar," Cori contributed.

"Conway is the eyes and ears in town. So when you ladies are pumping info from the women tomorrow, be careful," Deke said. "Cricket, you hear me?"

"I'm not talking to you anymore," she said and looked away from him.

"Back to this?" He shook his head.

"I can get photos," Cori suggested. "Photos might help."

"No!" Deke and Fort said in unison.

"Let us handle this," Fort said. "It's our job. You've already helped a bunch," he added and rubbed his hands up and down her arms. "You and Cricket need to be at the diner first thing to find out who might be missing cattle or getting some new heads in."

"I'm sorry," she said softly to him. "I'm really sorry," she told the others.

"I can't imagine whatever for," Cricket said.

"This is not your fault," Fort said.

Cori waved off his words. "Maybe not. But this isn't over, and if I know my dad, and I do, bad things are gonna happen if these guys catch so much as a hint y'all know what they're up to. These aren't guys who run away quietly and leave behind what they started. They'll try and get what they can before they split," she cautioned. "No, you'll have to be very careful. These guys wouldn't think twice of taking you out just to get the last of their count."

Cori's omen hung in the air, a thick cloud of icy cold truth that left goose bumps on her arms.

24

Heavy, gray clouds hung over Wolf Creek the next morning. Checking her weather app, Cori saw bad weather was expected. Finally, after months of dry days, a humdinger of a storm was heading their way, lightning and all. It felt like a sign from the universe that they should rethink everything.

Wearing a false smile, Cori met Cricket at the diner at the designated time. Mrs. Z and Mrs. Williams were waiting. Cricket had called them the night before, using the ruse of wedding planning to get them to the diner. She and Cori agreed to let Cricket bring up the missing cattle and hoped things would take off from there.

She and Cricket made it through the wedding talk, Cori deciding on a lavender dress for her bridesmaid, Cricket, because her friend happened to have a new dress of that specific color hanging in her closet. Flowers would be hydrangeas and food would be simple.

Secretly, the entire event sounded lovely. Perfect for her. Knowing it wouldn't happen made her want to burst into tears. In the short time she'd been here, she'd sadly experienced more days of happiness then she'd had over the last ten years. Even when fighting with Fort in the early days. If this pretend life became real, she wouldn't object. Secretly, she hoped it would. Not that she was expecting Fort to marry her. No, they'd need more than the few good days of sexy-time to build a foundation. Heck, she wasn't even sure she was needed anymore, or even if Deke was still planning on running. Maybe there was some way around this entire mess, a way that ended with her staying.

Possibly. Doubtfully. Hopefully.

Cori mentally pushed away the myriad of thoughts confusing her. She needed to stick to the task. Catching these cattle rustlers and finding out if her dad's hand was in it.

Her stomach was a mess of knots and twisting tension. Breakfast with the other women was difficult. Even Cricket appeared to be having a hard time focusing, so much that Mrs. Z point-blank asked them what was going on.

Cori used her lack of sleep to her benefit and yawned, touting a late night with a wink. Cricket brought up missing cattle from her family's ranch, which opened the door for the conversation they were trying to have.

Only Mrs. Z had anything to contribute, telling the others that her foreman was out of town purchasing cattle for her ranch. He wouldn't be back for a few days. Nothing that would help Fort and Deke with the current situation.

Cori noticed Conway sitting in the corner, nursing coffee. She was slightly impressed with his ability to drink so heavily and function the next day. Had it been her, she probably would still be in bed sleeping it off. At the very least, if she was tasked with scouting out incoming herds like she assumed Witty was, she would need to write down the info in order to be correct later when relaying it.

No one else took Cricket's bait, and the women had nothing to pass along to Deke and Fort. They excused themselves using the newspaper as their reason to leave.

"Okay," Cricket said as they walked to the newspaper office. "We suck. As detectives."

Cori grunted her agreement.

"What can we do to stay busy?" She'd texted Deke and Fort their dismal results.

Cori stopped walking. Across the square, small children were playing while their mother's chatted, businesses were opening for the day, and the streets of Wolf Creek were unrolling. People were trying to get their business done before the storm broke. She wasn't about to let her father destroy another town.

"Cori?"

"I've got to do something. I can't sit here and do nothing." She chewed her thumbnail. When her phone chimed, she pulled it out. She glanced at the screen and groaned. "Are you okay sitting in the office and waiting for Deke to tell you to come out from hiding?"

"What? What's happened?" Cricket said, then snatched the phone from Cori. "What's the National Picture Contest?" Confusion was written on her face.

Cori took her phone back and erased the reminder that she'd set. "It's a photography contest that I had hoped to enter." She tossed her phone back into her camera bag.

Cricket crossed her arms and arched her brow. "Why does it sound like you aren't going to enter?"

"Because I don't have anything good to send. A picture should tell a story, and everything I have needs more words to explain. Plus, many are landscape, and those don't really win. I'll try again next year."

Cricket's raised brow furrowed. "Have you entered before?"

Cori nodded. "A few times. Every year I get my hopes up that I'll have a picture that will knock their socks off."

"And not this year?" Cricket dropped her crossed arms.

"I've got more photos of Deke and Witty than anything." Cori rolled her eyes.

"What if I told you I know a place that merges old world with new. It's breathtaking. It might not be the picture you want to take, but it might be worth submitting."

"I'd beg you to take me to it." Cori grinned, excited for something purposeful to do.

They both looked up at the clouds. "We better hurry," Cricket said.

They rushed to Cricket's SUV, and while Cricket drove, Cori prepped her camera. They drove west, away from Fort's family's ranch, and turned off on a dirt road that pointed toward the foothills.

"It's nice to have the distraction," Cricket said as they bumped along. "Beyond those mountains is Yellowstone, but the springs aren't contained to that area alone." They crossed over railroad tracks and went off-road down a hill.

Cricket pulled the SUV to the side and pointed through some trees. "We're going that way."

More clouds had rolled in, and lightning arced across the sky.

Cori laughed. "Nothing like cutting it close."

They walked fast into the woods, a freshly trodden path leading the way.

"Do people come out here often?" Cori pinched her nose. The sulfuric odor was strong, putting her off eggs for the foreseeable future.

"We did a lot as kids. I suppose it still goes on. You'll get used to the smell."

The copse of trees broke open to reveal a hot spring. It was stunning. A contrast of vivid color and black and white. In the center, rimmed in deep golden yellow, was a spring of water that turned bluer as the eye drew to the center. Trees with white trunks resembling barren sticks surrounded the area. Shades of brown and yellow added to the desolate feel and yet, ten feet beyond were green hills, browned at the roots from the dry earth. Full evergreen trees stood tall surrounding the area like sentinels. In sunlight, the place would be breathtaking, sparkling. With the day being overcast, shadows hung near trees and whispered a foreboding message. Though the colors bounced off the landscape, the shadows clung. With the right lens, the landscape would be almost eerie. As if offering two paths of humanity, light or dark, only the choice was left to be made.

Cori took several shots from different perspectives using a variety of lenses, stopping only when a few large drops of rain splashed around her. Lightning cracked overhead.

"We should go," Cricket yelled and waved Cori to follow her.

"I want to see what it looks like in the rain," Cori called back.

But as soon as the drops began to fall, they stopped. Lightning arched across the sky.

"This isn't good," Cricket said while staring up.

No, indeed it was not. Rain was a wanted and welcome visitor, but the lightning with the dry earth was not.

Another flash.

Cori laid on her side and angled the camera to capture both the landscape and the sky, hoping for a shot of the lightning.

Thunder boomed, and she pressed the shutter. Another bolt streaked across.

"Cori!" Cricket had come up next to her and nudged her with her shoe. She waved for her to follow, then took off through the trees.

Cori jumped to her feet and, staying among the trees, wove her way to Cricket.

"I saw something," Cricket said and pointed through the trees. "Look."

Cori held up her camera and used the lens to bring the image in closer. "It's a truck," she whispered. "With a cattle trailer." Cori glanced at Cricket.

"I don't have phone service out here," Cricket said next to her, their heads together.

"I recognize one of the guys from Bruno's." Instinctively, Cori pressed the shutter.

"They're by the train tracks," Cricket pointed out.

"Do you think this is where they're loading them?" If so, then Fort and Deke were in the wrong place.

Uncertain, Cricket grimaced, then pointed to her SUV. Cori nodded.

They made sure not to slam their doors, which was pointless since Cricket had to turn the engine over.

"Wait for thunder," Cori suggested. They waited for the flash of light and the immediate following boom of thunder. Cricket's timing was perfect, and the engine purred to life.

"Can we get past them? Are they blocking our way out?" Cori asked, looking over her shoulder. She'd only seen the one way in.

Cricket nodded. "My dad used to let Laura, our brother, and I drive his beat-up old truck even before we had licenses. Sometimes he would take us out to the prairie and we'd do donuts and stuff. Or he'd take us out in the snow and teach us how to manage that. When we were old enough to drive, we'd go out with brother and do much of the same. So buckle your seat belt. It appears I've been training for this moment all my life."

She flung an arm over the back of the seat, twisting to look out the back window, then gunned it. Cricket backed down the trail at a speed that made Cori's stomach roll with apprehension and fear. They flew backward out of the trees and lurched to a stop on the other side of the path out.

Both Cricket and Cori looked out the driver's side window at the cattle rustlers. Cori lifted her camera and grabbed some more shots. The two men stood mouths' agape, staring at them for a frozen moment. Then one lurched, and another came running out from the woods, gun in hand.

It was Brody.

Cricket threw the SUV into drive and punched the gas. They sprung forward, jerked to the right, and shot out onto the path.

The SUV fishtailed, but Cricket kept it under control. They flew down the dirt path, hitting every bump known to man and some extras. Once, Cori's head hit the roof, her teeth banging painfully together.

"Keep checking for a signal," Cricket shouted as they crested up on what would be considered a speed bump in suburbia. The SUV caught air and flew forward only to quickly drop like a lead ball, slamming onto the ground on its tires.

Cori screamed. Cricket hooted with joy. They sped away.

They hit the county road at breakneck speed. Pulling out in front of another car in a squeal of tires, leaving it far behind them seconds later.

"I have a signal," Cori cried out and hit speed dial for Fort.

Lightning lit up the dark sky, thunder vibrated the earth, and the heavens opened up. Rain pummeled the SUV, making it hard to hear.

"He's not answering," Cori cried while hanging up. She redialed.

Nothing.

"Try Deke." Cricket handed Cori her phone.

She sent the call through and waited, desperate to reach one of them. "He's not answering either." Panic made her voice sound shrill.

The woman shared identical looks of fear.

"Oh, my word! What's that?" Cori pointed beyond the window where a streak of gray smoke lifted from the ground to the sky.

25

D eke and Fort parked their trucks a half mile past the cabin into the deep woods and hiked their way in, Deke splitting off to go toward the creek and railroad tracks.

Large thunderheads rolled across the sky, making the midday hour feel more like evening. Fort guessed the temperature dropped at least ten degrees. If he was to take the dark sky as an indication of how today was going to go, he'd cancel. Stay home with Cori, doing easy things like feeding the horses or changing out salt blocks. His gut was the second indicator that today was going to bring trouble. Like he'd known a building in Afghanistan was rigged, he knew this day would bring bad shit.

He picked his way around the cabin, looking for signs of people moving about, coming or going. Fort stopped and waited every few feet, being as still as the woodland animals, which was another bad sign. The wind whipped the tree branches around in all directions but the birds and animals were quiet.

The plan was for Fort to approach the cabin and confront the guys for illegally using the place. Force them into action. Last night, Fort had read Tinsdale in on the situation, and the sheriff had contacted neighboring county sheriffs. Deputies were strategically placed on all roads out of Wolf Creek in hopes of catching these guys red-handed.

Deke texted. *6 head down by creek. No tags or brands.*

The question to ask was if someone was bringing more heads as Deke and Fort waited, or was this the haul and tonight they would load it on the train?

Fort hunkered down next to an evergreen, hoping the branches would provide some relief from the impending rain. He glanced at the sky. He needed the rain to hold until these guys made their move. Twenty yards in front of him was the cabin. Parked beside it was the same beat-up white and blue truck Witty and Brody had been seen in. Inside, he could see a shadow moving around. Fort guessed they were using candles based on how the light flickered. It was too difficult to tell if there were one or two people inside.

All he needed was the go-ahead from Tinsdale before he could make his move. He checked his phone often, fearing he might miss a message since he'd put it in silent mode.

Thunder shook the earth, and Fort counted between the sound and the flash of lightning. Two seconds. The storm was upon them. He stood, moved so he was positioned facing the door, and pressed himself against a tree, hidden in the shadows. He supposed that was a silver lining from the storm.

He was given the go-ahead by Tinsdale and stepped out of the woods.

He walked briskly to the cabin. He was ready for this to be over. He banged on the door with the side of his fist. "Sheriff's Department," he called out.

He heard someone swear inside.

He went to bang on the door a second time when thunder boomed so close Fort thought it might be on top of him. Immediately following was a loud crack, much like the sound of a shotgun discharging, and Fort hit the ground.

Someone inside the cabin yelled.

The small hairs on Fort's neck and arms stood on end. The ground trembled beneath him and lighting cracked across the sky.

The cabin door was flung open and Conway ran out. He jumped over Fort and kept going straight to his truck.

Shocked, it took Fort a second to process what had happened. He sprang up, then ran into the cabin as Witty was peeling out.

No one was inside, but the back portion of the roof was on fire, as was the back wall, the bedroom engulfed in yellow flames. Fort ran to the kitchen. Under the sink was a fire extinguisher. He jerked it out, then ripped the plug out while running back to the fire. Flames were already nipping at the living room walls. Smoke filled the air and burned his eyes. Every breath ended in a cough, and his lungs screamed in pain. Covering his mouth with his sleeve offered no relief. There was no point in trying to save the cabin, half was already gone.

Fort did a quick sweep for people and escaped out the front door, gasping as he drew in fresh air. The sky split open. The storm that had been rushing toward him had arrived, and the cold drops of the rain were refreshing. He skirted the perimeter, spraying the grass that was on fire, working his way to the far back of the cabin where disaster waited for him. The fire had spread ten feet from the house, and a handful of trees were engulfed. Fort sprayed what he could, but the fire was jumping across the land, the conditions primed. The severely dry land was kindling. What rain falling would do little to bank the fire once the fire grew larger, and that was moments away. It would take hurricane level rains to control it. He whipped out his phone and called the fire department, ignoring an incoming call from Cori only because of the urgency of his situation. He made a mental to note to call her first chance to make sure everything with her was okay.

Flames licked at the walls of the cabin, burning it to the ground. His cabin. Going up in smoke. Another ten minutes, and it would be nothing more than ash and timber. A loud crack echoed through the space, and a large evergreen split, falling on what was left of the cabin.

After calling in the fire, Fort called Deke and warned him. Then, with a hurried pace toward his truck, he called Tinsdale to fill him in. Once off the phone, Fort ran the remaining distance to his truck. The rapid growing pace of the fire was frightening, and no amount of rain unless it was a flood, would extinguish it now.

In his truck, he called his stepfather with the warning and Mrs. Z since both homes lay in the path. The information now with them, the telephone tree would be activated. He also knew the fire department would have sounded the alarm.

As fate would have it, and heaven knows they needed a little help from the universe right about now, Witty was on the side of the road with a flat tire.

Fort came to a screeching stop behind him and jumped from the truck. Witty was leaning against the hood, head in his hands. He jumped when he heard Fort.

"Where were you going so fast back there, Conrad?"

"Listen here, Deputy—"

"No, you listen here. Did you start that fire?" Fort thought he knew the answer, but wanted to see how Witty would respond.

"Hell no. That was lightning. Hit that cabin with such force the whole place shook. Fire just appeared. Scared the bejesus out of me."

"So you ran instead of trying to put it out." Fort pointed over his shoulder where gray plumes of smoke filled the sky. It was then he noticed matching plumes on the other side of town. "Shit," he said. There was no time.

He grabbed Witty by the shoulder and spun him around. "I'm taking you in."

"I told you I didn't start the fire," Witty cried and tried to struggle, but the attempt felt halfhearted. Fort slapped a cuff on quickly then steered him toward his truck. "I'm arresting you for trespassing and destruction of property." He read him his Miranda Rights.

"I told you I didn't start that fire, and I was told I could stay there by Deke."

"You really going with that seeing as how we're gonna be seeing Deke in about five minutes?" Fort helped Witty into the truck and buckled him in. Witty's lips were pressed tightly into a thin line, his eyes averted.

"All right then," Fort said, slamming the door. When he got into the driver's seat, he waited until they were cruising above the speed limit before continuing the conversation. "It was a real gamble to come here pretending to be a campaign manager when the guy you're working for is a deputy. Must be something real important to make you do that." He glanced in the rearview mirror.

Witty's mouth opened then closed, returning to his tight-lipped stance.

"We know you're here rustling cattle, Witty. We've got the evidence, and it stacks up high against you. When I get you back to the station, I'm gonna run your prints. I'm betting that'll give me a whole treasure trove of information. Nails in the coffin for you. Right now, I've got an arm's-length list of crimes to charge you with and one is gonna stick. Back to the pokey for you." Witty's gaze shot to Fort's. He knew that would get the man's attention. He'd taken a stab at Witty's previous jail time, but the man's expression confirmed his suspicions.

"What do you want?"

"I want the name of the man in charge of this ring. I'm willing to pretend you didn't cooperate at all if it helps you save face. But your cooperation will go a long way." If he was going to name Cori's dad, it would be best if Witty said it now when she wasn't around to hear. He figured if there was bad news, it would be best coming from him.

Witty jerked his head in frantic disagreement. "He'll kill me anyway."

"He can't reach you in jail."

Witty's laugh was a short, brittle sound. "Jail. That's where he'll have it done. No." Witty wagged his head adamantly. "No."

They took the turn into town on squealing tires, Fort only slowing when he was close to the station. The truck hadn't come to a complete stop when he threw it into park and cut the engine. The town was empty. Businesses were closed. Many, it looked, done so hastily as their signs still read OPEN.

He jerked Witty from the truck and hustled him to the station. "Think fast, Witty. Time for you is running out regardless. If you think this person can reach you in prison, then you're a dead man anyway. Might as well do something right for a change. A good deed. Maybe it'll lighten the dark smudge on your soul."

Inside, Cricket and Cori were waiting. They brought him up to speed on what had happened out by the springs.

"And Brody was there," Cori said. "He shot at us."

Fort saw red. He wanted Brody something fierce. Fort turned to Witty, gathering his shirt in his fist and lifting, Witty going up on his toes. "Tell me where to find him!"

Witty met Fort's gaze with a panic-filled one of his own. "I already told you. He'll kill me."

Disgusted with Witty for being a coward and not having a definitive answer as to whether Cori's father was directly involved or not, Fort took out his frustration on Witty and shoved him into a cell without processing. He'd get to it. Right now, there were bigger issues.

Deke ran into the station. "We've got two fires, spreading in both directions." He pointed east and west. "They're gonna meet in the middle, Fort. That's you, Tinsdale, Mrs. Z and the Williams', plus, the handful of ranchers on the other side of the river. You need to get home and do what you can. I'll start notifying the other counties. This thing is gonna spread fast. The fire department is asking for manpower."

Cori gasped and brought her hands to her mouth.

Fort took her in his arms. "We don't have time to be sad or scared right now. People need to be evacuated."

"I'll go get Mrs. Z," Cori volunteered.

Fort held her tighter. "It's too dangerous. I'll go."

"You need to help with the fire. I'm going if I have to steal a car."

He set his jaw, searching her face. "Take my truck and bring her to Ma's. They will take care of her if they have to evacuate. Be very careful. You're gonna have to drive past the fires. If it's close to the road or has jumped the road, turn back. You understand?"

Cori nodded.

"If you get cut off after picking her up, drive out of here. Go someplace safe. Got it?"

She nodded again.

He pressed a desperate and firm kiss to her lips, holding her for all he was worth, wishing he didn't have to let go.

26

The fire raged uncontained for three days, sweeping across the dry land all the way to the foothills before they managed to bring some control to the situation. The devastation spread across more than twenty thousand acres. Mr. Phillips' barn, Mrs. Z, and the Tinsdales lost everything, home and herd. Fort and his family managed to save the structures and house but lost over sixty percent of their herd. As did the other handful of ranches caught in the fire's path including the Williams'.

The following week, Cori captured a photo of Fort's stepfather, Paul, the backdrop the charred land, a cow with severe burns at his feet. He'd just put the animal down, his gun smoking. He had knelt beside the heifer, his hand on the animal, his face, wet with tears, to the sky. The photo was not an original since the scene played out across the county as ranchers were called to perform the gruesome task repeatedly. It was the only humane thing to do.

Each night she and Fort would fall into bed, too exhausted to do more than hold each other, Cori often crying quietly against his shoulder. Deke had formally withdrawn from the election, citing how busy his insurance company would be getting everyone back on their feet. That left Fort set up to be the next sheriff and really no purpose for Cori to stick around other than to help out. Which she did every chance she got. Once things calmed down, she and Fort would need to have the exit-strategy conversation, but she was in no rush.

Wolf Creek, once a beautiful and scenic town with shades of blues, greens, yellows, and purples, was now barren and stark. Its color, black and gray, was accentuated by the sharp contrast of the baby blue sky.

Yet, for all the grief and loss, Cori had never seen a town rally like this one, neighbor helping neighbor. When she wasn't feeding animals on Fort's family's ranch, she was feeding them on someone else's while they were out looking for cattle. She mucked stalls, covered dispatch at the Sheriff's department, and worked alongside Cricket to get the paper out. Additionally, she and Cricket, alongside Mrs. Z, Mrs. Williams, and Ms. Saira, cooked copious amounts of food and delivered the dishes to those ranchers who spent all day in the field, or to the high school gym were many of the now homeless were temporarily sheltered.

It was a week after she submitted her photo, with Paul's permission, that she found out she'd won. The victory was bittersweet. She'd rather the circumstances that led up to the winning photo not have happened. Especially when the fire marshal ruled the fire at the cabin had indeed been caused lightning, but the one by the spring was caused by a human.

Brody. She knew it had been him. Instinct told her so. What she needed to know was if her father had a hand in it, if he was still running his business from behind bars, ranchers across the nation his target. Cori being in Wolf Creek would be a coincidence, having made sure not to tell her mother where she as going. If that was the case, then she thought perhaps it was a sign from the universe that she was meant to stop him. Why else would she be privy to this information?

Cori stared out Saira's kitchen window, amazed at the tiny flecks of green peeking up through the charred ground, the resilience of the people and the land, and felt the huge weight of guilt press down upon her. She wouldn't be able to live with herself if her father was involved. If he'd attempted to destroy another small town. How would she look people in the eye if that was the case? She would not spend another decade trying to right his misdeeds. To do so would break her.

"Cori," Saira said next to her.

Cori brought her attention back to the kitchen. "Sorry. I was thinking."

Saira smiled softly. "Must have been something deep. You look heartbroken."

"I was just thinking about what everyone here has lost." She blinked in effort to hold back the tears.

"It'll be hard, but we'll all rebuild. Or move on to other things. Like Mrs. Z. She's going to love living in town and have less to worry about. She's been lonely out there."

Cori nodded. "I hope you're right."

"I'm always right," Saira said. "Now, go put on a dress or something pretty. We're going to town."

"Are we taking this food to the gym? Do we have extra to take to Hannah?" Hannah had gone into labor the day of the fires and, thankfully, had been out of town. Even though the Jacobson's hadn't lost anything in the fire, the exhausted mom with two demanding infant boys was on the meal rotation.

Saira shook her head while pushing Cori from the kitchen. "Hurry or we'll be late."

"For what?" Cori called over her shoulder to no avail. She'd been shoved out the door, and it had been closed soundly behind her. She changed into a long peasant shirt and her cowboy boots. Then helped Saira finish loading the dishes into the backseat of the truck.

The sun was setting on what looked to be a beautiful night. A layer of golden yellow beams rose from the horizon with a slate blue sky resting above it. When they arrived in town, Saira parked near the newspaper.

"Do me a favor and go collect Fort. Meet us by the gazebo. We've all been working hard and need something good tonight," Saira said.

Cori nodded and slipped from the truck. She walked the block and half to Fort's building. Maybe now she should bring up their situation, much as she dreaded it. After all the town had just been through, it wouldn't be fair to keep pretending that she and Fort were each other's true love, particularly when only half of that statement was true.

When she entered the Sheriff's Department she found Fort, Deke, Sheriff Tinsdale, and the fire marshal sitting at a round table at the far end of the room. None of them heard her come in, and she was about to announce her presence when what the fire marshal was saying caught her attention.

"Yeah, there's no doubt that the spring's fire was deliberate. The bottle that was used to start it has been processed. Looks like he stuffed kindling into it and lit it. Set the darned thing against a tree."

Someone swore softly.

"The fingerprints off the bottle provided a hit to one Michael Brody." He handed the group a picture. Cori wished she could see it, but instinct told her she knew who it was. Michael Brody and Brody Fant were the same people. She didn't need a picture to confirm that.

"Do you have any leads?" Fort asked.

The fire marshal said, "Right now, he's in the wind. Last place we have him tracked was a State penitentiary in Texas. He went to visit a"—he looked at the paper—"Mr. Charles Walters. This make sense to anyone?"

Cori gasped. "No. Not again," she cried.

Fort spun in his chair. When he saw her, he leapt to his feet.

"Cori, you don't know anything yet. None of us do. Don't make this into anything."

She brushed away tears. Was there anywhere she could go where her father wouldn't show up? "Really? Do you really think that's true? Look at me and tell me you think he's not involved in this."

Fort sighed, and she could read the pity in his eyes. She didn't know what was worse, his pity or the town of Brewster's derision. Either way, they both sucked.

"That's what I thought," she said and spun on her heel. She didn't bother to close the door behind her. She was halfway across the parking lot to the square when she heard him call her name. She kept her focus forward, a plan forming with each step. She would bring justice to Wolf Creek if it was the last thing she did.

Fort caught up with her just as she stepped up onto the grass of the square. He grabbed her elbow and forced her to walk alongside him. "Slow down for a second," he said.

"No, I can't."

"Babe." He sounded exasperated.

They were walking around the far side of the gazebo when the park lights suddenly went on to show a large portion of the townsfolk had gathered.

"Surprise!" they said in unison.

A banner reaching from one side of the gazebo to the next swung in the breeze. It read *Cori and Fort* and had tomorrow's date.

Fort and Cori stopped short.

"What's this?" Fort asked and gestured to the banner.

Tables set in rows were covered with lavender tablecloths, flowers, and dishes upon dishes of food.

"Oh, no," Cori said, then covered her mouth in mortification.

"This is your rehearsal dinner," Mrs. Z called from within the crowd.

"We figured after the fire, this town could use something to look forward to, and what better than y'all's wedding?" Saira said.

"Ma," Fort said sadly.

"The Lutheran minister from Bison's Prairie is coming tomorrow at noon to do the deed," Mrs. Williams said. "I'm in charge of the cake." She clasped her hands in delight.

"No," Cori said, softly at first, then again louder. The generosity of the town was amazing and heartbreaking. Never was there a place filled with people she loved more, and all this time she worried about her father hurting them when she was about to do more damage.

But she would not go forward with any more lies. That was no way to live, and she certainly wasn't about to marry a man who had never asked her.

"Come on, give them some champagne and let's get to the eating," someone in the crowd called, probably Mr. Phillips.

"No," Cori yelled. "We aren't getting married."

A hush fell over the crowd. Fort squeezed her arm. She jerked it free and stepped forward, tears flowing like mad down her face.

"Why? Because you aren't ready? None of us are, honey. You just have to jump in," said the cashier from the quickie-mart.

Cori choked back a sob. "We aren't getting married because we aren't engaged. Never have been."

"I'm confused," Cricket said.

Cori wiped away the tears using her palm. She blew out a slow breath, hoping to steady herself, but failed. She shot Fort a look that hopefully conveyed her deep regret for what she was about to do. "I was—" She almost said hired but changed her mind. "I came here to help Fort win the election. It was a ruse." She held up her hand. "But before you think poorly of Fort, know this. He loves this town. He just didn't know how to show it. He loves each and every one of you, and if you find yourself doubting that, think back to the last week. You all wouldn't give him a fair shake because he keeps to himself. But he's shy. He's private." She turned to him. "I'm sorry," she said. "I had to tell them."

He stood tall, hands in his pockets, and nodded.

She faced the group. "There is something you should know about me. My dad is a cattle rustler. He's also a con man and is serving time in a Texas State Prison for crimes much like the ones that happened here and have been happening to good folks like you throughout the county. The man who set one of the fires works for my dad."

A few people gasped, and a murmur began to ripple through the group.

"Any chance your dad's an alien?" Mr. Phillips asked.

Cori gave a wobbly smile. "I wish. Unfortunately no. Just a bad man. I'm sorry." She said. "From the very bottom of my heart, I apologize to each and every one of you. My intention was to help a good man get into office." She clasped her hands over her heart. "I love this town, and I'm sorry for any pain I might have caused each of you. Truly." She sniffed, turned on her heel, and ran.

27

He went to run after her, but his stepfather caught him by the arm and stopped him. "Wait a sec, you need to do some explaining first." He pushed him to the crowd.

Fort looked at the faces of the people he was hoping would elect him sheriff. Confusion was easy to read on some, as was anger on others, but both his mom and Mrs. Z looked puzzled, and he didn't know what that meat.

"I'm sorry," he said. "All that time I spent in the Navy, whenever someone would mention home, I'd think of here. As a kid, I looked forward to coming here. Heck, even fighting with Deke was something that made me feel as if I belonged. I never felt that way in Texas."

"So why make up a girlfriend?" Mr. Phillips asked. "I knew there was something fishy about this."

"Of course, you did," Mrs. Williams said sarcastically.

"When I first got here, all I wanted to do was enjoy the quiet. Afghanistan was loud. And there was never time to be alone. Here. That's all I wanted. To belong and to have some peace and quiet."

"Except we kept trying to set you up," Mrs. Z said.

Fort nodded. "I didn't want to hurt anyone's feelings. I was in no place for a relationship."

"You could have said *that*," someone in the back said. Sounded like Sally.

"I think I did once. No one was really listening. Y'all think everyone should be married. Everyone should have kids. But that might not be for some folks. I didn't think it was for me." Fort tried to picture his life before Cori, but all he kept seeing was her. "Then this sheriff thing came up, and everyone was saying I should do it. I wanted to do it, but it seemed I'd have more luck getting kicked in the head by a horse than winning the special election if I wasn't headed toward wedded bliss."

A few people laughed.

"How do you feel now?" His mom stepped forward. "Are you okay with letting Cori go? Are you more than happy to go back to the way things were and give up the election?"

Fort gave it some thought. He had no regrets. Not for bringing her here, breaking the rules, or her confessions. All said and done, the last month and half had been amazing. Fire withstanding. He'd felt alive and energetic. So letting her leave was not an option. He knew that was unacceptable. He didn't need to be sheriff to be accepted; he needed to be himself.

She held up her hand and walked to him. "Before you answer, let me tell you a few things from a mother's perspective. You've had to be an adult long before you should have. I'm partly to blame for that for leaving you with your father. But you were never a child who wanted for anything. Don't get me wrong, you needed a lot, but you never felt like you deserved anything. If we went fishing and you caught the biggest one, you would throw it back or give it away. Like you didn't deserve it. Same with hunting. When I bought you clothes to take back to Texas, you'd leave them behind." She cupped his face in her hands. "If I could undo the past, I would. I'd make different decisions. But let me say this. Running for sheriff was the first thing I saw you reach for. And when you looked at Cori, it was the first time I saw you want something for yourself."

"We all saw it," Mrs. Z said.

"Yeah, duh," Cricket added.

Truth was, he'd been lonely, and the occasional time he spent with a woman he'd pick up out of town never left him wanting more, only satiated a need. But Cori, well, she left him looking forward to every day. Yeah, he could see now how he'd shuttered himself off, and now that he had a taste of what life *could* be like, hell, he wanted to eat at that buffet.

He ducked his head in happy defeat and quickly ran through his options before saying, "I'll admit that I was stuck in a rut that I called a routine, and if you all want, I'll withdraw from the election. We can go back to the table and see if there are candidates who might be better for the town. But if you'll have me, I'd like to be your sheriff." He looked at Mrs. Z. "I'd like to buy your half of the land the cabin sat on if you don't mind."

She laughed. "Son, I gave it to you."

"I know you did and I appreciate that but—"

"But nothing. It's yours. If you'd like to buy the rest of my land, I'm willing to sell to you first. I'm thinking I'd like to cash in my goods and do other things besides cows. Maybe cruises instead."

Bitsy Tinsdale cooed. "I'd love to take a cruise."

Fort was awed by her offer. The day he'd seen the deed, he'd known then he wanted his own ranch. "I appreciate that Mrs. Z. Let's sit down and see if we can't work something out."

His mom squealed with delight and rushed him, then threw her arms around him in a tight hug.

"Wait, there's one problem," Mrs. Z said. "Cori's name is also on that deed." She raised one brow and quirked her lips as if holding back a laugh.

Fort smiled. "I thought you said that wouldn't be a problem?" He detangled himself from his mom. "Now, if you all don't mind,

I gotta girl I need to chase and win back." He waited for anyone to grumble, but all he heard were cheers.

He spun to where his truck was parked and found it missing. "Well, hell. She took my truck." He tossed back his head and laughed.

"Here," Deke said and tossed him his keys. "Take mine."

Fort caught them and was once again hit with an overwhelming awe of how much had changed. How everything was better, except for his gone girl.

He hadn't been held behind long enough, but she'd managed to flee town remarkably fast. From the trail of clues she left, he pieced together what she did. She'd taken his truck, drove to the ranch where she collected her stuff, her camera and the majority of her clothes. Left behind were odd bits like a sock tucked between the cushion, her toothbrush in the bathroom, and her perfume in the air. She'd then caught the next train out of Elk's Pass, providing a factual text to tell him where his truck was, leaving the ring behind in the cup holder. She hadn't responded to any of his responding texts or calls. But he didn't need to talk to her to know where she was going. He made a quick call to Sabrina, threw a bag of clothes in his truck, and thanked Deke for the lift to retrieve his vehicle. Pointing his truck south, he pressed the pedal to the metal.

The drive to Texas took two days, and when he arrived, he was beat and in no shape to confront Cori so he crashed at Sabrina's where she handed him a small card with the poem *No Man is an Island* printed on it. They'd had a good laugh.

The next morning, he drove the forty-five minutes to Brewster. Cruising the main street, he was saddened by what had become of the town. Or maybe, for the first time, he was seeing Brewster in its true state. A handful of stores were closed up, boards on their windows. The vibe was nothing like Wolf Creek, where every season volunteers revamped the square flowers. It was hard for him to look at Brewster objectively. He'd worked so hard here, trying to keep their small herd going, fighting against Charlie Walters and his own father. There was no town center, no place for people to congregate for pleasure, only the church and the courthouse where the town meetings were held.

Trouble with Brewster was that oil was found on some of the land. Instantly, landowners became wealthy while their neighbor stayed status quo. Or worse, struggled. He'd often wondered what life would have been like had his dad learned there was oil on their land before losing it to Walters. Truth was, Fort was happy he hadn't. When he thought about life in Brewster, he didn't like it. There weren't happy memories for him here, but maybe there would have been if they had money. He doubted it, though. Worst thing to happen to a gambler is to suddenly strick it rich.

Fort parked by the diner near Main Street. The air quality was thick with dust, he was hot and sticky, and when he stepped into the small greasy spoon, the thick aroma of lard made him stop short. A handful of people were in the diner, only a few talking.

"Sit wherever," a flat voice called from the back. He scanned the place. It's gray tones and cheap laminate tops with burn marks spoke of the mentality of the town. He stepped back outside. No thanks. The place hadn't changed since he was a kid. He hadn't liked it back then and even less now.

Most of Brewster's businesses had shifted over near the super-center. A chain restaurant, bank, drive-thru ice cream shop, and a quickie oil change store had become the new main street. Charlie Walters was responsible for bringing in the superstore, and this is what Fort held against him the most. With the promise of improving the town, Charlie had instead taken away the small community that needed each other and replaced it with quick access. Yeah, superstores were in tons of small towns that managed to retain their charm and community, but Brewster had been different. Fort wasn't sure why, just that it was. He was glad that he had two goals. Grab Cori and get out of town sooner rather than later.

With the directions Sabrina gave him, he drove to her apartment, a square building of four floors, three apartments per floor. Cori's was on the second. The blue paint was peeling off the side, and underneath was a dingy white. Cement stairs jutted out from the center of the building, casting a dark shadow across the first three floors. He was depressed parking near it. He only hoped the inside was better.

He was about to get out when he saw Cori come out of her apartment and jog down the stairs to her car. The three days he'd been without her suddenly felt longer. Lonelier. He thought of all the things he wanted to tell her. About what the folks had said after she ran off. About the ideas he had for moving forward. She was adorable in her short skirt, boots, and her oversize shirt falling off her shoulder, her large glasses showing her the world but somehow missing what was right in front of her.

When she pushed the glasses up, Fort chuckled.

Cori drove a beat-up convertible. He'd put money on the old car living up to the name "rag top." He stayed three car lengths behind her as she zipped through traffic. When she pulled into the parking lot of the superstore, he made sure to obscure his truck behind others. He watched her sit in her car, staring at the large gray building, chewing her nail.

Now was as good as any to let her know he was in town, but his instincts told him something was about to go down, and he was too curious to stop it.

She threw her hands up in the air, likely talking to herself, then got out of the car. She kicked the door closed as she spun away. Head up, shoulders back, she marched toward the double automatic doors.

He had to see this go down. Fort jumped from the truck and followed, making sure to stay out of the reflection of mirrors and doors. All those times in the sandbox had paid off after all.

28

A handful of people were coming in or going out, and Cori didn't know any of them. Which was good. She didn't want to get sidetracked from her task. It had taken two days of staking out the joint, while trying to hide, to make her plan. She was exhausted from the sheer covertness of it. To give her strength, she would scroll through the many texts Fort had sent or listen to his voicemail. Her favorite was the one where he said, "Dammit, Cori. Pick up the phone." Then would growl in frustration before hanging up. In one message alone, she knew he wasn't mad, and therein lied hope. So she stayed focus on what she needed to accomplish here before she could tackle the problem of making Fort fall for her.

She made her way to the grocery section of the store and circled the aisles. Feeling much like a stalker, she grabbed a cart and began throwing the items from her mental grocery list into the cart.

She made another round and considered the milk she'd put in. It was getting warm from all her laps around the food section. Darn it all, she did not have all day for these people to show up. She debated putting the milk back, hopefully remembering to grab it again when she was done, but worried about the ethics of doing so. She didn't want to be *that person*, too. The one that walked around with a ton of perishable and then left them in the tampon aisle. Or worse, put them back where they belonged so the now spoiled food could make someone sick. She'd read somewhere that she had four hours before anything was considered "spoiled." If that was true, then she was safe returning the milk. This did not apply to her mood, though. It was going south fast. She needed her targets to show up already!

Cori talked herself down from the ledge of panic. The thing about growing up in Brewster and having spent the last 10 years trying to make it up to the town, she was really knowledgeable about the local's habits, and her stakeout over the past two days confirmed she knew the routines of people. It would be unlike Mrs. McAdams if she did not show up for her weekly milk, eggs, and bread. The milk truck came yesterday, the egg and bread guy today. Mrs. McAdams liked her stuff fresh. If she could get these deliverymen to bring it to her house, she'd totally do that. Mr. Miller was no different, only his prey was the beer man. He always came in for a six-pack. Cori made another round and found Mrs. McAdams in the bread aisle, her hand on a pack of sliders buns. Cori backed out of the aisle and peeked down the lane to the beer. Mr. Miller was coming around the corner, six-pack in hand.

She took a deep breath, then pushed the cart toward Mrs. McAdams, a pageant smile plastered on her face.

Mrs. McAdams glanced at her then back at the buns, clearly not registering who she was. But then she jerked her attention back to Cori. "What are you doing here?" Mrs. McAdams asked. "I thought when you left, you granted us a gift. Are you back to torture us some more?"

Cori smiled and faced the rack of bread. While pretending to study the bagels, she cut her eyes to the side to look for Mr. Miller so often she was getting dizzy.

Please let him walk by, she prayed. Time crawled.

"I'm talking to you," Mrs. McAdams said.

Finally, Mr. Miller came shuffling by and Cori called out his name. He jumped, startled, and gave her a puzzled look. She waved for him to come down the aisle.

"Did you need something for me, Cori?" he asked and shifted the six-pack to the other hand.

"Actually," Cori said while turning so she could see Mrs. McAdams and address her. "Did you know that Mr. Miller has a zero-turn lawnmower?"

Mrs. McAdams narrowed her eyes. Her already thin mouth was pressed tightly together. "So? Like I care. What's that have to do with anything that concerns me? That's your problem, Corinne Walters, you are in everyone else's business."

"I mention it because ever since Mr. Miller had to move to the trailer, he's had little opportunity to use his zero-turn. Mr. Miller sure loves that mower. Don't you?" She smiled widely at Mr. Miller.

"Sure do. Named her Peg. Used to date a woman named Peg who was fiery. The mower reminds me of her. Sure do miss using it. Miss it. Miss it. Can't bring myself to sell it."

Mrs. McAdams rested her hands on her lower back. "Again, I ask what this has to do with me? Why I should care?"

Cori pointed to Mrs. McAdams position. "That's why I think you should care. Your back bothers you. It's never been right since you had that accident twenty years ago. Has it? And with your son gone a lot, you have to do more work around the house."

"And that's your business, how?" Mrs. McAdams asked, though some of the bluster was gone from her bite.

"I was thinking," Cori said, "maybe Mr. Miller could come over and mow your yard every week. It would really help with your back."

"And why would he do that?" Mrs. McAdams asked.

Cori smiled. She knew if she got Mrs. McAdams to bite, there would be nothing left but to reel her in. "Because Mr. Miller loves your blackberry pie. Has said over the years how it is one of the best, if not *the* best, blackberry pie he's had his entire life. He misses your blackberry pie, Mrs. McAdams," Cori said.

"I sure do," Mr. Miller said, nodding then licking his lips. "I miss that pie."

Cori patted him on the shoulder. "Maybe Mr. Miller can mow your yard and you can make him a blackberry pie as payment. If I remember correctly, you love to bake pies. Used to always win at the fairs, too."

Mrs. McAdams puffed out her chest. "I took All-State three years in a row. Of course, any dumb-dumb can make blackberry pie. It's the easiest."

"That's not true," Cori said, throwing herself under the bus. "I've tried, and mine aren't good at all. I've tried others, too, but they're simply not as good as yours. There's something special about yours."

The corners or Mrs. McAdams lips twitched, almost as if she was going to smile.

"So what do you say? Mr. Miller misses your pie. The town does frankly. How about you get back to doing what you love and Mr. Miller can do what he loves with his zero-turn. Care to make a deal?" Cori crossed her fingers behind her back.

Mr. Miller stepped closer. "It is blackberry season. All those berries ready to be picked. Going to waste." He tsked.

Mrs. McAdams held up a finger. "What about when black-berry season is over?"

"Pumpkin," Mr. Miller said. "It's my second favorite, and then there's that mean chocolate pie you make with all those shavings on top."

Mrs. McAdams chuckled. "Oh Lord, I haven't made one of those in years."

It was the first time Cori had seen her smile in forever. "I'll let you two work out the specifics," Cori said and backed quietly down the aisle, leaving the two to talk. She walked right into what she thought was an end cap and spun to catch what she knew would be falling glass jars of something.

Instead, her hands found the rock-hard body of Fort.

"What are you doing here?" she asked and stepped back. Her senses reeled from being so close to him. She wanted to run her hands down his body, having missed touching him.

Arms akimbo, he looked down at her and laughed. "Is that what you're going with? What am I doing here? The question is, what are you doing here?"

"I..." She didn't want to say she couldn't face the good people of Wolf Creek, that she needed one more try here. After having spent those weeks in Wolf Creek, she knew what she needed to do for closure with the people and town of Brewster. But mostly, she couldn't say that somewhere along the line she'd fallen for Fortune Be-so-lame, and after having spent years in a town being unwanted, she couldn't bear to be in his wonderful town being unwanted by him.

He took her chin in his hand. "It's time to come home, Cori," he said, then lowered his lips to hers. It was heaven, familiar and kind, gentle and needy. His kiss spoke to parts of her that couldn't hear words. Reached deep into her soul and filled the empty space, the cracks and crevices.

Home he had said.

She heard someone gasp, and they eased apart. Fort looked over her head and smiled. "How ya been, Mrs. McAdams?"

"Well, not—"

"I'm sorry to hear that. Though it's like my momma always says, 'You can be a victim or you can be happy.' I hope you've been happy."

"What are you doing here?" she asked.

"I came to get my bride. She was staying away too long. I was getting worried." He brought his attention back to Cori and winked.

Cori searched for the right words. What to tell him first? She wanted to kiss him. She wanted to run because to stay one more second meant she was opening herself up to hurt. She was also opening herself up to love. There was so much to say she tried to sort through the multitude of words desperate to spill from her. There was only one thing she could.

"I love you. I tried really hard not to." Her heart was about to beat out of her chest.

Fort chuckled. "I know the feeling. What do you say about us trying really hard to do the opposite?" He wagged his brows and in one swift motion, lifted her and tossed her over his shoulder. She laughed and knew better to squirm. Instead she tucked her hands in his back pockets and waited to see what was going to happen next.

"It's been good seeing y'all, but we've got to go. I've got to get this girl to her wedding. She needs to make an honest man out of me." He turned foot and walked calmly from the store.

29

I t hadn't escaped Cori's attention that Fort had not returned her declaration of love by saying those special three words.

But actions speak louder than words, and she believed this sentiment with all her heart. The fact that he drove to Brewster to collect her. That he, literally, swept her off her feet to bring her home. Yeah, kinda caveman in nature, but sexy nonetheless.

And speaking of sexy. Well, secretly she dug getting it on in his truck. It was fun and awkward and rushed for fear of being caught, and the combination of those worked for her. So much that the normal two-day trip back to Wolf Creek took three. On the drive, he filled her in on what happened after she left. That he was running unopposed for sheriff with the town's support, including Deke's.

As they got closer to his home, the euphoria of being with him began to wear off, replaced by worry about what people would say about their future and how she'd be received. By the time Fort was slowing, preparing to turn toward the square, she was chewing her thumbnail.

He took her hand in his. "Relax," he said. "No one is mad."

"Right, they aren't going to be mad at you. You're part of the community, but I was an outsider who played them."

Fort pulled up behind the gazebo and turned off the truck. "I'm gonna need you to trust me on this, okay?"

She shrugged as if she didn't have a choice.

"If by the end of the day you aren't happy, I'll make every last bit up to you. Redo the whole day."

Cori knew she was giving him a weird look. Her nose was wrinkled in confusion. "What are you talking about?"

"You'll see." He opened his door, then slid out. "Stay put," he said when she reached for her door.

If she didn't trust him so much, she'd be worried he had a nefarious plan. Fort came to her side, opened the door for her, and offered his hand to help her out.

"This is weird," she told him. His only response was to laugh.

She continued, "Weird meaning I'm not sure I like it."

"That's because you expect bad things to happen to you all the time. You won that photography contest and didn't breathe a word of it. Just let it pass by. We had a cattle rustler come to town before you did, but somehow you managed to take responsibility for that as well. Even though you had nothing to do with it."

She stopped walking. "It feels like I did because my dad's involved."

"You think he's involved. Just because Body went there, doesn't mean anything more than he's still in contact with your dad." Fort took her hand in his.

"Did y'all catch Brody?" If they did, then maybe she would know for sure. It might not be important to them, but it was to her. She had thought if her dad was in prison, he'd be too removed to hurt others.

Fort shook his head. "He's in the wind. And your dad's not talking."

There was no denying her deflated feelings.

Fort led her around the side of the gazebo and stopped. The

setting sun was streaking colors of gold and slate blue across the sky. Twinkle lights beckoned from the gazebo and lined the shrubs that skirted the sidewalk. Crickets chirped.

Fort turned her so she faced him, the side of the gazebo in her direct line. He dropped to one knee, still holding her hand.

Cori's breath caught in her lungs.

"Short stuff, in the time that you've been here, we've been through some good and some bad, but through it all, we worked as a team. Until you ran off at the last part, but you're allowed a few missteps. Lord knows, I'm going to have plenty of my own. But one thing I realized through all this is that when I'm gonna face hard times, I want you there next to me. You give me hope for good times. When I face good times, I want you next to me. You give me hope for the unimaginable. Until you showed up, I was going along thinking life was fine. When you left, I realized life without you was empty. What I'm saying is that I love you. I want you with me for all the days. Every day. Forever. Will you marry me, Corinne Charlene Walters?"

Tears of joy rolled down her face. "How did you know my middle name?"

"Your mom used to yell it when she'd scream at you for not winning a pageant." His smile was soft, his eyes without pity.

"And you remembered it after all this time?" Her mind was processing all that he said, all that he asked, and she was finding it hard to believe it to be true.

"Short stuff, you called me out about all my misdeeds. Used to piss me off something awful, but only because you were right and I knew it."

She licked her lips as she sucked in a shaky breath and tasted the salt from her tears.

"Is it so hard to believe you are loved?" he asked, coming to his feet. Her hand still in his, he pulled her closer.

"Maybe," she said in a shaky voice.

"You have to have a little faith, babe. Take a chance. Take one on me." He squeezed her hand. "I mean what I say when I tell you I love you."

"I love you, too. That's what scares me so much." She took a small step toward him, her chest nearly brushing his.

"I'm going to hold on to you and never let go," he said. From his hip pocket he took out the ring Sabrina had sent with her. "This is real. It's the same stone my dad gave my mom. Sabrina's dad bought her ring from my dad after she left so he wouldn't hock it. Sabrina had it reset with you in mind. Just say yes."

Cori nodded, overcome with love and family and belonging. "Yes," she choked out. "Yes!" There wasn't much to life when one played it safe, and Cori had been doing that for years. Whether it was staying in Brewster, avoiding her parents, or never sticking up for herself. Whatever the reason stopped now. She was grabbing onto life with both hands and holding on for keeps.

She leapt into Forts arms and kissed him soundly.

Beside them, people cheered. Cori broke from the kiss and looked around. A large number of people had gathered near the gazebo and were watching them, many clapping. Everyone smiling.

"About this getting married thing," Fort said. "How about we do it now?"

With her still in his arms, he walked around to the front of the gazebo where Cricket waited in her lavender dress, two bouquets of purple hydrangeas in her hands.

He let her slide to the ground. "What do you say?"

She looked at the faces of people she'd come to like, even love, and smiled. She met Saira's gaze and saw the love waiting for her there. "I say why not? Why waste time?"

Someone hooted. Saira stepped forward with arms open. "Welcome home, Cori," she said.

Though the majority of the town was present, the wedding was small, quick, and full of laughter. It was intimate and personal and the people bearing witness were like family. Cori didn't care that she wore a flowy skirt in a patchwork pattern and a white peasant top or that Fort was wearing jeans with a button-down plaid shirt. None of that mattered. She had the love of a great man and his family and the acceptance of a town.

Mrs. Z had given her something borrowed by tucking a soft linen handkerchief under the strap of Cori's bra, Saira placed an antique family necklace of pearls around Cori's neck, Fort gave her a brand-new key and left her guessing where it fit, and Mrs. Williams gave her a blue garter.

"Every girl should have a garter that needs to be removed," she'd said in Cori's ear and followed it with a wink.

After the ceremony, they laughed and ate and celebrated the future, both the town and the people as well as Cori and Fort.

When the evening was gone and night heavy in the sky, Fort swept her up into his arms, thanked everyone, then dashed off to his truck, hooting and hollering echoing behind them.

"Still have that key?" he asked as he backed out his truck.

"Yeah, of course." She had tucked it into her boot and went about retrieving it.

They drove in comfortable silence, her head on his shoulder. When he pulled off onto the dirt road that lead to the cabin, she sat up.

"What are we doing?" She knew the cabin had burned, and though she would pretty much spend anywhere with Fort so they could get their honeymoon on, the charred remains of what was lost didn't feel like a good idea.

He pulled around the tree and hit his brights. In their beams sat a new, partially built cabin. Exterior walls were up but no roof. Fort cut the engine but left the lights on.

"Come on," he said and pulled her from the truck. He pushed her to the front door. "See if the key works."

It was silly on some level because she didn't need the door to get inside. She could tell there was no back wall yet by looking through the cut-out that would become a window. But she slid the key in the new door and turned the lock. The heavy wood door released, and she pushed it open.

Fort came up behind her and wrapped one arm around her waist while gesturing with the other. "This is all ours, the cabin, the acres that surround it. I bought more from Mrs. Z. We officially have the foundation for our own ranch."

Cori leaned back into him, her hands covering her mouth in disbelief, fresh tears on her cheeks.

"I had the crew leave the back of the house off because I thought maybe we'd want to extend it a little to add a few more rooms for future Besingames. Just need your input so we can move forward."

"This is all yours?"

"All *ours*, babe. Our ranch. Our home. Our future. Together."

Cori turned in his arms, then cupped his face in her hands, and said. "Can we call it Be-So-Lame Ranch?"

Fort tossed back his head and laughed.

They spent the first few hours of their honeymoon "christening" their ranch before heading into Elk's Pass to kick off the remaining portion of their celebration.

Hope.

One simple word brought so much in dreams, opportunity, and happiness.

ALSO BY KRISTI ROSE

The Wyoming Matchmaker Series

The Cowboy Takes A Bride

The Cowboy's Make Believe Bride

The No Strings Attached Series

The Girl He Knows

The Girl He Needs

The Girl He Wants

The Second Chance Short Stories can be read alone and go as follows:

Second Chances

Once Again

Reason to Stay

He's the One

Kiss Me Again

or purchased in a bundle for a better discount.

The Coming Home Series: A Collection of 5 Second Chance Short Stories (Can be purchased individually).

Love Comes Home

ABOUT THE AUTHOR

Kristi Rose was raised in central Florida on boiled peanuts and iced tea. Kristi likes to write about the journeys of everyday people and the love that brings them together. Kristi is always looking for avid readers who are willing to do beta reads (give impression of story before edits) and advance readers who are willing to leave reviews. If you are interested, please sign up for her newsletter. Aside from her eternal gratitude she also likes to do giveaways as well.

You can connect with Kristi at any of the following:
www.kristirose.net
kristi@kristirose.net

JOIN MY NEWSLETTER

AND GET A FREE BOOK

Hi

If you'd like to be the first to know about my sales and new releases then join my newsletter. As part of my reader community you will have access to giveaways, freebies, and bonus content.

Sound like you might be interested? Give me a try. You can always unsubscribe at any time.

Go to www.kristirose.net if you're interested.

XO,

Kristi

CARE TO LEAVE A REVIEW?

Dear Reader,

I am so honored that you took the time to read my book. If you feel so inclined, I would appreciate it if you left an honest review. You don't have to say much. Put the stars you feel it deserves and a few words. Some folks don't even put words. Reviews go a long way in helping authors in all sorts of areas including marketing.

Thanks again. You're a rock star!

Have a great one.

Kristi

CPSIA information can be obtained
at www.ICGtesting.com
Printed in the USA
BVHW071641050819
555095BV00014B/1972/P